Mary

(CALTER CREEK 4)

LizAnn Carson

Mary (Calter Creek 4)

© 2020, 2024 Elizabeth Carson

All rights reserved. No part of this book may be reproduced, stored, or used in any manner whatsoever without the express written permission of the publisher except for the use of brief quotations in a book review.

ISBN: 978-0-9949036-9-3

Cover photos used under license from:
Deposit Photos
"Mary" font: Stalemate, ©2012 by Jim Lyles for Astigmatic

Thank You

To the wonderful, supportive women of my critique group. Your varied and insightful comments helped me make *Mary* a better book.

Chapter 1

"Farewell to the bonds of society. I am a free spirit, a seeker of truth. Inthuthered."

Considering her light-headedness, at that moment Mary Boylan was more than a little free of the bonds of gravity, and possibly common sense. On a Friday night in late June, she and her two best friends had settled around a table in Libations, the principal watering hole in downtown Calter Creek, Ohio, a couple of hours earlier. "Untethered," she clarified.

"And you're what? Thirty-four years old? A little young to be untethered, seems to me," Bryony said.

"Or a little old." Mel snared Mary's purse and rummaged. "Got them," she announced as she pocketed the keys. "Lucky you, you're now freed from the bonds of transportation."

"It matters not. There's a chariot out there somewhere." Mary was aware that the s's weren't emerging crisply from her mouth. They seemed to be sliding, like the whoosh down a water slide.

"Any idea what we're celebrating?" Bryony asked Mel.

"Nope."

Mary hadn't finished. "I will not be chained," she chanted into her mojito. Then she waved a hand in the air to get the waiter's attention.

"Do we let her have another one?" Mel asked.

"Can we stop her?"

Bryony was snarky that evening, Mary thought. Not good company at all. This was a quest. Her pals could at least support her.

1

"Let's think about this," Mel said. "Free of the bonds of society, huh? Does this mean you're quitting your job?"

Mary hiccupped, then whispered. "Don't tell. I will *pretend* to sell houses. They'll never know."

"The joke's on them," Mel confirmed. "Do you own any tie-die?"

"What do you know about tie-die?" Mary shot back. "You're dating a *banker.* Boring, boring, boring."

"Hot, hot, hot. So I gather the mortgage isn't paid off?"

That stumped Mary. Experimentally she said, "I'm shedding the shackles of society." She suspected the *s*'s and *sh*'s had twisted around each other like in a mambo. Or tango. Or something. Great phrase, though, she'd have to remember it for later.

Was it even possible to do all that stuff with shackles if she had to make a mortgage payment every month?

"I'll deal with it," she said as the new mojito appeared in front of her. "Mortgages are boring. And you're not keeping up," she added accusingly.

"Someone has to get you home," Bryony said.

"Someone doesn't like mornings after," Mel said.

"Okay, smartypants," Mary said, pointing a finger at Mel. Is it 'mornings after' or 'morning afters'? Tell me that."

"She's not too far gone. Yet," Mel said to Bryony.

"I drove last time," Bryony replied. "Remember? She barfed all over my car. Not happening again."

"I think it depends on whether morning and after are hyphenated," Mel told Mary.

"Huh?" What was Mel talking about? Mary had a feeling she should know, but thoughts were slippery things, like eels.

"Forget I mentioned it," Mel said.

Libations was at its usual Friday night peak, and Mary was enjoying – if she could use the word in the context of this particular Friday night – her girls' night out with Bryony and Mel. "You're the besht friends in the world," she told them, noticing that the *s* got away from her again. Must need lubrication. She slurped at the mojito.

"Don't look now," Bryony said, "but we're being watched."

Mel shrugged. "Your deal, not mine." Mel was all ga-ga over her bank manager, although Mary didn't get the attraction. Sure, Ryan Pope was hot to look at, but he was so... ordinary. In Mary's humble opinion.

"Where?" Her head swiveled and locked on the gaze of... no one she'd ever seen before. And in Calter Creek, population next to nothing, this was remarkable.

The man sat two tables over, and alone. He had that nice guy look about him. Clean slacks, blue short-sleeved button-down shirt, cotton sweater over his shoulders. Brown hair trimmed and tidy. Nondescript, non-threatening. Not noticeably interesting, Mary thought. Not that she cared. Men hadn't figured in her world view in years.

"New blood," Bryony confirmed.

"Ordinary," Mary said. "Even more ordinary than—"

"Don't even think it," Mel warned her. Poor Mel was determined to make her bank manager into something hunkier than he was.

"Gonna check out the new talent." Mary got to her feet, sort of. It seemed to take a moment longer than it should before she located them confidently underneath her. Then, tethers to the earth re-established, she walked over to the new guy's table. "Hi," she shouted over the music, wondering where all the great pick-up lines hid when you needed them.

His smile was warm and open. "Hi," he shouted back. "I noticed you sitting over there. I wonder if you'd like to dance."

"I would." Proud that she'd avoided the pesky *s*'s, she watched the man get to his feet. He was a nice comfortable height, she decided, under six feet, but that meant you didn't go home with a crick in your neck from peering up at him. She couldn't sort out his eye color, not in the wonky light of Libations, but he seemed nice enough.

He took her hand and led her toward the little dance floor. The gyrating bodies did something strange to Mary's insides; her stomach sent out a warning signal, but she firmly swallowed it down. "I'm Mary," she hollered.

3

"Chris." On the edge of the floor he didn't let go of her hand, and he didn't attempt any mad gyrations himself. He moved, though, and moved well – seductively, Mary thought, apropos of nothing much. She moved in response, and it wasn't a good idea. "Thirsty," she shouted above the noise. "Have to go."

"I'll take you." Chris still held onto her hand, all the way back to the table where Mel and Bryony watched.

"This is Chris," she said. Three *s*'s in a row… drat.

"Chris Peterson," he confirmed as he handed her into her seat. They all introduced themselves and before she quite knew how it happened, Chris had become part of their table. An intruder into their girls' night out.

He waved at the waiter and got her a glass of water. "This may not be what you're thirsty for, but I suspect it's what your body wants."

Great, a do-gooder. She could bloody well attend to her own body, thank you. Chris nursed a Coors Light; Mary wondered what that implied about him.

Mel glanced at her watch. "I'm heading home," she said. Probably meeting Ryan for – Mary groaned internally. What could you get up to with a bank manager, anyway? Even if he looked like a surfer god, he was still… stuffy. That was the word. Stuffy. She repeated it in her mind a couple more times, because it seemed to come detached and vanish from her thoughts as if it had never existed.

They all indulged in farewells. Mel handed Mary's keys to Bryony and left. Mel wasn't much fun anymore, Mary thought. Her banker was chipping away at her devil-may-care.

Conversation was a challenge in the noise of Libations. Mary, Bryony, and Mel pulled it off among themselves because they'd known each other for so long that they pretty much knew what any one of them was going to say. Talking to Chris was harder. "New in Calter Creek?" Bryony shouted.

He shook his head. "A couple of years. Nice town."

"Conventional," Mary grumbled.

"She's casting off her shackles," Bryony explained to Chris.

4

"A noble goal, but could be challenging. What do you want to do? Once you've cast off?" he asked Mary.

Chris and Bryony both waited, but her brain seemed to have seized up. What would she do if she could be or do anything? At that moment she wasn't sure.

About anything. Abruptly her head swam. She could be in trouble here.

"What do you do?" Bryony shouted at Chris.

"Stuffy," Mary finally produced with some pride.

He hesitated, possibly wondering if her newly resurrected word had been directed at him.

"Not you," Bryony said, putting a hand on his arm to get his attention. "Ryan."

"Okay," Chris said slowly. "And Ryan is…"

"Not hers," Bryony said. "Mel's. And to return to the question of the moment."

The band hit a new decibel level. "Social work," Chris shouted. "Passages, that's the teen drop-in center. The Silver Threads Center for seniors, home visits." His fingers went to the neck of his shirt, where he played with the fabric for a moment. "You?"

"Dietitian out at the hospital. She's a real estate agent," Bryony added with a nod toward Mary.

"Goin' home," Mary said. She rose and sank back down. Because magic was afoot, and the ground wasn't where it was supposed to be.

"Steady." Chris's arm was under her elbow, and somehow Mary found herself on her feet. "You want to go home, right?" he repeated, as if maybe she hadn't heard herself.

She nodded and regretted it. "Very carefully," she explained. "Gravity. Dangerous stuff."

Bryony sighed. "This is unusual," she shouted at Chris. "Come on, girl, I'll call you a cab."

"No cab. Walk," Mary said. Irrationally, given that she had chosen three-inch heels for this night's get-together.

"I told you, I'm not driving you again. Not after last time."

5

"I'll take her," Chris said.

Bryony shook her head. "We don't know you, and my friend's drunk. I'll call a cab."

"You will not." Mary swayed but held onto Chris. "He's a good guy. I know. Free, that's what he is."

Chris smiled and met Bryony's eyes. "I'm trustworthy. Free, but trustworthy."

Bryony looked over at the bartender, who knew them. "Don! Good guy?" she shouted, angling a finger at Chris.

Don, who in the way of bartenders had no trouble hearing her above the noise, gave her a thumbs-up and settled in to watch.

Bryony knew when she was licked. "Call me the minute you get home. If you don't, I'll have the cops out looking for you." She tucked the keys into Mary's purse.

Mary looked up at Chris and slurred – shlurred?—"Good friends. Don't understand about shackles, though."

"I don't exactly understand, either, but I hope you'll explain. Don't worry, she'll call," he said to Bryony.

Chapter 2

Chris's first thought was that the light shouldn't be that bright. His second had more to do with the crick in his neck. Very carefully he opened his eyes.

Mary. Right. Her name is Mary.

He was slouched in a chair in Mary's living room. Full consciousness invaded his brain, along with an indelible memory of the most remarkable Friday night in years. The three women in Don's bar. Taking Mary home, barely in time for her to throw up in her own toilet instead of his car. Holding her hair, wiping her face. Feeding her water and aspirin, praying it would stay down.

And not leaving, because she had been horribly sick. He'd been worried about her.

Correct that. Worried, yes, but more was going on here than worry. Attraction, for instance. Her condition was a convenient excuse for sticking around. It hadn't happened in a long time, and usually didn't last, so staying at her place had made all kinds of sense.

Chris hauled himself to his feet, shaking out the kinks. The sun blazed in the window, giving a cheery yellow glow to the room. Not a cloud in the sky. They were in for another scorcher in a sweltering summer.

More memories surfaced. Using her cell phone to call her friend Bryony. Choosing the chair instead of the bed in her guest room, because he didn't want to presume.

In the kitchen he started coffee, making no effort to be particularly quiet. Okay with him if she woke up. Then he spent a hasty three minutes in the bathroom.

7

When he came out, Mary stood propped against the kitchen doorframe, barefoot and rumpled in last night's clothes, bleary-eyed, frowning at him and then, logically, at the burbling coffeemaker.

"Who are you?" she asked, but not as if she cared too much. Coffee interested her more than he did.

"Chris. And before you get any of that, you'll drink a full glass of water and take a couple more aspirins."

"Chris." She slumped against the frame and frowned at him, not being in the least subtle about it, but also as if she was trying to put the pieces of the night together. "I'm dying, Chris. Go away."

"I'm not surprised." He pulled a water bottle out of the fridge, twisted off the cap, and set it in front of her. "Drink. We need to get you hydrated. You know it as well as I do."

"Where'd you come from, anyway?" She picked up the bottle and stared at it.

From Libations, with her, but she'd sort that out on her own. "Kentucky, actually."

She took a tentative sip and groaned.

He pulled out a chair from the tiny table in the kitchen. "Sit. Drink. Do you want to go out for donuts, or shall I pick some up?"

"Wha?"

"It's Saturday morning. That's when normal adults eat donuts."

Mary managed a full swallow. Chris poured himself a coffee and sat opposite her.

Her eyes were clearing. And she glared very well.

"Think of it as torture," he said cheerfully. "Or an evil bribe. As soon as you get that water down, I'll give you a cup, too."

Another swallow. Good.

"So tell me, Chris from Kentucky. Why are you in my kitchen? I probably ought to throw you out."

"But you won't. I'm the lifesaver who got you home from Libations and held your hair out of the way when your stomach

8

rebelled. Besides, I'm your ride into town for your car. It's already too hot to walk."

"Oh. Yeah. Okay." Mary took a breath and chugged half the water. Chris allowed himself a healthy exhale of relief.

"About last night…"

When she didn't continue, he chuckled. "Do you have any idea how common that line is?"

That riled her. Good, he thought. Better than miserable and defensive and apologetic – which, to be fair, she had yet to be. "You're saying I'm trite?" she shot at him.

"I'm saying your brain isn't firing on all cylinders. You were anything but trite last night. Slipping shackles?"

"Oh." Her eyes went enormous; the scene in the bar must be coming back to her. They were blue, her eyes, but in some lights they shifted closer to aqua, like the photos he'd seen of tropical lagoons.

Those eyes pinched closed. "Oh, shit."

"That bad, huh?"

She held out the water bottle for him to judge, opened those remarkable eyes, and sent him a pleading look. She'd drunk about half, so he relented and grabbed the coffee carafe. "This cup's black. You can have cream at the donut place."

"You have no right to be cruel in my kitchen." She added a tiny bit of sugar.

"Consider it a kindness. Your system will. Less chance you'll upchuck."

"I need calories. Something solid," Mary grumbled.

"Bread?"

She pointed at a cabinet.

"Toast, coming up." While he worked, he talked. "Your first name's Mary. What's the rest of it?"

She looked better, not as likely to turn green as she'd been ten minutes before. "I'm not going to tell you that. I don't know you."

"True, but remember, Don gave me a thumbs-up, so that proves I'm a nice guy. Totally trustworthy. My last name's Peterson. Your turn."

Never had Chris been so glad for the trustworthy label that clung to him like bubble gum in his hair, something that had happened more than once in his formative years. Good ol' Chris, he'll take care of it. Taking care of business while everyone else went out partying. Story of his life.

Well, good ol' Chris had, just maybe, found himself in a situation he was in no hurry to clean up.

She'd finished most of the coffee, and she still hadn't divulged her last name. "I'm gonna shower. You can leave now." A statement, not a question.

After treating the toast to thin scrapings of butter and honey, he handed her a slice. "Eat this, then shower. When you're human we'll deal with donuts and your car."

She led off with a nibble, then bit into the toast as if it were manna from heaven. Her eyes rolled back in her head. "So good," she said around the bite.

He'd had the foresight to make two, so he crunched into his own. "Agreed."

It was quiet for a while. They ate, and she bypassed the dregs of her coffee in favor of water, and he watched. Because even pale as a ghost and still fighting queasiness, Mary was worth watching.

She stood. "You're really not leaving."

"Nope."

"Why not?"

"Why?"

"It's what guys do."

"Not the nice ones."

"Gonna shower."

"I'll clean up in here."

She stared at him as if he'd grown blue skin. "Weird."

Chris poured out the remaining coffee and squirted dish liquid into the sink. A lot of people thought he was weird. Take his parents and his older brother, for example. As for his sisters – well, arguments could be put forth that they out-weirded him every time, not that they'd admit it. But this was new territory, because he had picked up a hint of a compliment beneath the word, as if *weird* might be a good thing.

Situated just off the main street, the donut shop was a favorite stop of Chris's. The tiny apartment he'd rented when it looked like he'd be in Calter Creek for a while was near the park, on the edge of the downtown core, and Saturday mornings he allowed himself the luxury of a cruller and a cup of coffee he hadn't made himself.

By now they knew him. "Hey, Chris. The usual?"

"Sounds good. Morning, Jenna, Marlene. This is Mary. I won't swear to it, but I'm guessing she wants something involving chocolate."

"Boston cream?" Mary said a little tentatively. "And coffee?"

"Coming up." Jenna turned from them to fill the order, and Chris paid Marlene.

A table by the window came free, and he sprinted for it, narrowly beating a couple of teenagers. "Next time," he told them cheerfully, then handed Mary into a chair. "Be right back."

By then Jenna had their order ready. Chris put her donut and coffee in front of her and watched her eye his orange juice.

"That looks so good," she said. "I never thought."

"Not a problem." He shoved the juice across the table to her. "Tell me about shackles."

"Oh, God." Her hands covered her face. "Not my finest hour."

He pulled her hands down, holding onto them for perhaps a heartbeat longer than he should have. "I like the idea of slipping shackles."

She drank the juice in one go. Chris glanced over at Jenna, who caught his eye, saw his gesture, and appeared a moment later with two fresh glasses of juice. "Pay you later," he mouthed. Mary had gone off into her own world and hadn't even noticed Jenna at the table.

11

She turned her eyes to him, and he had no trouble at all fastening his attention on her. Her long, dark hair fell down her back; she kept pushing her bangs out of her face. A little more color had washed over her face, but she was still pale. Blue-aqua eyes, tiny pearl earrings. Mary had put on jeans and a faded purple t-shirt, with a pair of fancy sandals on her feet. He'd watched her maneuver into those sandals. Being more a sports sandal kind of guy himself, he didn't understand the flimsy, glittery things women wore on their feet. Overall, even after last night, Mary looked polished. Professional. Not like someone who was about to slip whatever bonds held her and make a bid for freedom.

"We can't, though, not really, can we?" she said.

Chris snapped back to the present from the insane daydream he'd been lost in. One involving her toes, nails painted royal purple, peeking out from the sandals. He couldn't see them now, but he remembered.

"Can't what?"

"Hello? Chris? You asked me about all that shackles stuff. I'm just saying it isn't really possible."

"I don't know. Depends on your definition, I guess. Drinking's one way."

"Not mine." She glared. "Look. I never drink like that. It was a one-off thing, okay? Don't lecture."

"Sorry, you're right. No lecturing. What's keeping you tied down? Why now? Or have you always wanted to escape and haven't been able to?"

"You're nosy."

"No. Sometimes. I want to know you better."

"Why?"

Why? Wasn't that obvious?

"Um, because you're interesting? Because I'm interested?"

And then you're going to tell her more about yourself? Problem.

Not going there today. Chris was used to incredulous negative reactions from women about his choice of profession.

12

Given how he'd met Mary, he expected rejection. But he could delay it, anyway.

Mary sighed. "I have a good life. I have a solid professional reputation, I work hard, I have good friends. Sometimes it just feels like Calter Creek's... small. I've been here fifteen years. Maybe I'm finding it a little confining."

"Not much new happening?"

"Nothing that hasn't already happened, at least once."

He grinned. "You haven't met me before. That seems to indicate that there are parts of Calter Creek you haven't explored yet. How are you feeling?"

"Better. Thanks."

What was there to say after that? A lot, but at the moment every conversational gambit he could think of had its perils. Mary stared out the window, caught in some vision of her own. Chris knew he was due at the senior center, but seemed to be fixed to the spot, watching her. His work allowed him that much leeway; he'd be late this morning, but they'd understand, especially if he told them why. The elderly crew expended a lot of energy trying to think of someone to fix him up with. Maybe he should snap a selfie so they could see Mary.

He chuckled. She looked at him. "Now what?"

"Dumb idea. Want me to take a picture? Immortalize the morning?"

"I'd kill you."

Too bad. He wouldn't mind having something to remember this morning by.

He settled the bill and they left, walking into town to her car. Standing in the lot, he put his hands on her arms. "I'm glad I met you," he said. "Well worth being late at Silver Threads. Busy day ahead?"

"Work. Saturdays are usually crazy."

"Can I call you?"

She twisted away, once again remote. "Thanks, Chris. Bye." She was in her car and gone before he knew what had happened.

13

Doomed. Once she learned his true profession, it'd be all over anyway. At least he didn't wear one of those dog collar things. She would have run for the hills.

~

Mary drove home, puzzled. Who *was* this guy?

She hadn't slept with him, she'd bet on it. As evidence, her Friday-night-at-the-bar clothes were tangled around her when she woke, underwires digging into tender flesh. Besides, the throwing-up episode ranked as a guaranteed attraction dowser. But she couldn't remember him trying. She expected guys to feel her up, but –

Oh, yeah, they'd danced. His hands well behaved. Perfect gentleman.

She could always have a word with Don, the barkeep. He'd give her the straight scoop on Chris.

But why bother? She knew better than to trust the nice-guy façade. Far better to keep her distance, avoid commitments she'd inevitably regret.

Not that she was in the market these days. Or had been for years.

Because really, a donut shop on Saturday mornings? Not her style. Even if she'd kind of enjoyed it.

Even if she didn't seem to have a *style* anymore.

Furthermore, she wasn't about to let anyone judge her. And that's what happened with men like Chris. They saw the body in the bar, and detailed – for her benefit, needless to say – the ways they expected her to change.

At home she phoned Bryony. "Opinion?"

"Good manners. Cute, in a preppy kind of way. You okay this morning?"

"So-so. He bought me a donut. Boston Cream."

"He stayed overnight? I'm surprised. Not the type."

"Yeah, I guess he slept in the living room." No need to share that she'd been sick as a dog. "He made coffee, before the donut. And didn't act as if I owed him."

"And that has you puzzled."

"It's… different."

14

"New experience, Mary. Slipping the shackles."

"Drop it with the shackles stuff. I'd checked my brain at the door."

Bryony guffawed. "Ya think?"

Mary sighed.

"Is he hot? I didn't pick up any heat. Can he kiss?"

"I don't know, not that it matters. It's not as if I plan to see him again. Chris is high maintenance. I'm not going to struggle to live up to his standards."

"You're selling yourself short. But if he's not hot, he's off the list?"

"Guess so."

Mary dressed for work, wondering what to do about that lukewarm 'guess so'. There shouldn't be any question. But Chris stuck in her mind, even though so far, the best thing to come of her Friday night was an immaculate kitchen.

He was... decent.

No. No, no, no.

She drew herself back from that particular precipice. A lifetime's experience told her nothing good lay on the other side of a relationship with a nice guy like Chris.

~

Chris arrived at Silver Threads just as they were beginning a singalong. He checked in with Wanda, the activities coordinator, a cheerful, heavyset woman in her fifties with a blond perm and a floral blouse sporting way too many colors. "It's been a quiet morning so far." She shot a warning look at him. "Around here, anyway."

"Sorry I'm late," he said. "Stop imagining my life's exciting."

"A little excitement wouldn't hurt you."

"It might." They exchanged a casual hug, and he dove into the crowd of seniors, helping them find the appropriate place in their songbooks.

Silver Threads had been a pleasant discovery when he moved to Calter Creek. Chronically shorthanded, they welcomed any help they could get. Chris enjoyed hanging out with the elderly men and women, and they in turn had adopted him, a virtual grandson. They were a feisty, spirited bunch. Some of them lived at the facility, but at least half of the thirty or so in the hall this morning came to enjoy the fun and camaraderie, and the lunch.

A lot of their recreation centered around strategies for finding him a wife.

He spent an equal amount of his professional time praying for their success.

"Hey, sweet cakes," Nadine said when he wandered over to sort out her music book. "What held you up?"

"Sorry. Restless night."

Nadine's eyes lit up – predictably. He'd walked right into that one.

"Got some nookie, didja?" She cackled and dug an elbow into his hip, the highest she could reach from her wheelchair.

Equally predictably, he felt his face go red. "No nookie. Let's find the next song in the book before the music starts."

"Look, everybody." Nadine's voice carried far better than it should for someone approaching ninety. "Our boy's blushing."

He treated himself to an internal sigh, turned to wave at the others, and went back to sorting out their songbooks.

At least this lively bunch considered his love life interesting. They'd line up every single woman under forty for his selection, given half a chance. He loved them all. And wasn't it a blessing they didn't seem to think it would be shameful for him to get some nookie – a cringe-worthy word if ever there was one. They didn't understand the high, seemingly impenetrable barriers he faced in his search for a partner, or even for a one-night stand. Not that he'd ever go there. Probably.

Chris held a sure conversation stopper in his arsenal – frustrating, but true. As soon as he admitted to being a minister, women wanted nothing more to do with him. They weren't interested in a goody-goody, they'd say, thank you very much. Or in heading up a church women's organization, or planning potlucks.

Like he'd expect his partner in nookie to do those things? And when had anyone who really understood him last called him a goody-goody? Did *lusty* and *minister* have to be a contradiction in terms?

But no point in speculating on the female mind. Evidence spoke more loudly than theory. Once a woman discovered his calling, she bolted.

Chapter 3

A week later, Mary slouched in her chair and poked randomly at her keyboard. The real estate office was quiet, typical of a late Monday afternoon, and browsing Find-The-Right-One.com provided as good a way as any to kill time until a possible client drifted in with a query, or a phone call came from a dreamer hoping to get an astronomical price for a shack.

She'd been playing around with Find-The-Right-One.com for days now but hadn't taken the plunge. Filling out the questionnaire was problematic, since strict honesty brought her to a certain dead end. "Mary Boylan, thirty-four, small-time real estate agent in a small town, leading a small-scale life, going nowhere" just wasn't scintillating.

"Mary Boylan, possessor of a honkin' big secret. To be revealed if you turn out to be the mythical right one." Oh, sure. They'd assume her secret was an STD.

And what were the odds? While she had picket-fence dreams in as glorious Technicolor as anyone's, she didn't believe in them anymore.

Although, inflated promises of the web notwithstanding, she just happened to know a good-guy type who might be interested…

The computer chimed. She switched to her email program and came down to earth with a thump. Because there it sat in her inbox. Her nineteen-year-old secret. Whose birthday she'd commemorated with a blazing drunk.

Now topping six foot two. And sending her a note.

Whenever Zach got in touch, she grew immediately wary. She read it once, caught her breath, and read again, but the words hadn't changed in the elapsed ten seconds.

Hi, Mary. I hope this finds you well.

I'm transferring to OSU. How'd you feel about me crashing with you for a couple of years?

Your brother,

Zachary

The formality of the note left her sad. The content left her panic-stricken. Because when Mary thought about her big secret, the emphasis was on *secret*. As in, no one in Calter Creek knew about her little fifteenth birthday catastrophe, the one that had resulted in Zach.

Zach didn't know, either. Her parents had forced her to put him up for adoption, then adopted him themselves and buried the truth. While Zach lived in ignorance, they never relented, constantly rubbing her face in the shame of his birth, making her feel like slime at every opportunity. Mary remitted money for Zach's upkeep, had avidly followed his athletic exploits in high school, and was present for most holidays, but none of that cut any ice with her parents.

Ever since Zach got to be old enough to send her the occasional email, he'd used that formal opening and closing. She supposed she should be grateful he communicated with her at all.

Ohio State. What on earth was she going to do?

What she wasn't going to do, she realized, was spend any more time with Find-The-Right-One.com. Sister or mother, what would her son think if mail-order men started turning up at the door?

Which led her straight to her second conclusion. Of course he'd stay with her. She'd been given a heaven-sent opportunity to finally get to know this boy of hers.

So yeah, there'd be a man around the house – the right one. Just not the way she'd expected it to play out.

Zach had been studying at Cuyahoga Community College up in Cleveland for the last two years. This new development, however awkward for her, at least suggested that her tall, handsome son wasn't directionless.

She should have cleared this up years ago. It wasn't as if she was ashamed; therapy and a realistic view of life had seen to that. But somehow days became years, and it got harder...

Mary drove home, mildly annoyed as thoughts of Chris invaded her mind. She regretted the necessity of fending off a nice, non-aggressive man who showed every sign of being interested in her. She didn't want to hurt Chris, he didn't deserve it. But she wasn't about to die of boredom for his sake, either.

But she hadn't been bored.

But she might have been bored.

Or had she been too hung over to tell?

Well, damn.

What was one more problem? And frankly, the Chris problem – if it was a problem – paled in comparison to the Zach one.

Ohio State. Whew. She'd better check on the cost of tuition.

Chapter 4

Mary was buried in a report on the local real estate market the next day when she heard a voice at reception.

A familiar voice.

Their receptionist, Jean, received new clients, ascertained their needs, and gathered preliminary information. She sorted people into serious versus browsers, buyers versus sellers, general requirements and price range. By the time Mary or one of her colleagues saw the client, they had a decent idea of what would be needed. And, not incidentally, the likely reward at the end of the transaction.

Although she couldn't distinguish the words, the tone of voice that filtered through her report on central Ohio sales stats was businesslike. And familiar.

Orange juice. Boston cream donut.

Mary left her cubicle and headed for the front desk. Protocol said to leave it to Jean to assign a new client to an agent. This time she was skipping the queue.

There he was, pressed slacks, button-down shirt and all. "Hi." Chris's voice switched from businesslike to warm. "I hoped I'd find you here. I saw the picture of Mary Boylan in the window."

"I'm it." She returned Chris's smile and belatedly remembered her determination to not encourage him. The smile faded.

Jean hit a button. "Form's on the printer. I'd planned to call Suzanne, but since you're here…"

Chris was all hers.

21

It took Mary no time to figure out that, first, she'd just complicated a situation that would have been infinitely simpler had she never seen Chris again; and second, her best option was to hide behind professionalism.

"Come back to my desk, and we'll discuss what you're looking for."

"You know I'm not selling?" he asked as he followed her.

"You told me you live in an apartment, so I concluded you don't own property." Mary waved him into a guest chair, said, "Excuse me a sec," and ran to the printer. When she returned with Jean's truncated report in hand, he'd wandered behind her desk to study her paltry collection of diplomas and certificates.

He turned when she entered the cubicle. "All work related," he said as he maneuvered around her to the guest chair.

"No choice. I couldn't afford a liberal arts degree. Whatever I studied had to be practical." She sat at the desk and moved them back on topic. "Now, Mister Peterson, it says here you want a condo. I need more information. Number of bedrooms and baths, age, part of town, yard, courtyard, balcony, adult oriented, and so forth. And price."

She'd never rattled off that list so quickly.

"Mary."

Damn. His pleasant voice cut right through her determination.

She took a breath. "Look, Chris. I'll help you find a home, but that's it. Okay?"

"Okay. Why?"

She closed her eyes for a moment. Couldn't he at least have the grace to make this easy for her?

He spoke again. "I mean, isn't it too soon to be dumping me? Before I even pick you up?"

Their eyes met, and then he laughed and the tension broke. "Boy, was that a mix of idioms. Thing is, if I'm the one to pick you up, how could you dump me? Visually it doesn't work."

22

"Bizarre." She dropped her voice. "You don't get privileges just because you've seen me puking my guts out."

"It's not because of that, but it might have to do with watching you the next morning. Your confrontation with that donut was sheer poetry."

She couldn't handle it. It was just too much... fun, she decided, and risky... to be around Chris. Mary rose. "I'll call Suzanne. She'll be better qualified to help you."

He stood, too. "No, she won't. Please, sit down and tell me what we do next for this condo business. You must realize that if I didn't jump you yet, it's unlikely I will."

They faced each other as Mary leaned over her desk and Chris leaned in toward her, his face as neutral as any she'd ever seen.

She cracked first. "All right. We'll work through this." She drummed her fingers on the incomplete form. "Then we'll review a few listings that meet your criteria, discuss getting mortgage approval, and go from there."

"Sounds good. Thanks."

Safely in their seats, she began the questions. "Let's start with the biggie, price range. That puts a boundary around everything else."

He gave her a number. "It's not much. I don't gravitate to the lucrative professions anymore."

"Enough to work with." She chose not to follow up on that tantalizing 'anymore'. "Mortgage?"

"Already arranged."

"Down payment?"

The amount he named was significantly greater than she'd expected. He had money... why?

She continued. "Physical requirements? Bedrooms, baths?"

He wasn't after luxury and had reasonable expectations given his budget. They talked for another ten minutes while Mary entered his data into their system. Two bedrooms, baths negotiable, lawn or trees would be nice, not decrepit, please.

"Not a handyman?" she asked him at that last requirement.

"No time. I'm good with tools, as it happens."

Chris in a toolbelt… Taken by surprise, she felt warmth creep up her cheeks. No way. No. Damn. Way.

Mary snapped her attention to the reality of the man sitting across the desk from her. A man who was still there, in spite of her aborted effort to get rid of him. Without further deviation into toolbelt fantasies, she walked them through the rest of the interview, then turned to her computer.

"I'll pull up the listings for the top five choices, to see if we're on the right track. Then we can fine tune and schedule viewings."

"That doesn't work for me," Chris said.

Now what? Mary prayed he wouldn't be the type of obnoxious client who knew more than the agent, expecting gold from lead or, worse yet, playing her along for the amusement of viewing houses with no expectation of ever buying.

But no. He gave every indication of being an up-front and honorable buyer.

"Why not?" she asked.

"Why don't you print them and we go get coffee? We can finish our discussion there. I need a coffee," he added. "Computer screens plus caffeine deprivation? Not a good mix."

"Oh. Well…"

Did she want to do this? No immediate answer came to mind. Because as soon as she stepped outside of strictly business with him, he'd start having ideas. And she'd shoot those ideas down, because…

Because…

Because what, Mary?

"Not a bad idea. How about the donut shop? It's only a couple of blocks."

"There's a problem," Chris said. "If we went there, I'd have a donut. With the visiting I do, I get far more desserts than I should. The Café in the Madison Inn's best suited for our purposes. Quiet, and booths."

24

"The bookstore across the street's planning a coffee bar, but that's not till the autumn."

"It's good to see new business moving into downtown."

Chris's skill at keeping conversation neutral matched her own.

Mary hit the button, and the printer clattered to life in another part of the office. She collected the papers and let Chris direct their steps to the Madison Inn, five blocks east, ignoring her self-preservation instincts the whole way.

Chris sat next to Mary in the booth to make it easier for them to peruse the listings at the same time, and wondered what kind of disaster he was bringing down on his head.

Calter Creek had several real estate companies. Seeking out Mary's was his own perverse brand of tempting fate.

Her desk provided a safe barrier in a nice, safe office. *And kept his hands away from that long, dark hair.*

His fingers twitched. He fisted them.

Nothing obliged him to suggest coffee, much less the subdued atmosphere of the Madison Café. If they'd gone to the Coffee Shack, the presence of half of Calter Creek whirling around them would have made it feel… less intimate.

No risk, no gain.

He paid attention while she walked him through the listings, pointing out the salient features of each. They sounded the same as his apartment, a sterile environment with little to recommend them in terms of style. Since mostly he slept there and nothing else, that might not matter.

There was one, though…

It was on the ground floor of a repurposed old house, with a yard, overgrown garden plots, and trees. It was more dilapidated than he wanted, but there was an allure to it…

"I'm warning you," she told him. "I've been in it. Tons of charm, but needs tons of work, too. That's not what you want."

"Cosmetic, or structural?"

25

"Cosmetic, I'd say, but you'd need a professional inspection. Only one bath – another negative these days. It's in the price bracket for a reason."

"I suppose. Still, can we arrange to see it? And this one." He pulled a second sheet out of the stack. "It has potential, and a decent location."

"It's a box, but you might be able to improve it. And a great deck for those crazy beer parties."

He grinned. "This is me, right? You think I have crazy parties of any kind at all?"

"Hey, you turned up at Libations. Maybe you have latent tendencies."

He wrapped his hands around his coffee mug, for ballast. "I got it out of my system years ago. I went pretty wild in my twenties, actually."

"You?" Disbelief dripped from the word. "You don't even look the part."

He shrugged. "Yeah, so I got picked on in my teens. My brother's three years older, works construction. He was always on my case to toughen up. That didn't appeal, which leads straight to the logical conclusion that girls seriously ignored me. My social life sucked."

"I went to school with a few guys like you. Great for help with homework, but beyond that, no."

"Fortunately – I guess fortunately – in college I unearthed another side or two of myself. Started working out and running, and… well, let's just say I discovered the greater riches of a university campus."

Mary chortled. "And you became a dog and made up for lost time? Frankly, Chris, that's hard to believe."

"Only because I've reverted to type. You get older, and hopefully wiser, and decide what you really want out of life. On that level, these days I'm more interested in finding one woman, one home, one community, than in leaving a mark on every bedpost in the city."

And isn't that a way to lure her into your web? You sound like a dweeb.

26

"You say you're never at home," Mary said, blatantly changing the subject. "What exactly do you do?"

"Well…" *Tread carefully.* "The senior center and the youth drop-in center, primarily, but there's home visitation, too. The elderly, shut-ins, sometimes a family where the teenager's at risk of going off the rails. I do tutoring, as well. It keeps me busy."

Not to mention parish functions, preparing Sunday lessons…

No, not to mention those. You already sound enough like…

Like what you are?

Mary interrupted his ramblings. "That sounds very salt-of-the-earth. You must be a good man, Chris Peterson."

"I try." He waited a beat and gulped his coffee. He hadn't been kidding; he did need the caffeine. "Why do I get the feeling that wasn't a compliment?"

Great. He'd stumbled into another conversation killer. Mary's smile deserted her; her eyes got that nail-him-to-the-lamppost expression that told him either he'd hit too close to the mark or he'd better back off, maybe both. Surely she'd clued in that she attracted him?

"It's just a question of whether we have anything at all in common," he continued, throwing caution to the wind. "We haven't got that part figured out yet, but I hope we will."

Out on a limb. Long way to the ground.

Mary nursed her coffee, no doubt wondering how best to tell him she wasn't interested, thank you very much. As he should have predicted.

Suffocating a sigh, he said, "Okay, we'll view these condos and leave it at that."

Her face took on an overly kind expression. He knew that look.

"Chris, you're a nice guy, really. It's just… right now's not a good time. My life is… complicated."

"Don't let it worry you." What had happened to those skills around women he'd mastered in college, then refined

27

during his hot-shot career days? Chris sighed. "I do play softball. I'm in the league at Fremont Park. Does that count in my favor?"

A beat of silence, then she smiled and shook her head, as if she despaired of him but yeah, he was a nice guy. Well, he guessed he was being a little ridiculous. He, the assistant minister in a tiny parish on the outskirts of Calter Creek, imagining he'd have a chance with this polished, self-contained woman?

They compared calendars and agreed on possible times to view the two condos, then Chris picked up the bill and escorted her back to her office.

Annoyed with himself and the world in general, Chris drove to his next appointment. He'd wanted Mary to see him as a whole man, and instead she saw a limp dishrag she'd never want anything to do with.

How was he supposed to get – or more accurately, regain – that air of urbane confidence he'd once used to intrigue the female half of humanity?

He smiled across the ancient furniture in the dark room at the elderly woman who was offering him a plate of cucumber and cream cheese sandwiches. One of his regulars, Mrs. Grierson always provided something, sandwiches or store-bought cookies, plus the inevitable cup of tea. Why did the world think ministers loved tea? He made the requisite small talk about her new great-grandbaby. Sandwiches eaten – and he made sure she also ate – he gave her a summary of last week's lesson at the Renewed Life Center and held her hand for a prayer. Then he watered the house plants and took her for a slow and careful walk around the back yard.

As always, he was perfectly pleasant – an attitude well suited to his features, he thought in a rare burst of cynicism.

Was Mary doing that to him?

Chris had a long history of facing up to his demons, especially the one that led him to abandon a burgeoning business career to pursue his ministerial calling. Mary showed every sign of introducing him to a whole new set of them.

Mrs. Grierson was in tears, so grateful for the forty-five minutes he'd spent with her, when he kissed her soft cheek and left. No way could he ever doubt the value of his ministry, much more meaningful than vetting bright, career-driven men and women to handle mergers and acquisitions.

He liked his work. He liked his life. His only regret lay in not having a partner to share it. At the moment, the life and the regret seemed irreconcilable.

This was all the more frustrating because he hadn't been kidding about his crazy twenties. He had more than enough worldly experience to recognize Mary's interest, in spite of whatever her mind told her.

The afternoon finally over, Mary shed her heels for practical sneakers, tossed her businesslike blazer into the trunk of her car in the lot behind the office, and walked the block to Libations. Since she couldn't solve the problems Zach's impending arrival raised – such as how she'd tell her circle of friends – she might as well get the scoop on the restrained, but pleasantly determined, man who had driven her home the previous Friday, supported her through a puking experience for the record books, and then bought her donuts and orange juice – and now wanted her help to buy a condo. Like it or not, Chris had been on her mind.

As a celebration of Zach's nineteenth birthday, the drunk wasn't something she'd repeat, but Chris… well. It didn't appear she'd be avoiding him any time soon.

She strode into Libations and spotted Don, as usual polishing glasses behind the bar.

He looked up and nodded as she entered. "You survived Friday?" he asked as she settled on a barstool.

"Barely. I should ask you to put me on a limit."

"Nah. Drink's not your issue."

No, men were her issue, or had been. In her early days in Calter Creek, she'd worked her way through the single male population – or at least, those with a hint of danger. One night stand, then it was hasta la vista, baby. And on to the next.

She'd been a slut, no question. But that was then. Truth was, she hadn't left Libations with a new man in years.

"Listen, Don, about the guy who drove me home…"

"Chris? One of the best."

"You know him how?"

Don shrugged. "Family member had some problems once. You could do worse, Mary."

She reared back. "Hey, I'm not looking."

"Perhaps you should be. He was in here asking about you."

She groaned. "Oh, great. He's decided to rescue the drunk he picked up Friday night."

"To hazard a guess, I'd say rescuing wasn't on his mind."

Their eyes met. Mary looked away first. In the half light of the bar, Don was inscrutable.

"Something to consider," he said. "Want anything?"

"Not today, thanks. Just on a fact-finding mission. It's unnerving when you wake up and there's a strange man in your kitchen making coffee."

Don raised an eyebrow. As he moved his hands mechanically from one glass to the next, he never even looked down to see where he'd lined up the polished ones. *And you consider your job routine.* But routine suited some people. Take Chris, as a guess.

She ignored the raised eyebrow and said, "Thanks. You're a pal."

"You watch out now."

She grinned. "Can't afford to lose such a good customer, right?"

He winked. "You got it."

30

Chapter 5

Chris met Mary at her office on a typically sunny Saturday afternoon. They took her car to view the two condos he'd selected, plus a third she'd added.

To say things were stiff between them would be an understatement.

So, what was going on with her? They'd left their coffee meeting on good terms. He hadn't given her any reason to believe he didn't understand and accept her wishes. Today his focus was on the condos. Her presence added to the anticipation, but that was his issue, not hers. The excitement clearly wasn't mutual.

"Okay," he said as she pulled the car up in front of the first condo, in a three-story block with no detectable architectural interest. "Something's bugging you. Want to tell me what?"

She hadn't said a word during the drive, other than to fill him in on the specs of the place, which he already knew since he held the fact sheet in his hand and had seen photos on the web. She was equally terse now. "Nothing's wrong. I've agreed to show you these homes, and here we are."

"You regret not handing me over to your colleague, don't you? I'm sorry I make you uncomfortable."

She glared – the first time she'd actually looked at him that afternoon. "This is my job. That's what you want, isn't it? To find your dream home?"

"You're not happy about it, and that's stressing me out. Come on, Mary. What gives?"

The glare died. Her hands clutched the listing in her lap. She took a breath. "You make me nervous."

"Why?"

"Just because… I don't know. That night…"

"Didn't mean anything. I get it. So why are you bothered?"

She sucked in a breath. "Don't push, okay? I'm sick of having to—" Her words cut off as if she'd chopped them away with a scalpel.

He sighed. "With me you don't have to. I agreed to your terms, but keep in mind that I'm a card-carrying man, and I'm not blind. Like it or not, I can't pretend not to have noticed you."

"Social workers aren't my scene, Chris."

"Got that."

Got a lot more, too. Worse.

"Can we just go look at this place now?" she asked, clearly between uncomfortable and annoyed.

Story of his life. He nodded and climbed out of the car. He'd play it her way, neutral, non-threatening, and try to make the afternoon at least comfortable.

~

Mary didn't misread vibes from men, and the vibe from Chris fell into the interested category. She'd done all she could to put a screeching halt to any ideas he might harbor in her direction.

And he seemed to acquiesce, but somehow he was still around, whittling at her defenses.

What was his game?

Mary had shut down unwanted attention from any number of men over the years. Her appearance or her attitude or *something* gave them the idea it was fine to hit on her. Heck, married men with families in tow and sagging beer guts turned their knowing looks on her, as if expecting her to arrange a hook-up after she'd shown the wife and kids a four-bedroom colonial with two-point-five baths.

32

No question but he'd bore her in the space of a single date. Wouldn't he? A social worker? Back in the day, she'd preferred worldly men, men who knew the score.

She frowned and let them into the condo.

He gestured for her to precede him, then stood in the miniscule living room and looked at the off-white walls. "Not terribly auspicious."

"I warned you not to get your hopes up for this one. Location and price are right, though. You need to see the full range to make a decent comparison."

They poked into the cramped galley kitchen.

"Room to serve corn flakes, but not to eat them. I wouldn't risk anything flambeed," he said. "You could have flaming cupboards. Mess up the woodwork."

The cabinets were as cheap as it got, and it showed.

When they turned to exit the room, they collided. She took a hasty step toward the door, leading them out of the ridiculously small kitchen, through the living room and into the master bedroom. Space for a double bed and a chest of drawers. The second bedroom was the size of a walk-in closet. The bathroom included a standard issue tub and a tiny counter surrounding the hardware store sink. What she'd expected, but depressing.

The total tour took under five minutes. They stood, a comfortable distance separating them, in the middle of the living room.

"Not even a balcony," Chris said.

"Nope. Or even a window ledge."

"Overpriced?"

"You can do better."

"Want to hear my ideas?"

Learning his thoughts was part of the job. How much harm could it do?

"Go ahead."

"Idea one." His face acquired a patina of innocence. "We paint forest murals on the walls. Install a portable fire pit in the middle and invite a troop of Boy Scouts to toast marshmallows.

The carpet looks like dirt, so it's kind of forest-y. It might work."

"Not Girl Scouts?"

"Not unless they come with a really foxy leader."

She stifled a giggle. She would *not* encourage him. "Is there more?"

"Idea two. We paint the walls black, and the ceiling and carpet. We hire a heavy metal band. Smoke something illicit. What do you suppose happens to a carpet if you paint it?"

Despite her best intentions, Mary found herself getting into the spirit of his absurd ideas for the depressing condo. "It might get scratchy. You'd have to dust instead of vacuum."

"Better than if the paint melted the carpet. All those synthetics. Naturally, we'd invite the neighbors, so they won't call the police. But what if some of them are eighty? I don't want to deal with a stoned eighty-year-old chilling out to heavy metal."

"The perils of your profession? You're a goof."

He grinned. "Moving on to idea three. We knock out the walls, all of them, except maybe the bathroom. Make it into a trendy great room. Paint it with earth tones and purchase fashionably neutral furniture. Invite the parents to come, as long as they don't mind no privacy."

"No way in hell I'd share one room with my parents."

"Mine would endure, politely, and the next day they'd move to a hotel. And my brother and sisters? I definitely need a spare room big enough to hold a bed. Soundproof, given my brother's proclivities."

"Music?"

"Ladies. Being in construction, he has ten muscles for every one of mine, and a lot more attitude. Caused friction growing up, I can tell you."

"Don't tell me you were jealous."

"No." Some of the levity left his voice. "He believed it was his job to bail me out of scrapes. He didn't want to, and I didn't want him to, but he did it anyway. I'm grateful now, but then? Not so much."

She wondered if he'd been bullied, and refused to ask. Too personal.

"Any other thoughts about this place?"

"Other than getting out of it as soon as possible?"

"Claustrophobic, isn't it?"

"Yeah. And it forces me into too close proximity to you."

That hung in the air. She sighed; here they went again. "I thought we were clear…"

"I've told you, you have nothing to fear from me. But at least you can get to know me. Who knows? You might even like me."

"Let's go."

The second condo, the one he'd asked to see, held more promise, with better sized rooms and a deck, but it was on the far southern outskirts of town bordering the industrial district, all manufacturing and office parks. Not run down or dangerous, but not in the heart of things either. Chris said less about this one, just seemed to struggle to dredge up enthusiasm. His shoulders had slumped a bit by the time they left.

"Reaction?"

"It's worse in a way, because it isn't bad enough to joke about. But I hope I don't end up here."

"You won't. My job's to make sure of that."

Two down, one to go. She drove into a neighborhood close to downtown. The lots were deep, and a row of maples lined the street. Almost all the grand houses had been converted to apartments or condos.

Chris exited her car before it was fully stopped in the driveway. She thought of a coiled spring as she came up beside him.

They stood looking at the old mansion. "This is the one," he told her with absolute confidence.

"You're not even inside yet."

"Doesn't matter. When it's right, it's right. How many units are in the building?" he asked as they followed the walk up to the door.

"Five, two on each floor and one tucked under the eaves with the storage." She led Chris up the steps and used her pass key to let them in.

The lobby had once been a grand entrance. The floor was inlaid, and a majestic staircase rose from the right side. Wainscoting and a carved ceiling completed the picture. Now, of course, the floor was scuffed, an industrial runner covered the stairs, and metal mailboxes had been attached to the wall. Mary led them to the door next to the foot of the stairs.

The suite's main room probably had been the original dining room. Bare floors were stained dark brown and were desperate for polishing, if not refinishing. The walls were uneven, Mary guessed paint over multiple layers of wallpaper. The windows faced east and south, looking out over grass and barely maintained gardens. An old-fashioned radiator sat silent; according to the fact sheet, the building still used hot water heating.

Chris reacted by walking through the space as if enchanted, tracing the elaborate finish around the doorframe, trailing fingers over the window ledge. "Wow," he said.

"Did you grow up in an older house?" Mary caught his attention and directed them toward the back, into a narrow hall. On their right the kitchen looked out on the side garden where shrubbery hid the view of the neighboring property.

"No, ultramodern A-frame affair. Not a bad kitchen." He raised the flap on a large hatch that opened the kitchen to the living room. "Better. This will be coming off." Then he turned to study the room and nodded. "There's space for a small table. Convenient for breakfasts."

"You'd have to put your dining suite in the living room," she pointed out. "It'll be tight."

"Keep things on a smaller scale, even though this room's crying out for furniture that makes a statement. Not that my sofa would know a statement if one came and sat on it."

The unexpected, goofy side of Chris was fighting to emerge again. "Come on. Get the stars out of your eyes. I have three more to show you next week, remember."

"So you say. You may not need to."

She led him farther down the hall to a windowless bathroom on the left, obviously part of the conversion into suites. It tucked under the staircase, with fixtures not old enough to be interesting. "You'd have to learn not to hit your head," Mary said.

"Just storage at that end. I learn fast."

Two bedrooms came next, the master in the right-hand corner, the other on the left facing the back garden. The hall dead-ended with a door to the outside.

"The second bedroom's small."

"Big enough for a desk and a bed, or maybe a wall bed. It'll do for the siblings."

"Soundproof?" she asked, grinning.

"I wouldn't mind if my brother took his recreation elsewhere."

His voice came from outside; while she'd been poking into the bedroom, she'd heard the building groan when he unlocked the back door and forced it open. He stood on a flagstone patio that ran the width of the building with a low wooden divider separating the two suites. "North facing," he said. "Challenging for gardening, but then I've never been much of a gardener." When she joined him, he flung an arm around her shoulders and gestured toward the yard with his free hand. "Imagine kicking back out here with a beer on a hot afternoon – do the other owners get access?"

She took a step away; he barely noticed. "Only the other ground floor unit, I think. I'll check."

With a final, enraptured look, Chris steered them back inside, using his shoulder to shut the door. Walking back to the front of the house, he said, "Any woman looking at this would be itching to upgrade the kitchen and bathroom, I suppose."

"Too true."

He shrugged. "Good thing I'm not a woman, then. I'm in no hurry. The rest, though… I'd love to refinish the floors. I could rent a sander…"

"Earth to Chris. Not a lot of free time? Masses of work needed?" Mary nudged him, and belatedly realized that he'd lured her under the spell of his enthusiasm. She hadn't even objected to his casual arm around her shoulders, out in the back yard.

"So I'm a dreamer. But after those boxes... I bet any others you could show me would be boxes, too. Can you blame me?"

She fought to regain her dignity. "No, but I'm the professional here. I need to caution you about aging plumbing, weird room configuration, questionable insulation, oddly placed electrical outlets that'll blow as soon as you plug two things into the same circuit—"

"Caution away. Come on, I'll buy you an early supper and you can tell me what we do next."

"Chris." Mary pulled him to a stop at the door to the condo. "Are you listening to yourself? My read on you is that you're not a spontaneous guy. You'll want to consider your options, think things through."

"Don't know where you got that idea."

"You've only seen three properties—"

"Plus the ones on your website. Nothing compares."

"Okay, fine, but face it, they might suit you better. These old places... some of them were renovated well, others were thrown together."

"Sounds as if an inspection's called for, but it'd have to be something major to stop me loving this. I can handle the occasional blown circuit."

She locked up and trailed him out to her car. "You're in a hurry to leave, for a man newly in love with a house."

"Sure. I'm ready to fill out whatever forms you need." He stopped and turned back to her, serious. "I want this place, Mary. I rely on you to get the best price you can for me. We need to sit and talk, and, in case it slipped your notice, it's closer to dinner time than working hours. So let's go to Joe's and get this done."

She clicked open the car, and they both climbed inside. "Joe's. Are you a burger guy or a pizza guy?"

"Both, but not at once. They do a nice roast chicken, too."

38

"I'll have to call in at the office to pick up some forms."

"That's fine, we can walk from there."

Driving back into town, Mary wondered about the wisdom of having supper with Chris. The man kept surprising her. Joking in the ghastly first condo, making it blatantly clear he was interested in her despite keeping his hands to himself, then this instant love affair with the suite in the old mansion. She'd have to list the flaws more forcefully, try to make him believe that it might not be the bargain it appeared to be on the surface.

In parallel, she thought grimly, with his other blatant interest.

She left her car in the office lot, and they walked through the heat of downtown Calter Creek. Neither of them said much of anything until they'd been seated in one of the age-worn booths. Which was good, Mary thought, because it gave her time to reflect on the afternoon. She enjoyed her work and always found something to interest her in the houses she showed, but today had been... different. As if Chris brought a new set of eyes and a new life to her daily activity.

But she couldn't let him make an offer on the condo after a single short viewing, after seeing only two other properties. It wouldn't be right.

Despite the way pure delight had washed over his face when they'd stood outside the house. Despite the absolute conviction in his voice when he'd said, "This is the one."

Despite the way he'd draped his arm around her when he imagined a beer in the shaded back yard. She'd stepped away from that casual embrace, and he'd been so lost in his dream he hardly noticed.

He waited until the waitress left with their orders, then said, "Tell me what we do next."

"Next." Mary paused, took a breath, and began the litany. "I'll put the word out to see if there's been any serious interest. You need to spend more time there, so you go in with your eyes open."

He slouched back and drank down half the water in his glass before answering. "Rather than in a lovesick daze, huh? You think I'm an idiotic dreamer with a vision that doesn't match reality, don't you?"

Something about his innocent grin raised all manner of protective instincts in her, a totally unfamiliar reaction. She shook it off. "I'm both practical and ethical, and I'd be unhappy putting in an offer now. There weren't any other agents' cards on the kitchen counter, so I doubt anyone else is actively looking at it. That means we have time. And we need to take that time, Chris," she said with a thump of her fist on the table. "It may be your dream place, but I won't let you buy a disaster if I can avoid it. Are you free tomorrow?"

In the hazy light of Joe's, she thought he blushed.

Their beers arrived. Chris took a sip. Good. She hated when guys swilled the stuff like it was a mark of manhood.

"Sunday won't work. How about Monday?"

She put down her mug and pulled out her phone to check her calendar. "Morning's okay."

They agreed on a time to meet at the condo just as their food arrived.

For a few quiet minutes they both focused on the food, then, "Tell me about yourself, Mary Boylan," he said between bites of hamburger. "Brothers and sisters? Ever married?"

Should she come clean?

Hornet's nest.

She finished a bite and took a drink, buying time, before replying, "I have a kid brother. He's a lot younger than I am, so we don't see much of each other. Nothing in common."

"Your family doesn't live here?"

"No. Outside of Cleveland."

"I'm the youngest of four. You've heard about the muscle-bound brother. My sisters… they hover, if I let them. I suppose it's because they virtually raised me, since both our parents worked."

"You like them." She could hear the affection in his voice.

40

"Yeah, I do. Susan's five years older than me, Abby's seven years older. They know me way better than I'm comfortable with. The good and the challenging about families, I guess."

"Once upon a time, I dreamed of having a sister. Someone to talk to, share my life." Mary stirred a fry in the paper cup of catsup, watching its progress through the thick red sauce.

"I expect it's different when you're a guy. Going to big sis with your issues? But I was such a late bloomer where girls were concerned, they proved their worth. However embarrassing." He accompanied the words with a self-deprecating chuckle. "Now it's, how are the kids, what's new, that kind of talk. There does come a time when you have to cut the apron strings."

She reluctantly remembered her own dysfunctional youth and rigid, uncompromising parents. "I cut those strings years ago. I've lived in Calter Creek for fifteen years now. I don't go back very often." It hurt too much – but she didn't say that.

"Not close to your family, then?"

"Just the opposite, in fact. They made me feel like I'd never amount to anything, and I was bound to get into trouble."

His warm hand covered hers; he gave a squeeze before he moved it away. "That's sad. My family don't understand the way I live my life, but they can see it's what I want to do so they're not in my face about it. Or maybe at first," he added, "when I threw over a nice, plump corporate salary with benefits. But that was practical. They worry."

"I envy you." *Was that where the hefty down payment came from?*

"The sibs descend on me periodically. You'll like them."

The prospect made her stomach clench. Meet his family? A net, ensnaring her... "I expect we'll find you a condo, then probably never see each other again."

His face turned serious. "Do you really believe that?"

For a moment, Mary felt as if his eyes were a sanctuary, a home base to come back to. She couldn't remember being so comfortable around a man. When you threw in his quirky sense of humor and his tolerant attitude toward life, the package was…

Tempting. But it won't last. It never does.

She answered him briskly. "It's the way it is. Business."

He sighed and waved to the server for the check.

❖

Chris didn't say much as they walked back through Calter Creek to the parking lot, his mind turning over their dinner conversation. She'd revealed more about herself than she'd intended. After a less than ideal childhood, she now considered herself alone in the world. Did that account for the barriers she insisted on throwing up between them? Perhaps, if the wounds went deep enough.

He didn't have a clue where that left him, except that the interest was there, despite her words.

Halfway to the parking lot, he took her hand. Possibly he'd managed to knock her off balance, because she didn't resist.

At her car, surprising himself, he turned to her and kissed her.

And things got interesting in a hurry.

To say she hadn't expected it would be an understatement. But then he hadn't expected it either. He caught her gasp and held her against her momentary panic as she tried to twist away from him. Then he felt the resistance fade and…

Holy cow.

He hadn't been kidding about his reputation and experience. He'd more than sown his wild oats. But nothing had ever hit him the way kissing Mary did. He got his arms around her, pulling her in closer and allowing their kiss to deepen while his heart tried to pound free of his chest and what little blood it wasn't using flooded directly south.

Which she noticed.

"Chris…" She sounded short of breath.

"I'm here." His mouth was close to her ear, so he whispered, then kissed and explored.

42

She trembled.

Dear God, she trembled in his arms.

And then she stepped back, giving herself plenty of leverage when she hauled off and slapped him.

Did he deserve that? Probably.

There was still plenty of daylight for him to watch the play of emotions across her face. From stunned bewilderment – at the kiss or the slap? Shifting to happiness, even desire, followed by... fear?

"Listen." He ignored the flare of pain on his cheek and put his hands on her arms, not holding her, just touching her. "You don't have to be afraid of me. You know that by now."

"It's not you." She blurted the words and wheeled from him. He heard the car door click open; she'd had her keys clutched in her hand, and as a result digging into his back, as they clung to each other.

"I'm here, Mary. I can help."

He knew it was the wrong thing to say as soon as the words were out of his mouth. Her eyes flared as she looked over the car door at him. "Don't try to be a damn social worker with me. I don't need you."

She'd driven out of the lot before he recovered from that verbal attack. Whatever was going on with Mary went much, much deeper than he'd imagined.

Mary arrived home before she got herself under control. Sort of under control.

He'd kissed her. He'd actually had the *gall* to... and she'd... she'd damn near melted. Then hauled off and clobbered him, and his response was that gentle touch on her arms, no anger or harsh words, and his... Jesus, his offer to help. A freaking rescuer.

He had no right. And if he was capable of triggering this kind of reaction in her, keeping him at bay became even more critical.

But his kiss...

43

If her life weren't so screwed up, Mary would be floating on air, drifting through a limitless cosmos with celestial music that gripped at her heartstrings and...

Bread? Sure, why not? Her impossible world included the scent of bread baking, or maybe cookies... all the things she'd dreamed of and knew she'd never have.

Because that's what Chris did to her. He made her feel special.

As if she'd come home.

Mary hurled her purse at the floor instead of placing it carefully on the table beside the front door. *Damn him, anyway.*

Nice, innocent Chris.

To her amazement, he knew his way around a woman's body. And that kiss had affected him as much as it did her. She'd felt it – and panicked. Because his undoubted physical response upped the stakes yet again.

The way he kissed and held her, using his hands to subtly explore without seeming to...

Mary stood at the door to her condo, staring at her purse where it slumped on the floor, and wondered what to do next. And how, and with what justification.

She was, in a word, terrified.

Chapter 6

Two days later, Mary stared at the phone in her hand and sank onto the couch, unsure what she thought or what to do next. The old man was dying and would probably be gone before she got to Cleveland to say goodbye. She hadn't missed the note of censure in her mother's voice at her absence from the deathbed.

Whatever, her presence was demanded. Stat.

Offhand, Mary couldn't think of anything that thrilled her less than attending her father's death and funeral. The man who'd taken his belt to her when she'd fled home from that party after enduring what she now recognized as date rape? The man who'd barely spoken ten words to her since Zach's birth and made every visit, which she only ever undertook to see Zach, into a concentration camp experience?

But she had to go, for Zach's sake. And there went her Sunday afternoon. Instead of kicking back and relaxing, maybe catching up on laundry, she'd phone clients to clear her schedule for the next week – because no force on earth could make her stay longer than that   before driving up tomorrow.

She poured a glass of wine and began phoning. Saving Chris for last.

"You just caught me," he said cheerfully. "What's up?"

His voice set off little cascades of happiness through her, but she ignored them. "Nothing good. I need to cancel for Wednesday."

He turned serious in a beat. "That's too bad. Is there anything I can do?"

"You don't even know why yet."

45

"No, but you're upset. And irritated, maybe?"

"You can't help this one, social worker. My father's dying. May be already dead, for all I know. I'm on my way to Cleveland."

"Oh, Mary." She could hear Chris swallow as he switched gears. "I'm so sorry."

"You're extrapolating from your family to mine. It's an obligation. A command performance."

"And you'll be there. I admire that. I get that there's no love lost. Let me know if there's any way I can help."

"Thanks, but I can handle it. We'll reschedule when I figure out what's happening. In the meantime, I'll pass your file to Suzanne, in case anything comes up about the condo."

"That's fine. But you take what you need, time, space, whatever."

"I always do. Have a good week."

Mary tossed her phone on the dresser and started throwing pieces of her wardrobe on her bed, trying to put together an outfit that might be acceptable to her rigid mother for a funeral.

It would be raining.

The next day, after an uncomfortable drive, Mary pulled up in front of her parents' house, dreading every moment of the upcoming few days, except for time with Zach. She hauled her rolling on-flight bag out of the trunk and dragged herself and it up the gravel driveway.

Inside, all hell was breaking loose, although it took a minute to manifest.

In the kitchen she found her Aunt Claudia – Claude – her father's sister, the woman who had given a home to a fifteen-year-old desperate for love and support. And who had taken her tiny baby Zach and carried him from Halifax to Cleveland, where he'd forever be a charity adoption, her parents' new son.

The best thing for everyone.

Sure.

46

"Darling." Claude swept up from the table, where she appeared to be brooding over a coffee, and folded her in an embrace. "Good you're here, but I've put the cat amongst the canaries, I fear. No worries, though, I'll defend you."

Claudia wore her thick gray hair pulled back in a long ponytail. A floaty, loose caftan with odd symbols printed on it – chosen to enrage her mother, if Mary guessed right – draped her lanky body. Given her aunt's unflappability, her words sent flutters of worry along Mary's nerves.

She returned the hug and nodded at the mug. "Is there more of that stuff?"

"It isn't advisable, but if you must… Your mother buys the cheapest coffee, and she actually tried to limit the number of scoops I put in the machine." Claudia pulled a mug from the cupboard and poured her a cup.

As she located milk and sugar, Mary said, "What happened, Aunt Claude?"

Her aunt hesitated long enough that she never got a chance to answer. Footsteps pounded in the hall, then Zach stormed into the kitchen. When he saw Mary his face went red, and muscles bunched around his jaw.

Her tall son had a light blond crewcut, a strong, square face, and, at the moment, a seriously pissed-off expression. A born athlete, from the time he could hold a plastic bat he'd been involved in sports. Every girl's dream, because he was also fun-loving, responsible, and polite.

Not today.

"Zach, dear…" Claude began.

He rounded on Claude. "Don't say anything. You've done enough damage."

"Hardly damage," Claude shot back. "The truth will out."

Mary got it. She sank into a chair, the coffee sloshing over her hand. "You told him."

"And you." Zach's furious gaze speared her. "You never said a damn word. You ran off to live your own fairy-tale existence and left me stuck here to deal with *them*."

His heavy sarcasm bit into her. How often since his mid-teens had she resolved to tell him? And chickened out, every time.

But Zach, unhappy? Not that she'd ever seen.

"What were you so afraid of, *Mom?*"

The disdainful emphasis on the word just about killed her.

He went to the fridge and began tossing lunch meat, cheese, tomatoes, and lettuce on the counter. "Let's keep the ball rolling, shall we? Since we're having so much *fun* here. My *grandparents* adopted me and made it into some great big secret? Whose kid am I, anyway? A teenage mom who doesn't want me and an old couple who don't even like me? What kind of a deal did you people set me up for?"

His back rigid, he slammed the fridge door, turned from them, and began making sandwiches.

"He needed to know. That woman's clueless," Claude said. Her aunt and her mother were oil and water, repellant forces.

Mary's trepidation vanished in the wake of Zach's fury, leaving her detached from the drama. She fiddled with her mug. "When did all this happen?"

"Last night," Zach said. "I went out for a while to escape the fake misery around here – as if anyone's going to miss the old man. I come home and *pow*. Right between the eyes."

"Lots of weeping and lamenting yesterday," Claude said. "From your mother, needless to say. Thank God, she's gone somewhere to make funeral arrangements."

Zach carried his sandwiches to the table, fixing a glare on her. "It's your turn," he said. "*Mom.*"

In the grip of her eerie calm, Mary laid it out. "I'm sure you've done the math by now. I got pregnant on my fifteenth birthday – and not with my willing participation. My parents blamed me and sent me off to Halifax. They intended to adopt you out."

"But my brother and his wife realized that Mary's supposed transgression meant good fortune for them," Claude put in. "They never wanted a girl, and here was a ready-made boy,"

"You were two months old when Claude brought you here. I stayed in Halifax until the start of the school year, supposedly doing a cultural exchange."

"Mary's parents completed a legal adoption— "

"And forced me to sign the papers," Mary added bitterly.

"And here we are. I'm sorry, darling," Claude said, turning to Mary. "But I couldn't stand it another minute, with that woman ranting at Zach about not showing proper respect and expecting weeping and wailing and gnashing of teeth. The mismatch was simply too great."

Zach's cold gaze stayed on her. "You might have told me. You might have got me out of this dump."

"Legally, they're your parents," Mary said.

"Legally, I can vote," he pointed out. "I can join the military and go off to defend my country. How am I not old enough to be told the truth about my gene pool? Are you ashamed of me, *Mom?*"

Again that heavy, sarcastic emphasis.

She straightened, took a deep swig of the appalling coffee, and looked him in the eye. "I've never been ashamed of you. They made it my fault, but—"

Her mother crashed through the back door. She'd aged since Mary's last visit in the spring. Thin, graying hair hung around her gaunt face. "I always knew you'd add lying to your transgressions," she said, her bloodshot eyes radiating hostility.

"Nice to see you too, Mom," Mary replied.

"Betty, settle down," Claude said. "We're talking this through."

"It sounds more like you're speaking ill of Herbert and me, and him so recently gone." Mary could see spit pooling at the corners of her mother's mouth as she hurled the words into the room.

Mary clung to her sense of calm. "For the record," she said to Zach, "when I came home from that party in tears because I'd been raped, my mother gave me a lecture fit to curl

49

my hair, then my father took a belt to me. They'll never believe it wasn't my fault."

"Peace, everyone," Claude said. "This isn't solving anything."

"There's nothing to solve." Not surprising for a man still in his teens, Zach's primary focus had shifted from his family to his sandwich. He took a giant bite, then spoke around it. "You all lied to me. Fact."

"Not complete facts," Mary said.

"No?" Zach had inherited her eyes, blue but with streaks in them that tipped them closer to aqua in certain lights. Not today, though. Today they were arctic ice.

But he wasn't done. "And what else is there? You gave me up." He swallowed and stabbed a finger at Mary. "And you tried to make me into something I'm not," he said to her – their – mother, who stood quivering by the door. "You never liked or approved of me." He wheeled back to Mary. "While you waltzed away into your own world, leaving me stuck here."

"Until you came of age, I had no choice."

"You damn well let it happen in the first place."

Mary had heard enough. "Zach, I was fifteen. *Fifteen.* Remember fifteen? Do you really think I had any control over my life?"

That silenced him. After a pause in which no one moved, he scooped up his remaining sandwich and stalked off.

"You're not welcome in my home," her mother said to Claude.

"And miss the fun?" Claude dismissed the statement with a limp wave of her hand. "Mary, perhaps we should go somewhere else to catch up. Is there a Coffee Shack anywhere near this godforsaken place?"

"A ten-minute drive." She stood and scooped up her purse.

"I'm with you. Come on, darling." Claude swooped them out of the kitchen with a swirl of her mystical symbols. Mary found herself dashing through the rain to her car to drive her aunt to the Coffee Shack, leaving her termagant of a mother standing at the back door.

Mary collapsed into the hard chair at the Coffee Shack while her aunt got them each a decent coffee. Nothing fancy, no lattes for Claude, just straight, basic drip. She shoved a mug across the table. "Drink this. We're both going to need fortification before this funeral's over."

"Will he ever stop blaming me?" Mary blurted out the first thing that came into her mind, to the only person in her family she'd trust with the question.

"I think you got through to him. No one's in control at fifteen. Was Zach?"

Mary shrugged. "Mostly he lived in his room with the music turned up. Drove the folks crazy. I figured it was standard teenage defiance. I didn't know he wasn't happy. He seemed okay, and they doted on him…"

"Knowing my brother and that shrew of a wife of his, I'd say they put on a show for you. How superior Zach is compared to you."

"I'm not sure I'll ever be able to face him again." Mary ignored the coffee – she'd never liked the stuff black, and the thought of drinking the bitter liquid curdled her stomach – and buried her face in her hands.

"No dramatics, missy." Claude sighed in resignation, then stood, claimed Mary's cup, and carried it to the milk-and-sugar station. When she returned, the drink was half milk.

Mary pushed her hair out of the way and took a cautious sip.

Sweetened. Thank God.

"I can't help it. When I'm here it's as if I'm fifteen all over again."

"Happens to everyone," Claude said cheerfully.

A baritone voice spoke from behind her. "There you are."

Mary looked up. Her heart made a painful shimmy. "Zach. We were talking—"

51

"About me, I assume." He shrugged out of his wet anorak, hooked another chair from an adjacent table with his foot, pulled it over, and settled into it. "I guess I ought to tell you, fifteen's when I tried shoplifting. I got away with it, but *they* overheard me boasting. He never dared to hit me after that."

"A good age to rebel," Claude commented.

Mary felt anger sizzling up from a place near her appendix. "I never broke the rules." She snorted. "The original good girl. It was a date rape, Zach."

"That's not what *she* says."

"She never believed me. She always figured I'd led him on, based mainly on the fact that the hem of my skirt hit above mid-knee. They concluded I must be a slut."

"Were you? A slut?" Zach's question didn't carry any offense, and he had a little trouble getting out the last word, as if it embarrassed him.

"No. I was a total innocent who got in over her head."

"I hate that morality thing of theirs. All that yelling. Makes me want to go out and do what they tell me not to."

"I hated it, too, but I reacted by shriveling in a corner. The party on my fifteenth birthday was almost the first one I'd ever been invited to. They only let me go because the minister's son hosted it. I didn't even realize the punch was spiked."

Newly minted mother and son stared at each other. Mary hoped Zach could tell she was leveling with him, but she wouldn't let herself be optimistic about it. Fifteen was a bitch, true, but at nineteen you know everything, and uncomfortable facts be damned.

But maybe he believed her. He didn't seem as angry as before.

Maybe.

He turned to Claude. "She asked me to be a pallbearer. I said no. I suppose you're going to tell me I should do it."

"Frankly," Claude said around sips of her black coffee, "I couldn't care less whether you tote my brother to his final rest. You're grown up. Make your own decision."

"It might be best to give in."

"It's possible she's actually mourning, you know," Claude said. "But whatever you want." She used the same tone that Mary remembered from those months in Halifax. Calm, wise, supportive.

Mary set down her empty mug. Funny how things seemed easier to face after a decent cup of coffee. "I'm tired. I want to take a shower, then lock myself in my room and unwind."

Zach got to his feet, returned the chair to the other table with an easy, one-handed movement, and said, "See you later. Is either of you a good cook?"

Mary shrugged. Claude laughed. "Probably better than what you live with," she said. "I'll walk you to your car."

"I cycled."

"Whatever. It's irrelevant." The older woman stood in a flurry of bright robes and odd symbols, wrapped a hand around Zach's forearm, said, "Wait for me," to Mary, and sashayed out of the Coffee Shack.

Despite her upset, Mary couldn't help but notice the eyes following her flamboyant aunt as they left. She also noticed that her son hadn't said goodbye to her.

Later that day Mary caught Claude on her way out the door. Claude had been uncommunicative during the drive home from the Coffee Shack, and Mary figured she had a right to know what passed between her aunt and the young man who had now been outed as her son.

"Where are you off to?"

"Anywhere but here," Claude snorted. "This place is a mausoleum with your mother looking for ways to assign blame."

"I'm with you. I want answers, Aunt Claude."

"You're entitled. Come on, let's get while the getting's good."

The rain had let up. Dodging puddles on the aging sidewalk, Mary asked, "What did you say to Zach?"

53

Claude wore hiking shorts instead of her swirly dress, revealing impressive calf muscles. Mary was already struggling to keep up with her aunt's pace. After a minute Claude said, "I wanted to be sure he understood that you're not responsible. You were even more an innocent victim than him, because being a guy he's had more resources. They didn't turn their overbearing morality on him until he hit his teens and started to show an independent streak. Two neat, well-behaved kids, but were they happy with that?"

"Aw." Mary squeezed her aunt's hand – although she had to hustle a step to catch up with her first. Claude walked at a pace suited for power walkers. "That's sweet."

"Believe me, there are days I wish I'd kept him in Halifax. Or both of you."

"Makes me wonder how life might have been different."

"You've done okay. Calter Creek sounds like a good place to live."

"It is. There's a small town vibe, but it's big enough to have the schools and hospitals and such, and Columbus next door."

"I'd like to think that you'll get to know each other, now that the dam's burst."

"I hope so. Right before Dad died, Zach sent me an email. He wants – wanted – to stay with me for a couple of years while he's at Ohio State."

"Perfect. Give you two a chance to reset the clock. You would have done okay as a mother, Mary. You were young, but you're strong."

"It's up to Zach now, I guess."

"Trust yourself. Make it clear he's welcome. That you're willing to sort it out."

Mary walked on in silence. She doubted both Claude's assessment and the advisability of Zach's entering her world, however much she longed for it and would let it happen if that's how the cards fell. She'd forged a career, but look at the rest of her life. Not that there was much. Since the early days in Calter Creek, when it had been as if she'd set out to prove her parents right, she'd become so self-contained that no one got through her defenses.

There hadn't been a man in her life at all in five years, and that hadn't been serious. So where did the fun come from now? Short answer, it didn't, at least where men were concerned.

Except for Chris. Chris was fun. And that kiss…

But dammit, a social worker? Come on.

Chapter 7

Few things elevated Chris's spirits, or calmed him, as successfully as driving up to the classic white clapboard church beside an old but lovingly tended cemetery. Northwest of town, the building once had been a Methodist church and was now home of the Calter Creek Renewed Life Center, his spiritual community. Inside, the simple sanctuary resonated with eighty-plus years of worship. However often he reminded himself that it was only a building, it fed something in his spirit.

He needed ballast, and he was sure of finding it here. Mary's phone call the day before, the hint of dread in her voice, had rattled him. He wasn't happy with her on the road alone between here and Cleveland, not to mention facing whatever demons awaited her there.

And it mattered, on a personal level. That was the true source of his unease.

The offices were in the basement, adjacent to the fellowship room. He parked and entered by a side door. As he'd hoped, Rodney Bradshaw, his boss and mentor, sat hunched behind the desk in his cubbyhole of an office. Chris admired and respected the elderly man who was senior minister to their congregation, whose place he would take some time in the next few years. Both Bradshaws had been like parents to him since he'd arrived; he loved and trusted them.

"Rodney, got a minute?"

Rod looked up and smiled. "Come on in. Coffee?" He put down his pen. Rod never wrote his lessons on his computer, explaining that he connected to his ideas better through pen and paper. Chris didn't get it, but figured it was generational. To each his own.

"Not for me, thanks. I've hit my limit." He dropped into a guest chair. This chair and he were old friends. He'd spent hours here, especially when he was still getting his ministerial feet wet. Even now, whenever he needed to sort something out in his mind he counted on Rod for a sympathetic ear and worthwhile advice.

"I hear you lost one of your seniors," Rod said.

Chris plucked a pen from the desk, shifted it from one hand to the other. "Not unexpected, but it's hard. Herb turned up for the singalongs, always chatted up the women. He'll be missed."

"Are you taking the service?"

"No. He belonged to a congregation downtown, so the family wants their own minister." Chris slouched back in his chair, a casual posture that Rod had plenty of experience seeing right through.

"So that's not what's bothering you."

"Wish it were that simple." He hesitated, because this was treading into territory more personal than anything he'd brought to Rod in the two years he'd been at the Renewed Life Center.

"Easiest to just say it."

You're here for a reason. Spill it.

"Okay. I met someone."

The corners of Rod's mouth twitched, but he kept his face serene. "And?"

"Suppose I were to have an affair."

Rod studied him with his faded blue eyes in their nest of wrinkles. Chris met his gaze.

"You care about her?"

"This wouldn't even be a question if I didn't. And nothing's imminent. I'm in the realm of supposition."

"Officially there wouldn't be any censure, you know that. All the Center asks of us is to be discreet and maintain the highest standards of probity. As I'm sure you do."

"Yes, or at least I try to. That's not what I'm asking."

"Then what are you asking, Chris?"

He'd considered this, wanting to get the words right. "For openers, what would the parish say?"

"None of their business," Rod said comfortably.

Chris grinned. "And you believe that's sufficient to stop the talk?"

"Most of them accept that we're human, and given how desperate they are to see you paired up, I expect we'd hear hosannas, not condemnation."

"So, I should discount that particular worry."

"Be aware of it and behave with scrupulous honor. I assume she's not a member of our congregation."

Chris smiled. "No. Probably never will be, no matter what happens." He gave himself a minute, which Rod didn't interrupt. "I guess I'm worried about the potential for harm, if it doesn't work out. Nothing like this has come up before, not since I started seminary. I'm trapped between being a minister and being human. It leaves me a little off base."

"Falling in love can do that."

"Yeah." Had he? Fallen in love? He admitted to obsession. Whether that might lead to love... Chris ran his hands over the battered arms of the chair, as if by smoothing the wood he could smooth his thoughts as well. "But what if I've misinterpreted this? What if it's just sex? It's been a hell of a long time. I may be reading things all wrong."

Rod ignored his language, as usual. "You've surely desired women before this."

"Women, sure. Never a specific woman."

"I have to assume you won't act until you're certain. You don't get a pass on that one."

Chris shook his head. "That's not the issue, either." He paused, thinking, then huffed air out through his nostrils. "Love and lust," he said reflectively. "I suspect it'll end up being both. Maybe that's why I'm worried."

"Harm happens. Pain happens, and not only for her."

"That worries me, too."

"We rarely intend it, but that's the reality."

"She's carrying a load of some kind, but we aren't at a point where I can ask her about it. I don't think she's led a very saintly life."

"Would you want a partner who has? I know you, Chris. You'd be bored within a month."

"Who, me? Mister nice guy?"

Both men chuckled. Rod knew his history and fully appreciated why Chris's current 'nice' reputation drove him a little crazy.

"So, what is it I'm supposed to say here?" Rod always prodded him, forcing him to answer his own questions.

Chris's grin widened. "How about, be honest, take it slow until I'm sure that it's more than sex. In this case, that'll be a challenge." The memory of kissing Mary zinged through him.

"And if it does turn out to be only sex?"

Chis shrugged. "Hands off." He'd dealt with his own needs for years, since he first started training. At the thought of his occasional relief in the shower, he felt the heat rise up his throat to his face. He'd give a lot not to blush so easily. He must have blushed a thousand times in this office.

Rod nodded. "Treat her honorably. That's the most any of us can do."

"I hope it'll be enough."

"Which leads to another interesting point. Have you told her yet?"

Rod was well aware of his reluctance to admit to his vocation when confronted with an attractive woman who might – just might – be interested. Because it was a bone of contention between them, the blush, which had been cooling, now flared. "I haven't exactly told her, no. She thinks I'm a social worker."

Rod said nothing, merely steepled his fingers in front of his face and looked over them.

"You know why," Chris stumbled on. "I want half a chance before… well, before I throw that into the mix."

"Coward." He heard the affection in Rod's voice, but also the criticism.

"It's not as if I'm ashamed. People make assumptions."

"And?"

"You think I should tell her."

"It won't get easier or go over any better if you wait."

"I know. It's a dilemma."

Rod shuffled the papers on his desk into a pile and clicked his pen closed, a sure sign the conversation was at an end. "Come for supper. Sadie's been complaining we never see you."

"I'd love to. I'll give her a call to arrange a day." No point referring practical matters like dinner scheduling to the minister. It was his wife who ran both their household and the parish.

Rodney stood and circled the desk while Chris got to his feet, and the two men embraced. "Be safe, son,"

"You too."

Chris left, aware that he hadn't learned anything new, but that by laying the issue out before Rod he'd become clear in his own mind about Mary, making love to Mary, drawing Mary into his life.

As for telling her the truth about his calling... that required more consideration.

The next Thursday, Mary shut herself in her childhood room at her mother's house. Her plan: to set up appointments with her clients for the next week. She hoped that if she anchored herself in something normal and concrete, she might survive another day of her family.

Over the last three days she'd avoided her mother, sat stoically through the funeral, hung out with Claude whenever possible, and watched Zach. Watched, and waited. But it appeared her son had no intention of discussing his mixed-up parentage further, or of having anything to do with her beyond polite, pass-the-salt-please conversation.

She didn't blame him. She had been pretty badly screwed up at nineteen, Zach's age. Having acquired a truer picture of his life with her parents, she conceded her kid was probably a mess.

Claude was leaving for Halifax Friday morning, breaking up their little party. Mary planned to tough it out until Saturday but might flee before then. Being in this depressing house with her mother, even for Zach's sake, threatened to drive her to drink.

Not that drink was an option. Not here. No point adding fuel to her surviving parent's bitterness.

Halfway down her need-to-phone list was Chris, and the old condo he loved so much. She tapped in the number, then ended the call before it could ring. Chris... Holy Hannah. She'd been absorbed in family drama since the weekend, but now, faced with the reality of next week, how did she plan to play this?

What did he think he was doing kissing her?

What possessed her to haul off and slap him?

She hadn't forgotten the kiss or the slap, but had been forced to set the memory aside while she grappled with her dysfunctional family. With the phone in her hand and the probability of Chris on the other end, it roared back with a vengeance.

It wasn't only the kiss. It was how decent he'd been that horrible Saturday morning after she'd puked her guts out the night before. It was his quirky sense of humor, how comfortable and right it felt to relax with him at Joe's. She tossed the phone on her single bed. How was she supposed to conduct a calm, businesslike viewing of a condo in an old building that even she admitted had charm oozing out of its non-parallel walls and cracked ceilings, when Chris raised every red flag imaginable?

Chris of the hot kisses. As if she needed to remind herself.

Calling him to arrange an appointment opened a minefield of all that could go wrong, or right depending on your perspective. Really, she should pass his account over to Suzanne.

Not going to happen.

She focused firmly on the task at hand, punched in the number, and managed to swallow the lump blocking her throat before he answered.

"Hi, Chris. Mary. I'll be back in town soon. Are you free Monday?"

"Mary. How are you?" His voice conveyed both pleasure at hearing from her and concern for her well-being.

"Fine, thanks. Looking forward to getting home. Monday morning work for you?" If her voice held an element of brusqueness, well, she couldn't help it.

"Sure. What time?"

"I can meet you at the office at nine thirty."

"Okay, great. We can do all the checking you think we need to, then sign the offer and go for a celebratory lunch."

No! No more meals, no more kisses, no, no, no.

"Sorry, I won't have time for lunch. It's going to be a busy day. See you Monday."

She ended the call before he could answer and huffed out a breath. Done. Without giving him a chance to say anything skirting the personal.

A relief? Sort of. But business or no, his voice had been right there in the room with her. Cheerful, kind, lyrical –

Lyrical? Seriously?

She completed the calls on her list, then returned to the kitchen. The war might swirl around her, but that didn't mean they couldn't eat a halfway decent supper.

Mary dreamed that night, and her dream revolved around a nice man. Who kissed her, and then did other nice things with skill and determination, things that involved getting naked and…

And then something crashed in the kitchen and it was morning and she woke up, sweaty and horny and more confused than ever.

By Friday afternoon Mary couldn't stand life in her mother's house another minute and failed to come up with a good reason to try. Zach had disappeared into his own world of sports and friends, so she seldom saw him. And when he was around, he radiated an impenetrable aloofness. Her mother's fumbling attempts to be nice had ended in vitriol about Mary's ruining their lives and how they'd always known she'd come to a bad end.

So, she left.

One day, Mary thought as she navigated back to Calter Creek, she'd figure out just what had convinced her parents of her unremitting badness. She remembered being a timid teenager without friends, who wanted desperately to be accepted. She'd been effectively abandoned by those who were supposed to love her.

Well, it all happened a long time ago. Zach knew the truth, and surely some good would come of that.

And now she had this chance to get to know him, assuming he still planned to crash with her while he attended OSU.

Friday evening, she lounged around her condo, catching up on laundry, determinedly not thinking about her parents, Zach, or Chris. A tall order, especially since she didn't really have that much to do. But being in her own space, in the quiet of her home without either hostile or seductive voices bombarding her, was its own kind of heaven.

Saturday, she put in a shift at the office, covering walk-in inquiries and reviewing changes to Calter Creek's housing market over the last week. Normal was good.

Very good, she mused as she worked her way through the weekend, showing houses to a couple with a pair of obnoxious, bored kids, eating alone at her own table, sleeping alone in her own bed...

Very good, until Monday when Chris arrived at her desk, right on time for their walk-through of the condo. Then, out of the blue, a supersonic missile crashed through the roof and lodged behind her breastbone, and gremlins invaded her voice box, leaving her with an uneasy premonition that her reputation as a calm, detached real estate agent was about to be shot to smithereens.

Chapter 8

"I've driven by this place daily," Chris said as Mary pulled up in front of the old mansion, "and checked the online listing more often than that. Nervous wreck, expecting someone else to snap it up."

"I couldn't help being out of town." After saying virtually nothing on the drive, Mary's voice was pitched to put distance between them, as if he'd insulted her. "And I did arrange with Suzanne to keep an eye on things. She would have been in touch with you if there was any urgency."

He had the car door open before she disengaged her seat belt. "Just telling you I'm keen," he said over his shoulder as he climbed out of her sedan.

She caught up with him, and they approached the house together along the long driveway. "Brace yourself," she retorted. "This time, with luck, you'll be aware of the flaws you missed before. While it's not quite a dump, it's going to take some serious attention to bring it up to date."

"Probably." He knew he sounded cheerful out of all proportion to the actuality of the place, but at that moment the prospect of refinishing walls, laying flooring, the things a man did when he owned a home, filled his head. In a pinch he could get in touch with his brother for advice, but Barry and he orbited different suns; his brother would laugh until the cracked ceiling fell down when he learned of Chris's reno plans.

He spent the next hour happily wandering around the sprawling condo with the wonky layout. Mary, he noted, failed to share his enthusiasm. She made the right comments, followed him with a notepad and pen, and pointed out every flaw she spotted, but he got the definite vibe that she'd rather be anywhere else. He worried he'd caused it himself with that totally inappropriate – and totally hot – kiss. The impulse to kiss her had escaped from his brain to his hands and mouth before he had a chance to capture it and stomp it down, something that had never, ever, happened before.

Not only hands and mouth, either. Which she was well aware of; he was sure of it.

Still, done was done. He couldn't call the kiss back, even if he wanted to. And at the moment he needed to forget that Mary was a female person, because the condo, in his eyes, cried out to be loved and pampered and turned into a home, and being here alone with her... talk about distracting.

Mind on business, kid.

Great. Now he was channeling his brother. Barry was the only person who ever called him kid.

Their last stop was the door to the back yard, at the end of a hall that shot out from the living room, with kitchen and one bedroom on the right side, bath, storage closet, and second bedroom on the left. The hall itself was utterly featureless, other than doors. "Not much you can do with this," Mary said as she watched him struggle with the recalcitrant lock. The back door was out of alignment, so even when he conquered the mechanism it didn't want to open.

"Good for the muscles?" he asked. "If you're planning to sit around all afternoon out here in the cool, laughing at the poor jerks in their airless, balcony-less places, escaping to the outside counts as exercise."

He almost got a laugh out of her. Almost. He tried a hard yank with upward lift and the door popped open.

"Come on." He stepped from the concrete stoop down onto the patio, and from there wandered out into the yard. Trees and shaggy hedges defended the property line, fronted by flower beds hosting weeds among tired-looking flowering plants – perennials? He had a lot to learn.

Mary followed him and looked around. "This could be great," she said, making it sound like a concession, "but not enough reason to buy the place. We need to go over the list. Estimate what it'll cost to fix it up. It might prove to be a money pit."

"It's livable now. A little at a time." He glanced at her face, tight-lipped and serious, and changed his mind. "Okay, tell me what worries you. I'm going to buy it anyway, but you're welcome to try to warn me off."

She heaved a loud, frustrated sigh, and settled on the stoop, tucking her legs demurely to the side. "Here goes."

As he settled next to her, he was aware – as he shouldn't be – of positively itching to lay her down in the soft grass and kiss her senseless.

She launched into her diatribe. "Wiring's sound, according to the listing, but inadequate. You'll be running extension cords everywhere. Speaking of which, there's only one cable outlet, in the large bedroom. Kitchen and bath, hopelessly outdated. Poor quality bathroom fixtures, as evidenced by the way the enamel's chipping in the tub. Lighting, appalling and old-fashioned. Cracks in the ceilings in living room and kitchen, and the start of one in the bedroom. Floors… no point going there. They might come up nicely if you sand and varnish them, but they'll never be level so you may be better off replacing them. Good news is that there's a market for old flooring, so you could recoup some of your investment. Walls need stripping, then deal with whatever's underneath. The original walls are plaster, not drywall, so they'll be a bitch to work with, not to mention the hundred years of wallpaper underneath the paint. The new ones… well, let's say they did the finishing to minimum specs. You can see the taping and mudding."

She stopped to take a breath; she'd been talking rapid-fire, as if to emphasize the impossible state of the condo. "Do I need to say any more?"

"What's urgent?" Chris figured nothing was. He'd tested the shower, which flowed fine, so he could live with the bathtub. The kitchen, while outdated, was functional as long as he avoided the peeling laminate countertop. As for the bedrooms, the master looked out on both the side and back gardens, promising a great breeze on hot nights.

Mary took a minute, making marks next to the items on her list. "In priority order, I'd deal with electrical. More outlets, and new overhead fixtures, to be sure you can actually see when winter comes. Probably means ripping out some walls, but given the state of them, that might not be a bad idea. Then kitchen and bath, especially that kitchen counter. They scream for updating."

"What about the fireplace? Do you suppose it works?"

"It's supposed to. There's no smoke staining, but who knows how much use it's had? I'd get it cleaned."

"Add that to the list, then. Want to ballpark the outlay?"

Mary shot him a look of pure exasperation. "I'm no builder, Chris. I sell real estate. If this worries you, get a contractor in."

"Oh, I'm not that worried. I'm content to play it as it comes." Sitting beside her on a beautiful summer afternoon, looking out over the soon-to-be-his backyard, felt so right that he once again draped a loose arm around her shoulders.

Mary tensed but didn't move away, although she knew she ought to. Something threatening was going on here, something she hadn't bargained on. His arm didn't pin her down, force her into anything or even imply anything. It simply felt... right.

Like friends, she assured herself, and sighed. "You're determined to buy this place. I'd hoped to discourage you, because it's a lot to bite off. But there are a couple of agents' cards on the kitchen counter, so if you're serious we'd better make an offer soon."

"Want to hear my vision?" He didn't wait for her to acknowledge the question. "I'm thinking about my seniors. Even the dreaded Nadine," he added with a grin, glancing at her. "I'll build a ramp to cover the stoop and improve access around the outside of the building. Too many of them don't get much chance to be outdoors, never mind a backyard like this one. We can set up tables, serve afternoon tea. And something in the

67

autumn, with pumpkins. I reckon twenty people, half of them in wheelchairs."

Oddly, she could imagine it. "Nice dream. Who's Nadine?"

He turned pink. She wondered what there was to blush about. Nadine, senior cougar?

But his smile was amusement more than embarrassment. "Nadine's the head of the find-Chris-a-woman brigade. They canvass their friends, family members, the staff. At the first hint there might be someone wearing skirts in my life, she announces it to the world. 'Nookie,' she'll say. 'Our boy's getting him some'. Happened in spades the day we had donuts. All I have to do is be late on a Saturday morning and they're on it."

"That's kind of sweet. They must care about you."

"I think they do. Family visits are in short supply for a lot of them, so I'm the son or grandson who never drops by. I don't mind."

She settled into the vision. "Not only seniors, though," she said. "You could entertain."

"Invite friends for a barbecue, hang out. And indoors... I hope the fireplace works. Sitting around with that magnificent window, watching the snow..."

"Dreamer."

"It's good to have dreams."

A vision. Not a throwaway man, a keeper.

Admit it. You like him.

Going nowhere.

And why not?

Simple. Because years of experience had taught her not to trust men, any men, even a seemingly sincere man like Chris. Next thing she knew, he'd either leave or start trying to change her, remake her into his own image of the ideal woman.

Besides, there was Zach.

She shrugged out from under his arm and organized the papers on her clipboard, a sure sign she was done with this conversation.

❖

68

All business, Chris thought. Fair enough. "I'm buying it, Mary."

"All right, you're the client. Let's go to the office—"

Except... He grabbed her hand and interrupted her attempt to rise to her feet. "Hang on a minute."

No point giving her time to back away. Twisting sideways on a concrete stoop wasn't his favorite way to make out with a beautiful woman, but he'd take it. Unless he somehow got her horizontal...

Don't go there.

His vocation. He'd never regretted it more. In fact, he'd never regretted it at all.

Her clipboard slid from her grip; he heard it hit the patio, followed by her pen. As he'd hoped, her freed hands found their way to his back. He pulled her closer and intensified the kiss, deeper, tongues tangling, no time or space to breathe. His arms locked her as close against him as she could get, given their awkward side-by-side sitting position on the stoop.

Nirvana.

Mary created space between them, smacked a hand on his chest, and pushed. Hard. Either she'd run out of oxygen first or she'd returned to her senses. He hoped it was the oxygen; both of them seemed to be temporarily short. Her breathing was as labored as his.

"You were saying about the office?" he asked.

He didn't get the laugh he wanted this time. Instead, she snatched up her clipboard and pen and fled into the apartment.

Chris followed, pausing only to give the door a vigorous shove back into its frame and throw the lock... and think hard about baseball stats, car engines, anything but what had just happened, giving his body a chance to cool down. "Hey," he called out to her. "Wait."

"Are you coming with me?" She stood by the front door, all but tapping her foot. "It's under a mile into town if you'd rather walk, but I'm leaving. Now."

"Then so am I." He took a last look around, regretful because he'd willingly have lingered in this space for hours more, then followed her out the door and to her car.

The drive to the real estate office gave Chris plenty of time to wonder what had seized him. In his wildest days – heck, in his wildest daydreams – he'd never behaved like this, and now… every move she made told him she was unavailable. Except when they kissed.

Besides, when she learned his true vocation, she'd bolt. Guaranteed.

For the moment, she wasn't talking, but her knuckles were white as she gripped the steering wheel tighter than warranted by the five-minute cruise downtown.

Unfortunately, pulling into the parking lot behind her office triggered a memory of that first kiss, every bit as tantalizing as the more recent one.

Are you a kid who's never kissed a girl before? What's the big deal?

He didn't have a clue. His only certainty was the chemistry between them, that they both knew it and she was fighting it, so far successfully.

And he was about to buy a condo, if the Good Lord's willing and the creek don't rise.

Great. Now you're quoting your mother.

Between them they managed to fill out an Offer to Purchase form without once touching or meeting eyes. In Chris's business, this would count as a rarity. In Mary's, who knew? He suspected intimacy didn't rank high on her priority list.

Chris left the office with a copy of the offer, a promise she'd be in touch within twenty-four hours, and a regret that he'd be going home alone. Again.

Way of life.

He cheered himself up by thinking that soon the trip home would take him to a quirky condo surrounded by shrubs and trees.

❖

70

Abby phoned that evening. Chris considered not answering. Then he accepted the inevitable, namely that his sister wouldn't give up until she possessed all the facts anyway, so why not now. She might even dole out some useful advice.

"Hi, sis."

"Baby brother. Long silence. How are you?" He could almost see Abby settling in a chair at the other end, twiddling an end of her wavy, brownish hair and waiting for whatever confession or confusion he presented her with. In another day and age, not to mention an alternate universe, she would have sat in a little box listening to lisping confessions through a grille and dispensing absolutions and penances right and left. She'd missed her calling.

"Good. Everyone okay there?" He used his hearty voice.

It didn't work. "What's wrong?"

"Nothing, nothing at all." He paused, seeking the right gambit to get Abby off his case. "Tell me about Doug and the kids."

"Doug's putting on weight. Ben's my height and Ashley's a princess. Come visit."

"How about over Independence Day? Rod's got the service that weekend."

"Perfect." There was an ominous pause. "Spill, brother."

He hedged. "Well, I'm about to buy a condo, I hope. Old building, lawns. It's pretty run down, but there's a charm about it."

"Spare bedroom?"

"Of course. May double as an office."

"Who is she, Chris?"

He sighed and gave the silence a chance to take root. He knew better than to think he'd bamboozle Abby. "Her name's Mary. She's a real estate agent."

"Ah. She showed you the condo. That's kinda romantic."

"I picked her up in a bar, actually."

71

Now it was her turn to be silent. Finally, she said, with a hint of disapproval, "You're not supposed to be hanging out in bars."

He shrugged, although she couldn't see it. "I know the owner. There's no rule against stopping in for a beer."

"Really?"

"For heaven's sake, Abby. They treat us like grownups these days."

"Sorry, soothe your feathers. What else?"

"Long, dark hair, blue eyes like the ocean."

"Hot?"

"Naturally. When did I ever go for frumpy?"

Abby snorted. "I haven't been too sure lately. All that sanctity."

"Oh, come on. You never get any sanctity from me. That's not how it is."

"How it is, brother, you're suffering from a serious lack of social life. Are you sleeping with her?"

"Can we leave it that I want to?"

"You don't sound quite on top of this relationship," she said carefully. "She may not be interested."

"So far she is."

There was the kind of pause Chris had come to dread, because it meant Abby was putting the pieces together. "You haven't told her, have you?"

He hesitated. "Only that I work with kids and seniors." Even he picked up on the defensiveness in his voice.

"So, you're going to tumble her, then say, by the way, I'm a minister? Bad plan, brother."

Nothing like having your thoughts echoed by your big sister. "Believe me, I know."

"Can't wait to hear about her first church social. Anyway, are you even allowed to have affairs? Would they kick you out of your pulpit if you did?"

Chris capitulated. "Yes, I'm allowed, if it's serious, and no, they wouldn't. But I'm in a no-win situation, Abby. I can't figure out how to tell her, and I keep putting it off because it's so damn fine to kiss her, and—"

"And you're toast. You know that, right?"

"Yeah," he said glumly. "Totally screwed."

"Hey, have hope." His despair seemed to brighten up his sister. "Maybe she's hiding deep dark secrets of her own."

"There's something she isn't saying, so it's possible. But I'm not holding my breath."

"Come for a visit. You need perspective, and the kids would love to see you. Seems you're Ashley's favorite teddy bear."

He groaned. "That is so unfair. Why can't I be dangerous, like Barry?"

"Because Barry's not a nice guy. You are. One day you'll find a woman who'll appreciate the fact."

That wasn't the problem, he thought glumly as he hung up. He'd already found the woman. A woman with a hidden gentleness protected by barriers a mile high.

Chapter 9

Zach had sent her a brief email, so Mary knew to expect a weekend visit sometime on the Friday following Independence Day. It would be the first time he'd come to Calter Creek, the first time he'd set foot in her domain.

Worrying about this visit for the last two days meant that it hadn't been a fun week. The shift in the relationship, and hence in the power balance, left her unsteady. Because right now the son held all the cards, the mother none. And this time she couldn't turn to Mel or Bryony, much less Chris. Because they didn't know.

What did Chris have to do with anything?

As she waited for Zach to arrive Friday afternoon, she cursed herself for a fool. Why hadn't she told anyone? Even ten years ago it wouldn't have seemed like that big a deal. But keeping it a secret until she was thirty-four implied she was embarrassed, ashamed of having her son. And now just look at him, someone to be proud of, to strut and show pictures of, to brag about. She'd cut herself off from everything he might have offered to make her life richer.

When the doorbell finally rang, she jumped a foot.

Zach was unsmiling as he stood there in her doorway, duffel bag in hand and not in the least happy to be there. She stepped aside; he strode in. Neither of them had said a word.

"So, you still plan to stay here for school," Mary said after he'd dropped the bag on the bed in her spare room.

"I can't afford anything else. I just know I need to get out of there before I go out of my mind."

Their eyes met, briefly. They both knew where 'there' was.

"It'll be tight, but we'll figure it out. I just wasn't sure…"

"Whether being my mother as well as my sister makes any difference? What did you expect? I don't even know who you are anymore."

"You never did," Mary said sadly. "And that cuts both ways. We're strangers. The most we share is that we've both survived life in our parents' house."

"Yeah, tell me about it. I don't have any intention of letting their constant criticism hold me back."

"What do you intend, Zach?" Mary went into her kitchen and poured them each a glass of tea. At least she'd learned that much about her son. Apart from his appetite, he drank prodigious amounts of iced tea.

"You really want to know?"

"Yes, I do. All I've heard is sports so far. But where's it taking you?"

He settled at her dining table and finally seemed to relax. "Sport management, but it's a master's program, so there's still a lot of school to go. I'd thought sport medicine, but science isn't really my thing. I'm not sure if I should do a physical education degree or a business degree first. A business background might make the master's degree more manageable."

"Which do you want to do? Are there prerequisites?"

"I'd sure as heck rather not spend two years in business courses when I could be out playing baseball. I've enrolled in the Sport Industry program, but I could switch, I guess. If it makes more sense."

"I expect it's worth talking to a faculty advisor, sooner rather than later."

"Yeah, Mary. I'm not dumb."

He'd called her Mary, not Mom.

She looked across the table at her son and suddenly saw the vulnerable kid underneath the cocky college student. Zach was only nineteen. Life at the university wouldn't be anything like the community college he'd attended. He was about to get a lesson in growing up.

And she'd be the mother who helped him along, if he'd let her. The whole thing felt as alien to her as it must to him.

"How'd you feel about going over to OSU?" Zach said. "Tomorrow, maybe? Look over the campus, get an idea of what's where."

"I'm showing a house in the morning. We could leave right after lunch."

"Sounds good. I'm going out." Zach stood abruptly and carried his glass to the kitchen.

"I'm not sure what's available for—" She bit her tongue. She'd almost called him a kid. "I mean, you're still underage for the clubs."

"You don't need to remind me. Don't worry, I've done some research. Do I get a key?"

"Of course." She'd had shiny new ones cut the day he sent the email saying he wanted to stay with her. Since then she'd been holding her breath, hoping to have a use for them. She went to her room and came out with the keys on her palm. "Square one's downstairs, curvy one's the condo. Make this your home, Zach. I'm glad you're here."

He gave her a terse nod and wheeled toward the door. She watched her golden son leave and sighed, as only a mother, even an absentee mother, even a too-young mother, can.

As the door closed behind his broad back, Mary collapsed in a chair, well aware that her carefully cultivated way of life was a thing of the past. For Zach, the prospect of OSU had to be more intimidating than he'd let on. He might be from Cleveland, but they'd grown up in the outer suburbs, and she doubted he'd spent much time in the city. He wasn't as worldly as he wanted everyone to believe.

Typical guy. Mary thought about the upcoming two years and wondered how many challenges lay ahead of them.

Easier than thinking about the next month or so, and how she was going to explain this hunk of a son to her friends in Calter Creek. And how she would ever, ever, explain to her son that she'd never told anyone of his existence.

❖

With a mind entangled in thoughts of Mary and his new condo, Chris's Saturday morning at Silver Threads provided a respite of sorts, although he'd never consider his group of feisty seniors restful. He ducked Nadine for as long as he could, but finally there was no ignoring her waving hand. As he made his way over to her wheelchair, she launched her opening volley.

"And don't you look smug, young man."

"Just bought a house, Nadine."

"Not much point in that until there's someone sharing it."

If thoughts of Mary and the condo weren't so hopelessly enmeshed, he'd have been safe. Chris cursed his fair skin. Nadine had done it again. Her voice filled the room. "Listen up, everyone. Our boy's got a gal."

"I don't," he protested, but it did no good. The whole posse joined in.

"What's her name, Chris?"

"Is she hot?"

"Is she moving in with you?"

From Ralph, one of the blustery men, "You getting any?"

Respect your elders? Whoever said that didn't have to deal with this rowdy bunch. He tried a new approach, the frontal attack. "Are you?"

It backfired. "Me and Bernice, Sonny. Every night."

The room erupted. His face progressed from blush to flame.

Chris really didn't want to know about the sex lives of his seniors, so he beat a strategic retreat. He'd reached the office, hoping for a breather, when his phone vibrated. He fished it out of his pocket, nodded when Wanda gestured to her coffeemaker, and answered.

"I'm five miles out of your podunk town," his brother boomed through the ether. "You got a spare key hidden anywhere?"

"Barry. Good to hear from you, but what are you doing in Calter Creek?"

77

"Felt like a break. It's a nice day, so I drove up. Where's the key?"

"In a drawer in the kitchen. Come by the senior center and you can use mine, as long as you don't clear off and lock me out."

"Would I do that?" Barry's laugh forced Chris to shift the phone another few inches away from his ear.

"You have before. Are you telling me you've grown up?"

"Nah. It'd drive the sisters crazy if I got responsible. Where's this seniors' place?"

Chris gave him the address and waited while Barry punched it into his GPS.

"Later, bro." As quickly as Barry had disrupted his already disrupted morning, he disconnected.

What difference could one more complication make? Chris accepted the coffee and once again braved the maelstrom, a devil in him anticipating the moment his seniors laid eyes on his handsome brother.

Saturday night, Mary and Bryony had settled at their usual table at Libations, sharing an order of nachos. Mary sipped her wine cooler, knowing from experience that she could make it last all evening.

"How's Chris?" Bryony asked.

For once Mary wished her friend occasionally pulled her punches. "Good, as far as I know. I haven't talked to him since the condo sale. Why?"

Dangerous question.

"Come on, Mary. Don't play coy."

If you can't deny it, downplay it. "Not my type, Bry."

"Maybe you should rethink your type."

"Or… check it out." A man had just walked up to the bar. A stranger. T-shirt stretched over muscles, blond hair in a short cut, tanned, tight tush… it was almost like a checklist as she enumerated the new guy's attributes.

Bryony followed her assessing gaze. "Nice. Any idea who he is?"

"Nope."

Both women sipped, crunched nachos, and surreptitiously watched as he accepted his beer and turned around, leaning his back against the bar and surveying the room.

It was still relatively early, and she and Bryony were the only unattached women in the place. Inevitably his roving gaze alit on them.

With interest. He drifted over.

"Ladies."

"Hi," Bryony spoke up. "Join us for a few minutes?"

"Sure. I'm Barry. Up from Kentucky for the weekend. You?"

"Lived here forever. Bryony…" Mary gestured to her friend. "And Mary."

Mary watched Barry survey them and make his choice. He turned incredible blue eyes, in a nest of lines like you got when you're outdoors a lot, on her. "Dance?"

"Not yet, thanks. Tell us more about yourself. Why are you here, of all places?"

"Visiting my baby brother. He needs me to keep him on the straight and narrow."

"Are you sure it isn't the other way around?"

And so it began, the banter that lead to a dance or two, a drink or two – or five – and ultimately to his bed, or hers, and a more or less satisfying tumble.

And an empty, solitary Sunday morning – although this time, it might involve getting to know her son, who tonight had rejected her company in favor of some kind of pickup Frisbee game at one of the parks.

Anyway, the whole solitary Sunday thing was once upon a time. Mary hadn't played the game in years. Perhaps distance gave her clarity; she found herself as much observer as participant as she and Barry followed the steps in the dance of courtship – or hook-up-ship. She didn't take Barry seriously or see him as a long-term prospect, even if she were seeking one.

79

Which she wasn't. After the disgrace of her pregnancy and the wild, loose life she'd lived in her twenties, she'd learned to value both herself and her solitude.

So she danced, and even had a second drink. But she went home alone.

When he groped his way into the kitchen Sunday morning, Chris was surprised to find his brother already up. "Thought you went out partying."

"Thought you planned on an early night. You aren't exactly bright-eyed and bushy-tailed this morning."

"I'm not. I didn't sleep all that well."

"Are you doing the sermonizing thing today?" Barry waved a mug of coffee under his nose.

He accepted it gratefully. "Are you coming to hear me?"

"Should I?"

"Given that you never have, I'd say either you're missing something profound in your life, or there's no point breaking your record." The coffee went down well. He needed its help to find the energy – and the focus – to get through the morning service.

"Too many words, Chrissy. Use simple sentences. You're talking to your big, dumb older bro."

"Far more than that. You want a cooked breakfast?"

"You have time?"

"Sure. Service isn't until ten thirty. Eggs?"

"You got sausages?"

"Check in the freezer."

Conversation waned until the two men were sitting across from each other at Chris's small table. "So, what did you do last night? There aren't that many places to go in Calter Creek."

Barry looked up from his plate. "Dropped in at a place called Libations, downtown. Met a couple of hot chicks."

Chris grinned. "Does anybody say things like that anymore? The only time I hear expressions like 'hot chicks' is when I'm at Silver Threads."

Barry groaned; the seniors had been as enthusiastic about the new 'beefcake' as Chris had predicted. "I threw that in to rile you. Funny thing, though. One of these gals acted like she'd analyze me half to death. The other one – long dark hair – she seemed interested, then she turned right off. Odd to be tossed aside like that. I was gearing up for an interesting night."

Mary and Bryony. Had to be.

And she'd rejected Barry. His handsome, confident brother.

"Just as well. I don't need you cutting a swath through the single women in Calter Creek. Too many pieces to pick up afterwards."

"Hey, I'm the one who picks up after you."

"No, you're the one who picks me up when I get knocked flat on my back."

"Do-gooder, Chris. That's what you are. It's a miracle you're still alive, the way you get in the middle of things that aren't any of your business."

"Not true. Only when it's not a fair fight."

"Our very own crusader against injustice. But my point holds." Barry shoveled in the sausages and eggs as if he hadn't seen food in a week. Chris idly wondered if he should have cooked double.

"Got plans for today?"

"Thought we might hang out a little," Barry said. "Once you take off your ministerial halo. Haven't seen much of family in a while."

"Sisters boycotting you?"

"Nah, busy with their own stuff. All the munchkins."

"Ever consider a family, Barry?"

His brother put down his fork and was silent for a moment. "Actually, yes. I thought we had something good, but..." He shrugged, gave Chris a twisted smile, and picked up his coffee.

81

That explained the sudden visit. His sisters were nothing if not opinionated. Abby would cluck and comfort. Susan would give him a dissertation on what he'd done wrong. Barry must realize that Chris would do neither. He'd just be there.

"Let's do lunch. There's a world-renowned burger joint in town. I'm free around twelve thirty."

"Think I'll come along this morning. See what it is you do in this church of yours."

"Always welcome."

His brother was three years older and had long been Chris's rescuer, but his life trajectory had concerned parties and short-term affairs rather than anything serious or settled. Maybe, just maybe, he was in the company of a new, more mature Barry.

Chapter 10

Mary had office duty Monday morning. She was grateful for the anchor of work, because the weekend with Zach had unsettled her. Not only because of the looming decisions – make that confessions – ahead, but because she really had no bead on where his head was, on their relationship, or his enrolment at the university, or something else.

He'd carefully avoided calling her Mary or Mom or anything at all. They'd had a pleasant time on the OSU campus, but no meaningful talk. Zach had left after lunch Sunday. Part of Mary felt relieved, part deprived.

Around ten o'clock Suzanne came into the office. A colleague, Suzanne was mid-forties, one of those women whose blonde hair, possibly permed, never moved an inch, even in a gale. Mary liked her well enough, but she wouldn't classify them as friends.

Uncharacteristically, she stopped in Mary's cubicle. "Did you hear about Ellen?"

"Oh no." Mary didn't have to ask. The look on Suzanne's usually unperturbable face said it all.

"Saturday afternoon. I'll post it on the notice board. The funeral's Wednesday. Her husband says it's at some little church out of town, so we can get a carpool together."

"Count me in. Jean can hold the fort. She didn't know Ellen, so she probably won't want to go."

Mary returned to work with a faint, but real, sense of loss. Ellen had staffed their front desk for years before the cancer that took her from her job, then killed her. She'd only been in her fifties, young enough to have expectations of an old age, grandchildren growing up, lots of meaningful events still to come. Another thirty years, Mary figured, snatched away.

It could happen to anyone. To you.

True. And what was she doing with her own life?

Somehow her father's death didn't seem half as significant. Apart from the lack of caring between them, he'd been in his seventies. The normal course of things. This was different. None of her acquaintances in Calter Creek had died before. It was a new experience, one she didn't quite know how to handle.

Wednesday afternoon, Mary and three of her work colleagues, including Suzanne and Robert, the owner of the agency, sat near the back of the packed church. The place had a certain charm about it, with simple lines and light pouring in through a pattern of clear and frosted glass in the rectangular windows. Not a lot of trappings, either. A raised platform, a plain table with a single candle, and a lectern. The room was white, the pews a blond wood, the flooring dark and scuffed, but clean and well maintained. A woman played an old upright piano. Pop tunes, oddly enough, not hymns. The coffin rested on a bier in front of the platform.

The church was full. Because she and her colleagues were seated to the side, Mary's view of activity along the center aisle and on the platform was partially blocked. But she wasn't really paying attention anyway, letting her mind focus on Ellen, her life and her challenges...

Overall, it felt good to be in the positive energy of this small space. Ellen had been a regular here and often praised the warmth of the ministers and relevance of the message.

"Nice church," Suzanne whispered beside her.

"Good energy," Mary agreed.

There was movement up front. The family coming in, she supposed. Then a quiet but carrying voice said, "Thank you for being here today. We'll begin our remembrance of Ellen Murchison by singing 'Morning Has Broken', which was one of Ellen's favorite hymns."

Mary heard the first sentence, and at some level the rest of the words must have sunk in because she could replay them in her mind later, but they didn't register at the time. She stood with everyone else and ignored the song.

Because she knew that voice.

Mary shifted in tiny movements until she got a better view of the platform. Two men stood side by side, both in white robes. An older man and...

It couldn't be.

He would have told her.

He hadn't told her.

Maybe he was just some kind of layperson, a friend of the deceased or something. The older man had to be the minister. Not Chris.

When the hymn ended, everyone sat. Chris exchanged a couple of words with the minister – *the other minister* – then he stepped up to the podium and began to lead them through the simple service.

Oh, God.

No wonder he seemed so nice. He'd met her and decided to fix her.

He was the same as her parents, just with a different coating.

But those kisses...

He'd lied.

There was no way to get out, and nowhere to go if she did, since the church was on a country road and she'd carpooled. Mary closed her eyes, then forced them open to stare at the apparition that was Chris, in full ministerial regalia, leading Ellen's memorial service.

Tributes and music filled the next hour. Entangled in her own thoughts, Mary heard none of it... until one moment near the end. Chris paused after the short talk he'd given and looked out over the audience... congregation, she corrected herself. And their eyes met.

85

He turned red and swallowed. Then he spoke quietly to the older man, who announced the closing hymn and wrapped up the service.

Good. Chris deserved to be shaken.

As the people surrounding them filed out, Mary excused herself, telling Suzanne she was feeling a little faint with the heat and would meet them at the car. She made her escape through a side door. Once outside, she leaned against the white clapboard and tried to breathe normally.

Not such a great catastrophe. You hardly know him.

He's not the only one who omitted a fact or two.

What's it to you, anyway?

She'd never trust anyone who believed he had the moral authority to sit in judgment of her. Never. She'd had enough of that growing up. Her parents had been rigid in their religiosity, making life miserable for their daughter.

Mary laughed to herself. Cynically, she figured if there was a god up there, she deserved bonus points for already having endured a fair share of hell. Given her history, why on earth had she believed Chris was different?

Chris found her a few minutes later. As soon as she saw him rounding the building – no robes, thank heaven, because that really messed with her mind – she started walking through an old graveyard beside the church. It was quiet, grassy, surrounded by a low stone wall, and few of the tombstones stood at a straight angle anymore.

He moved quickly. "A place to be silent," he said from right behind her. "To decide what matters. I come out here when things get to be overwhelming."

She wheeled on him. Her voice, to her, sounded shrill. "How dare you? You pretended to be... You made me believe... how could you even... what you did, the..." The words tumbled out without coherence.

"How dare I what? Kiss you? Let you know I'm interested in you? Is that what you're saying?"

Was he mad, or upset he'd been caught out? "Just go away, *Reverend* Peterson. Leave me alone."

He shook his head. "Not until we straighten this out." He looked steadily at her, but she wasn't about to meet his gaze.

"You lied," she said viciously. Her hands balled into fists. "Who do you think you are, anyway? Don't imagine you can drag me to this church of yours. I'm not some project you can fix, like a dog from the SPCA."

If he was upset before, now he looked bewildered. "No, of course not. I'd never try to lure you—"

"Go away. You're the last person on earth I want to talk to right now."

"Mary, listen. I can explain."

"Oldest words in the book, buster."

He reached out and put his hand on her arm, his fingers barely moving against her skin. "Please, give me a chance. There were reasons. I never wanted—"

She virtually hissed at him. "What you want is nothing to me. Zip, zero, nada. You're nothing, Chris Peterson. Stay out of my life."

"Honestly, I was just—"

"My friends are waiting. *Good* friends, who don't deceive people." She shrugged his hand off her arm and bolted for the parking lot, weaving through the ancient graves.

This time he let her go. Mary caught a glimpse of him as she climbed into Suzanne's car. He stood by one of the gravestones, running his hand over it as if comforting it. He didn't look up as they pulled away.

"I guess you were close to Ellen?" Raymond, the owner of the agency, asked. "You're quiet."

Mary would rather be almost anywhere than stuck in a car with her boss and two other women she knew just well enough that they'd feel entitled to ask questions.

"Not so much. There was something about that building. Peaceful."

87

"Yeah, I got that too. That young minister, he put on a fine service."

Did he?

Mary was grateful they'd left Jean back at the office. She was the only other person at work to have seen Chris, and at the moment she intended to keep their connection under wraps.

It would come out eventually, of course.

Another thing to explain away at some future date.

Not avoidable, either. She couldn't talk about Chris today. To shut out further conversation, she turned to her window and watched the Ohio countryside unfold as she and her colleagues made their way to downtown Calter Creek.

Apart from it being Chris, she knew why his appearance in that ridiculous white gown thing had triggered her so strongly. It stemmed from the rigid, hellfire church her parents had dragged her to, and the related disgrace, of being called out from the pulpit, of being pregnant at fifteen. Didn't they use to stone fornicators? She shuddered.

She had been so certain Chris was one of the original nice guys – but what did she know about nice guys? Nice guys had never had any use for her. Nor was he the sort of man she could sleep with and never see again. She'd worked that out the night at Libations, when that guy named Barry tried to get it on with her. Barry had everything she'd lusted for in a hook-up, back in her crazy twenties. Tall, built, good-looking, and with that vibe going that told her to expect a heck of a ride if she allowed the attraction to develop.

Attraction? What attraction? Sure, she was interested. No, she *should have been* interested. But all she'd really wanted to do was chat with Bryony, then go home for a solid night's sleep.

Anyway, Chris deserved the lambasting she'd given him. He'd deceived her, hiding his true occupation. Furthermore, ministers were in the business of condemnation, making you feel small so you'd come crawling for absolution.

Chris?

And exactly where did a minister learn to kiss like that?

The pieces didn't quite line up. She didn't care. Even though all the evidence suggested she mattered to him, he'd treated her like… like he didn't respect her. Somehow, he'd seen through her façade and set out to save her. A *minister*. No human species more feared, or despised.

Her life was devolving into one impossible situation after another. She'd long since lost her taste for the bad boys. Now she found herself drawn to a man who inevitably would despise her or, more likely, try to reform her. The web of secrets kept getting denser, the way out less and less obvious.

Chapter 11

Passages, the teen drop-in center, was housed in a wing of a local Baptist church, all red brick and clean lines, with parking for five hundred at least. Chris was on duty Wednesday afternoon, something he could have done without. He'd already endured not only the funeral that morning for a church member he'd genuinely cared about, but also his confrontation with Mary.

He hoped one day the feeling of equanimity, previously imparted by the old graveyard, would return. After the words she'd hurled at him, he feared the memory would override any sense of peace he might find there.

What did she think he was going to do? Try to make her wear her hair in a short perm and host meetings of some women's auxiliary? She hadn't even given him a chance to explain.

Your own fault.

Sure, he knew that. But he had his reasons. He'd bet he'd never have pulled off burgers at Joe's, those kisses, if she'd known.

Still, she didn't go off with Barry. Which, to hear his brother tell it, was a first. Chris might have sown his share of wild oats back in his twenties, but nothing like the way Barry plowed through the female population. Insatiable, that was his brother. With the proverbial cold shower here and there, Chris was surviving the absence of a woman in his life, a fact his sisters bemoaned.

Not that he liked it either. Especially since Mary.

The kids started turning up around four o'clock. Most of them were in their early teens, thirteen to fifteen. He was wary when the older ones dropped by. He supposed it was demographics, or pushing boundaries, but he'd confiscated too much alcohol and broken up one too many fights to be sanguine about their presence.

They'd organized a table tennis tournament, and the turnout was good. Chris stayed on the sidelines, chatting with the occasional teen who wandered his way but otherwise letting things unfold.

A mistake, as it turned out.

"Get off!" The voice was female, high, and frantic.

He left the gym. A little knot of kids had formed in the entrance. One girl and three boys, and the boys were crowding her. He nodded to Peggy, the receptionist, and strode over, catching the tail end of one of the boys' speeches. The young people were so engrossed in their own drama they didn't notice him.

"...about you and Ty, the stuff you did."

"Yeah, out in the smoking area after everyone else went in."

"Carry knee pads around with ya, bitch?"

"It's lies. Get your hands off me." Her voice veered toward panic. He'd only seen the girl a couple of times and couldn't remember her name, if he'd ever known it. But she was in trouble. Whether she *was* trouble remained to be discovered.

"You know you want to." This was from the tallest boy of the group. Jarrod must be sixteen now. "I can show you—"

"Show her what? How manly you are?" Chris forcibly inserted himself into the group, in the process releasing Jarrod's grip on the girl's arm.

Up close he could see that Jarrod's eyes didn't look right, unfocused, pupils mere pinpricks. The boy was high.

"Why, if it isn't Rev. Peterson. What a surprise. Why don't you get Tessa here to blow you? Bet she'd love it. Not many girls get a chance at a virginal priest."

"If you meet a virginal priest, let me know." Chris put a hand on Jarrod's shoulder to move him away, but the boy shook him off.

This kind of problem occurred rarely but could escalate in a blink. Chris risked looking to his left, immediately caught Peggy's eye, and signaled her – two fingers, meaning police and ambulance both. She nodded and picked up the phone.

He didn't want Jarrod to leave the building. The boy wasn't in his right mind, and there was no telling what he might do. But Chris couldn't let him interfere with the other kids, either.

"The rest of you. Vamoose." He barely touched the girl's arm to get her attention. "Hang out in the office for a few minutes. The receptionist will give you a drink."

"Thanks," she mumbled, and slouched off, her body language conveying that she wasn't grateful for his interference. She'd probably rather fight than be rescued by an adult.

A burst of noise came from the gymnasium. A table tennis match must have concluded. Time to finish this, before more kids were milling around, forming an audience.

"Jarrod, how'd you get here?"

"None of your fucking business."

"How do you plan to get home?"

"Not going home. Bastards." The boy's eyes were darting all over the place, as if boogeymen might start crawling out of the walls.

All he had to do was keep things under control until support arrived. "Want a pop? I could use one."

Jarrod twisted away and headed for the front door.

"You're not interested in table tennis? Usually some of the guys shoot hoops once the tournament's finished for the day." Chris moved more quickly than Jarrod, placing himself between the boy and the door.

Jarrod tried to shove him aside, and failed. He wobbled on his feet, but the attitude was as strong as ever. "Fuck off, old man."

"How about telling me what the problem is?"

The boy gave a snort.

Chris didn't expect an answer, or even rationality. He just wanted to keep Jarrod in one place. "Got any plans for the weekend?" Meaningless chat.

"Gonna get myself... real... go get..."

Chris pulled a chair over an instant before Jarrod dropped.

Wheels sounded on the pavement outside. Thank heaven, because this would be a run to the hospital, not to the lockup or to Jarrod's family home. He was pale and covered in sweat. Bad reaction. Chris kept his hands on Jarrod, keeping him still and preventing him from falling off the chair, until the policemen got into the building. Chris knew these two; they regularly patrolled this stretch of Calter Creek.

"Hey, Chris, how you doing?"

"Better before this."

"He give you any trouble?" The policeman knelt beside Jarrod and began a quick assessment. Jarrod tried to shake off the invading hands and mumbled incoherently.

"Escalating. Then the full force of the drug hit him."

"Ambulance is right behind us." He stood. "We'll come back once we know what we've got. Witnesses?"

"Peggy, and the girl in there."

"Get 'em to write down what they can."

The ambulance screeched to a halt outside. Several of the teens, alerted by the activity, drifted into the entry and watched. Without further ado, the paramedic team set to work. Chris herded the other kids back into the gym while they completed their assessment and loaded Jarrod in the ambulance.

Chris joined the girl in the receptionist's office. "You catch that?" he asked Peggy.

She gave him an uneasy smile. "Some day one of those big guys is going to hurt you, you know."

"Hope not. Keep your fingers crossed for me anyway." He squatted beside the girl, slumped in one of the office chairs and trying to look bored. What she actually looked was undernourished, underwashed, and definitely underappreciated.

Maybe she and the unknown Ty had been up to something at the high school; Chris suspected she'd do anything for attention. But that was irrelevant.

"Tessa or Teresa?" he asked.

"Don't matter to me."

"Teresa, then. Are you willing to talk about what just happened?"

"Nah," she mumbled. "Bunch of jackasses."

"True. But they might have hurt you."

"I take care of myself, Priest."

Not a priest, Chris thought. Minister, but not a priest. The distinction, to him, was significant. He wasn't in the business of judgments or absolutions, or providing a conduit to some deity out there. But many of the kids called him Priest, either with disdain or affection. Teresa's intonation suggested somewhere in between, as if she hadn't made up her mind.

"You don't want to file a report with the police, do you?"

"Nah."

"Peggy?"

"I'll take over from here." He and Peggy had worked together for two years now, and they had a firm understanding. First, she'd see to Teresa, since at the moment Chris wasn't the best choice. They kept emergency packages for girls like her, shampoo and conditioner, some female supplies, something nice from their small supply of donations, a scarf, piece of jewelry, or – most popular – a stuffed animal. Then Peggy would fill out her own report about the situation in the lobby.

Chis headed for the gym. He surveyed the twenty or so boys and girls there, some watching a hard-fought table tennis match and others standing around in groups talking, until he spotted one of the boys who had been hassling Teresa. He strode over and cut the boy out of the pack. "Gotta talk to you," he said quietly. "What kind of pill did Jarrod take?"

The boy's eyes shifted, looking for an escape. He was about fourteen, overweight, miserable. Chris touched his arm lightly. "You aren't in trouble, don't worry. But Jarrod's in a bad way. He's having a reaction. If we can let the hospital know

94

what caused it—" He broke off. He wasn't about to tell the boy he could save a life, because if by chance Jarrod died, the kid would live with it forever. "It could help."

"I dunno," he mumbled.

"Where did it come from?"

"Dunno."

"I think you do. Something bad's going down. You can help or be a part of the problem."

The boy squirmed some more. "He don't want anyone in his business."

"This is just between you and me. What was the pill?"

"I really don't know. Honest." He was terrified. Chris could smell it, the acrid scent of fear.

"Then tell me who's the supplier. Now." His tone, which he seldom used with the kids, commanded both respect and compliance.

The boy shook in his trainers, but he finally gave up the information. "He's called Mac. I don't know if it's a first name."

"He go to your school?"

"Nah. Hangs out on the street."

"You're in middle school."

"Unh."

"Jarrod's in high school. Look around. Plenty of middle school kids here. Why don't you get to know some of them?"

As if it were that easy. The boy squirmed. Probably he took his friends wherever he could find them.

"I never saw you or talked to you," Chris assured the boy. "I don't even know your name, okay?"

The boy fled as Chris headed for the office.

He asked Peggy to phone in the information about the dealer, then completed his own incident report and left it with her. At least two more rounds remained in the table tennis tournament, so he returned to the gym.

Later he joined the young people in the snack room for juice and cookies. They were good kids, here to socialize, have fun, avoid going home to an empty house.

He wouldn't mind avoiding going home to an empty house himself. But it didn't look like that was on the cards anytime soon.

Chapter 12

By Friday, Chris still hadn't been able to reach Mary. Understandably. There were so many ways she could have found out. Better ways.

You could even have told her yourself.

She wasn't at her office that afternoon, so he tried her cell. He left a message.

Another one half an hour later.

After a third message, he went to her condo. To his surprise, she answered the buzzer.

"Wait there. I'm coming down."

Given the sound quality through the speaker, he couldn't get a bead on her mood, but he'd bet it wasn't friendly.

She appeared at the door tight lipped and distant. "The sale goes through in two weeks. Call me at work if you have any questions."

"Not good enough. There are things I need to say. You didn't give me a chance Wednesday. I get that, but it's not Wednesday anymore."

An arrangement of curved concrete benches bordered the small lawn in front of Mary's building. He took her hand and led her to one of them. "I messed up," he said as they sat, more air between them than he wanted. "And I'm sorry. There's a reason, but I'm not sure you'll think it's good enough."

She removed her hand. "Let's just—"

"Listen. Please."

"There's no point in this, Chris. Our worlds are too different. It would never work." The anger had been replaced by

97

a resignation that said – or so he suspected – that she hated to hurt him, but she'd do it anyway. Because who ever dated a minister?

"Bull."

Her eyes widened.

"Want me to swear? I know how, just ask my mom. *Language,* she'd say. Good thing she loved me. And by the way, have you seen my halo recently? I seem to have misplaced it. Maybe I left it at your place the night I spent in your chair."

"You sound bitter."

"I am, a little. Can you imagine what it's like? Women hear what I do and they run, not walk, for the nearest exit. As if I'm trying to condemn them to a lifetime of church bazaars. Among other things, church bazaars terrify me. That's not how it is. Or who I am."

Yeah, he was bitter. Was a fair chance too much to ask?

He reclaimed her hand… her cool hand, even in the heat. Calter Creek was its usual sticky summer self. Outdoor activities were for those who relished the heat and humidity.

"Have you eaten?"

"No."

"Then let's walk into town. We can stop in at the sandwich bar or Joe's, grab dinner, and talk. I'll tell you anything you want to know about my work. It's a job, Mary, same as working at Silver Threads or Passages."

"It's not the same."

"Why not?" He stood and pulled her to her feet.

"Because… just because."

"Tell me about it." He started them walking toward town.

"About what?"

"What you're convinced I'm going to judge you for."

She jerked her hand free of his and stopped. "You've got a nerve—"

"Point of fact. When people meet me, they expect me to have an opinion on their morality or their faith, or at a bare minimum to come over as holier-than-thou. I hope I don't do any of that."

He could almost see her trying to get mad. She failed. Instead she squared her shoulders and fixed her gaze a long way in the distance. "Once... well, I was young and dumb. But I got tired of being used. I learned, and I keep to myself."

This time, as they walked, Chris didn't touch her. "Everyone needs other people," he said. "The lucky ones need someone special."

Mary snorted. "I stopped believing in that soul mate stuff years ago."

"Then it's my job to convince us both that you're wrong. I'm thirty-five, and it hasn't happened in my life so far, either." They walked in silence for a minute before he spoke again. "I never told you my brother's name is Barry."

He watched it sink in. she went from puzzled, through comprehending, to horrified in a split second. "That was your *brother*?"

"Sure was. Next morning he told me he'd met these two women. From the description, it could only have been you and Bryony. It stunned him to strike out." Chris grinned. "Barry's usually the man who gets the girl."

"Your brother?" Her voice almost squeaked with disbelief.

"Not very alike, are we? He used to be my defender. I was always going around rescuing people, animals, whatever. Sometimes they took exception to my interference. After a couple of incidents, Barry stepped in. Mostly I was left alone after that."

He hadn't planned to say that much about himself, or Barry, or his youth. No guy likes to admit to being the one who needed a champion to defend him. But his verbal flood gave her time to recover.

She was silent.

They were approaching downtown, a twenty-minute walk, when she finally spoke up. "I guess my reputation's not so great."

"Isn't it? Does it matter?"

"Lesson learned." Now she was the one to sound bitter.

"Don't beat up on yourself." He stopped them in the shade of a tree-lined building and turned her to him, reclaiming her hand. "I'm doing the confessing tonight. Yes, I'm a minister. No, I don't usually wear those robes. Ellen and her family wanted it. No, I don't hear confessions or try to save people. And yes, I was wrong not to tell you. I'm ashamed about that, but I just wanted you to get to know me first. As I said, far too often I don't get that chance."

A line appeared between her brows, as if he were an enigma to be solved. "You're a strange man."

He shook his head, a half smile on his lips. "No, I'm not. Not really."

"You are." She turned from him and pulled him along as they continued through town.

"How about we hit the takeout window at Joe's and go to the park?" he asked. "We could sit on the grass and watch the ducks."

"Sounds okay."

They got their meals and found a shady patch near the small lake. After eating a few bites of her burger she said, out of the blue, "Barry's the type I used to go for. This time… it was nice to be noticed, but… I don't know. The whole scene wasn't working for me," she added, as if she needed to clarify.

"This is, though."

"You flatter yourself."

"I like kissing you." He dropped his voice, to be sure it stayed confidential. "One day, I want to try it naked."

His declaration threw her. "But you can't… I mean, you're a minister."

"Therefore I'm asexual? Not quite." He laughed. "Didn't I tell you about my wild past? Trust me, Mary, I'm no innocent." Chris sighed and flopped onto his back on the grass. Mosquitos were starting to put in their nocturnal appearance; they wouldn't be able to hang out here long.

"But now…?"

He gave her question due consideration. "To be honest, even if I weren't a minister I doubt I'd be the dog I was then. It's just not the way I want my life to go anymore."

"I see." He'd given her food for thought. As he saw it, all he'd done was grow up. Sex was an optional extra.

With Mary, say. He'd give a lot to experience that particular optional extra. But it wasn't going to happen. Not until they both agreed they had a future.

They walked back to Mary's place as the evening cooled marginally. This time he sensed the handholding was mutual, not merely his determination to maintain contact.

Until, at the outer door to her condo building, she freed her hand, gave him a sad smile, and said, "Goodbye, Chris."

She never looked back as she waited for the elevator.

"Hey, Mom," Chris said. Phoning Abby counted as a last resort, but he had to talk to someone.

"Don't you start that with me, Christopher Peterson," Abby retorted on the other end of the phone. "I'm not your mother."

Good. Abby wasn't feeling all melting and maternal tonight. He wanted the comfort of her voice, but not necessarily the easy way out.

"I've got a problem, Abs."

"You're your own problem. Your vocation's messing with your head again, baby brother. Am I right?"

"Not with my head. With someone else's."

"Ah." Abby could breathe more meaning into a simple syllable than anyone, other than his other sister, Susan. But Susan would be acerbic and possibly sarcastic. Abby always tinged her comments with kindness. Even though they might well kick him right in the butt.

"The new woman."

He confirmed. "Mary."

"The real estate agent."

101

"I move in two weeks. Wait till you see it, Abby. The guy's already booked to check the fireplace—"

"Deflecting, Chrissy. What's the problem? No, wait. Tell me about the place while I make a cup of tea."

Chris spent five minutes giving Abby a verbal tour of the new condo. Some she knew; he'd sent out the online listing, with photos. What the snaps failed to convey was his vision, the way he'd actually live in it. The sense of home it gave him.

"Like the folks' old place, before they moved to the A-frame?"

"I barely remember the old place, but yeah. That kind of feel. Outside, anyway."

He heard some clunking and shuffling through the receiver.

"There, I'm settled. Reveal all."

"She found out. You were right, I should have told her up front. She came to a funeral and there I was, right down to the stupid robes."

"Her reaction?"

"Furious. Insulted. Defensive. As if I'd betrayed her."

"That sounds about right. And now?"

Chris sank onto his brown leather sofa. "I think we've got past the funeral. I did a whole confession thing, said I should have told her, said why I didn't. But now it's like she doesn't know how to relate to me anymore. I haven't changed, Abby. But she sees me differently."

"As a man who keeps facts from her, or as a minister?"

"Maybe both. Tonight she made it pretty clear there's no future. But she let me hold her hand. Talk about mixed signals."

She chuckled. "Then you've got some figuring out to do. Are you sure you aren't buying yourself grief?"

"I'm not sure about anything. But damn it all, Abby. No woman's ever affected me this way. I can't just let it go. Now her brother's coming to live with her, and that's going to change the dynamic. She isn't easy about it. Not unhappy, but definitely uneasy."

"Shut up a minute."

He detected faint sounds as Abby shifted around in whatever room of her commodious house she was in. He knew her. She'd be thinking about the best way to deliver bad news.

"Time's up, sis. Just say it. I already know anyway, so you may as well get it over with."

"It's always been so hard to hurt you, baby brother. You're so gracious in defeat."

"You don't want another Barry, do you?"

"God, no. So, assuming you're a single act again, it's not the end of the world."

He chuckled. "Platitudes will get you everywhere."

"Except that if you're calling me, it's hurting. Are you liable to see her again? Just around, with friends? All the final stuff about the condo?"

"Yes to both. I've already got crews of volunteers from the Renewed Life Center waiting to move me, by the way."

"Always suspected your job would come in handy," Abby said dryly. "When you're around her, talk to her. But no moves, okay? She needs to learn to relate to you as ordinary folks."

"Love you, Abs."

"Love you too, Chrissy. But I have kids to strong arm into bed. Call me."

"I will."

Abby kept him grounded and gave him love. He'd dumped a lot on her over the years. Less so on Susan, because she wasn't inclined to be gentle, even when she told him what he needed to hear. Even less on Barry, but Barry had always had his back. He valued his big sisters and brother, sometimes wished that they could all start seeing him as a fully fledged adult, and turned to them whenever times were bad, or good. His first line of defense, this tightly woven family his parents had crafted.

Chapter 13

Chris had debated whether to attend the Saturday backyard barbecue at the Smiths' house. He had met a few of the probable attendees through Sven Larsen, who was on the board at Passages, and liked John and Debbie, the hosts.

He certainly needed to get out of his half-packed apartment, to think about something else.

The fact that that Mary was a probable attendee didn't figure into his plans. Not at all.

It wasn't only the move that had his mind whirling. Friday night, eating in the park with Mary, had left him with an absurd amount of hope. And an equal share of uncertainty. Because this thing between them couldn't be serious until she bought in. Right?

Which is why your mind fills the new condo, not with furniture or friends, but with her?

Yeah.

Even his morning at Silver Threads hadn't distracted him. So, to tie his rampant mind to something more down-to-earth, he'd turned up at the barbecue, intending to keep a low profile. Perhaps he'd have a chance to follow Abby's advice and chat with Mary like ordinary people.

The rain held off despite the overcast day. Gray sky didn't inhibit the people around him. A babysitter kept the younger kids busy, and the adults unwound and played.

Across the lawn, Mary stood with a group of the women. He'd never run into her socially before and kept his distance now. She didn't seem to be unwound at all.

Debbie joined him as he propped up a corner of the garage, watching a volleyball game, husbands against wives, unfolding fiercely across the lawn. "I hope you don't mind," she began tentatively. "When we eat, well, some people here would be put off if we said grace. I'd ask you to do it, but..."

He grinned. If only this were the most complex issue facing him. "No problem. I'm not here to convert anyone."

Debbie gave him a wide, innocent smile. *Her* universe seemed to be unfolding very nicely. "Thanks. Having fun? You're not mixing much."

"A few things on my mind. It's all good, don't worry about me. Have you heard about my new place?"

Condo raptures filled a few minutes and gathered a group around them. A couple of the men volunteered to help the church crew with moving. He made a mental note to stock beer and order a lot of pizzas on the day.

Chris estimated twenty adults filled the Smiths' back yard. Conversation meandered from the approaching heat wave, to the economy and lines of credit, to the free entertainment at the bandstand in the park. This type of casual interaction suited him, but through it all he kept his eye on Mary. She mostly stayed with the other women, disappearing into the house or wandering the flower beds that lined the lawn.

Around four o'clock, when perhaps a quarter of those present were in the kitchen putting the finishing touches on the food and preparing the burgers for the barbecue, another single man arrived. He looked oddly familiar, yet not. Chris was close enough to overhear snatches of the ensuing conversation.

"...looking for Mary Boylan."

"Probably in the house. John Smith, I live here. And you are...?"

"I'm Zach." He said it like everyone ought to recognize the name.

But John clearly didn't. "Zach...?"

The young man – not much past a boy, Chris realized, for all that he was fully grown – looked puzzled. "Boylan. Mary's son."

Astonishment, quickly suppressed, flitted across John's face, and the faces of three or four others gathered around Zach. "Really? Well… gosh. Welcome to the barbecue."

The sky, in the form of a crashing realization, fell down on Chris's head.

When his mind came back online, the catastrophe was well underway. Zach, the admitted brother, the unacknowledged son, had become the center of an increasingly large group of people. He looked as confused as everyone else.

That little hesitation when she talked about her brother…

It made sense now. Knowing he planned to attend OSU, Mary must have been a child herself when she gave birth. But why keep him a secret?

By then word had reached the kitchen. Mary appeared in the door, looking like she might bolt any moment. Chris started in her direction.

A spasm crossed her face, telling him she'd seen Zach. Then she turned and fled back into the house.

Chris had reached the patio by the time Zach extracted himself and entered the house through the back door. He came out a minute later, looking bewildered. "She's got all these women surrounding her," he said to no one in particular. "Babbling."

Chris fell into step with the young man as he crossed the patio. "Good," he said casually. "They're her friends. And as far as I know, no one here knows about you, so she's got some stuff to deal with." He introduced himself. "I'm a minister, and I'm not prying, but it sounds like there's something that needs to be resolved here. Do you know where she lives?"

"Yeah, of course. That's how I got here. Her planner was open on the dining table. So I looked up the address and gambled."

"And didn't find what you expected."

"Why wouldn't she tell them? I thought she was proud of me. She said so." Zach shrugged. "Just my dumb assumption, huh? But with coming to live with her and all…" He shook his head, clearly still puzzled by the turn of events.

106

"You'll work it out, when you both have some private time to talk. This isn't the best place."

"I don't need to work anything out." The boy was moving from bewilderment to anger. "But she sure as hell does."

Chris could hear in his tone that for Zach, Mary was more a sister than a mother. He picked up none of the residual deference that still followed him and his siblings in their dealings with their parents.

As they exited through the back gate, heading for the road, he touched Zach's muscular arm. "It may not be instant, but it'll be worth it in the long run. Here, take this." He fished a business card from his pocket. "If you ever need to talk, give me a call." His card listed his role at the Renewed Life Center, his work at Passages and Silver Threads, and his training in mediation, dating from his earlier career in corporate human resources, well before his ministerial calling.

Zach pocketed the card without looking at it.

"Until school starts, have you considered volunteer work? The teen center could use someone like you, a younger man who knows his sports."

He'd caught Zach's interest, and deflected it from Mary. "Maybe. My program talks about community involvement."

"Drop by. See what you think."

Zach headed for his car, and Chris turned back to the party.

~~

Mary stood on her deck, expecting Zach to storm in any moment. She had left the party early, soon after being swarmed by her friends, every one of them praising her son to the skies, his looks, his manners... and dying to know, in the politest possible way, what the story was.

Zach wasn't a secret anymore. And damn, it felt good.

Even Chris, *Reverend* Chris, had said nothing negative. But experience had taught her what to expect from a minister.

None of which eased the tension twisting her gut into pretzels. Because she still had to face Zach.

For half an hour or more she paced the balcony, keeping herself on a tight rein. But it had meant so much, for so long... when she heard Zach's key in the lock, her eyes flooded. As he entered she turned away and dropped into one of the patio chairs.

He arrived on the deck in an instant and looked down at her, exasperated. "Jeez, you don't have to go hysterical. All I did was try to find you. Is that so bad?"

"Ye..." Hiccup. "Yes. I mean no. Be... because..."

"You never told them about me."

She shook her head.

His dander was up. "Yeah. And guess how that makes me feel. School starts in a month. When exactly did you plan on telling them? Or did you figure I'd keep it a secret?" His voice got louder. "Let me be your kid brother forever? Thanks a bunch, *Mom*."

The familiar, heavy sarcasm on the last word.

First she'd lacked the courage to acknowledge him, and now he'd probably refuse to acknowledge her. Mary wearily rubbed away the tears with the heels of her hands.

Zach sighed as only an impatient male could, recognizing the utter hopelessness of the state of affairs. "I'm out of here. Get a grip. We'll talk tomorrow." He frowned at her. "You okay?"

She nodded and stood, following him inside. Zach scooped up his car keys and left. The door closed none too gently behind him, leaving her standing at a loss in the middle of her living room.

A murmur of men's voices sounded from the corridor, then the door opened again. She fully expected to see Zach returning. But the man coming in wasn't Zach. Chris crossed the room, pulled her down on the sofa with him, and wrapped his arms around her.

He didn't say a word, he just held her, one hand cradling her head, the other around her back. Settling her against him, stroking her hair.

"What are you doing here?" she mumbled into his shirt.

"Sitting beside you. Later I intend to wash your face. It's kind of streaky. And hope you'll tell me what's going on."

"I don't want you here." She heard the petulance in her voice, but she made no move to push him away. Even in her current, messed-up state she recognized the incongruity of the situation.

But being held by Chris felt like being in shelter from a hurricane, where nothing could hurt her again.

"Too bad. I snuck into the building on the heels of one of your neighbors, and I'm not wasting a perfectly fine break-in. Your building does need to beef up its security, though."

"You met Zach."

"I did. At the party, in fact. He's still young, he hasn't had time to develop the tools to handle any of this. He said he yelled, but he doesn't know how to say he's sorry. Actually, I'm not sure he is sorry. He feels wronged."

"With justification. He got a rotten deal."

"Your world hasn't ended, Mary."

Defenses flared. "So you say. But that's what ministers do, spew lies and platitudes."

As soon as she flung the bitter words at him, she longed to retract them. The look on his face... stunned, and hurt. But if he thought she'd ever trust a minister....

Chris swallowed. "I do my best to live those platitudes. There's not much point if you don't believe what you say."

She pushed herself away. "Have you done the math?"

"Of course. Fifteen, right?"

"What kind of girl gets knocked up at fifteen? Only one kind, and you know it."

"I don't know anything of the sort." Chris left the sofa and headed for her kitchen. "Grilled cheese?"

"Why not." At the barbecue she hadn't been able to eat much, between the knots in her stomach and the bevy of friends wanting to praise Zach... and get the real scoop.

"Intense lack of enthusiasm might be one reason." When she followed him, he studied her, then said, "First things first, though. Come with me." He tossed the cheese on the counter and led her along the short hall to the bathroom, where he seated her on the toilet lid, ran her washcloth under the faucet, and knelt beside her, supporting her head as he bathed her face. "Good?"

She didn't answer. He was involving himself with her, and it wouldn't end well. If she had a scrap of morality left in her, she'd give him the boot, but fast.

She couldn't do it. She closed her eyes to savor the cool on her overheated skin.

So she was caught unaware when the washcloth stopped and his other hand tunneled into her hair. "Mary…"

When she opened her eyes, the washcloth had vanished, but Chris's face was no more than six inches from hers.

He stood, pulling her up with him. His hands shook, but that didn't stop his mouth from finding hers with the assuredness of a magnet.

And she responded with the hunger of a woman who hadn't allowed herself to care about anyone in her entire adult life.

His kiss deepened, and if he'd blown her mind before, now she experienced the true meaning of need. Because she couldn't have stopped him if she wanted to, and beyond a doubt she didn't want to.

When he let her go, worry lines had appeared at the corners of his eyes. He must have seen something in her expression because he stepped away from her, took her hand, and guided her back to the living room. He settled her on the sofa, then stood before her like an abashed schoolboy. "I'm sorry," he said, "that was inappropriate. Lousy timing. But you looked so…"

Needy? Yeah, she knew a lot about how minsters handled to that species of need.

"Can I make you coffee?" Chris asked. "Iced tea? That sandwich?"

"No."

"Okay." He sat and put an arm around her. "Now, let's disentangle this. It sounds as if you expect me to judge you for having Zach."

"It's your job, isn't it?" she said bitterly. "To keep the sinners in their place."

He sighed. "I don't believe in hellfire and damnation. That's not who I am, or what my spiritual community teaches."

He sat forward and turned to her, his eyes reflecting the earnestness in his voice. "Having a child isn't a sin. It's a blessing. You're beating yourself up because someone planted the idea in your head.

"And don't I sound sanctimonious," he concluded with an edge of self-criticism. "I try to save talk like that for Sunday lessons. But you asked, and I need you to understand. I'd never condemn you for anything, much less an event half a lifetime ago."

She'd never heard of such a creed. And frankly, she doubted its reality.

Again he drew her to him, brushing her hair back with his free hand. "Zach's solid, from what little I've seen. And I want you and me to continue down the path we've started on – oh, yes we have," he interrupted himself when she struggled to escape his arm. "I like you, Mary Boylan. I may fall in love with you, if I haven't already. Give me a chance."

She shook off his arm and twisted to look at him... really look. She saw nothing she expected. No hint of judgment or criticism. No suggestion that the newly revealed relationship with Zach made him any less respectful of her.

She shouldn't do it, but she touched the side of his face.

He gasped, then reached up and corralled her hand. He raised it to his mouth and kissed her palm.

They stared at each other. As if, Mary thought, we're both waiting...

Then they were clinging to each other, his mouth desperate on hers... and then they weren't. Before she could figure out what was happening, he'd pulled back. But the evidence of the effect she'd had on him, even with one kiss, was

111

blatant, as was his heavy breathing. He pinched his eyes closed. "God, Mary."

But for once in her life she'd encountered a desirable man who treated her with respect... so far at least. Maybe he was just what she needed right now. "Chris, let's... I mean, let's go. Back to my room."

He shook his head. His eyes on hers were desperate. "I'd give almost anything to. But I can't."

She recoiled as if he'd slapped her. Why did she ever hope he was different? After making a big show of his superior morality, he'd hardly sully himself with the likes of her.

She broke free and stood over him. "You're not welcome here, Chris."

"But—"

"Maybe a miracle will happen, and I'll be washed clean as new fallen snow. Until then, why should you contaminate yourself, right? So *get out*!" Her voice had risen to a shriek, but she couldn't help that. She wasn't about to put herself in his power to judge her forever.

He stood. "That's not it. That's not why."

"Sure," she sneered. "Your message came through loud and clear."

Unable to take any more, Mary fled to her bedroom, slamming the door closed. Chris could damn well find the front door and get himself out of it.

Chris gave himself a minute to let his heart rate settle, then sent a quick text to Zach – they'd exchanged numbers earlier. "*Better. Now she's furious at me instead of worried about you. I'm leaving. Come home.*"

Mary's reaction was more than simple embarrassment at having Zach revealed in such a public way. It stemmed from him, or more specifically, his calling. But why? And how the *hell* was he going to convince her to trust him?

112

Mary didn't leave her room when she heard Zach come in. She'd curled up small on her bed and thought she just might stay there for a lifetime. She'd had more than all she could take.

She traced his movement by the heavy sound of his footfalls and wondered if he was storming around in rage or if his size made him so noisy. A full-grown man, physically.

Eventually, he knocked on her door. When she didn't answer he opened it; the condo hadn't been blessed with locks on the doors and she'd never bothered to have them installed. "I made grilled cheese. Come eat."

"Chris was going to make grilled cheese," she muttered, but didn't leave the bed.

"Yeah. He left the stuff out."

From her position with her head half buried, she could sense more than see Zach's uneasiness. He shifted from foot to foot. Mary sighed. "I'll be there in a minute."

He closed the door behind him. She rolled out of bed, feeling as if she'd aged fifty years in the last handful of hours.

The bathroom mirror told her she wasn't far off the mark. She allowed herself a full five minutes to wash her face again and make a stab at putting herself back together.

The sun was sinking when she got to the living room. Her apartment was in shadow. The door to the deck was open, and outside she could hear voices, people on the street, off to enjoy their Saturday night.

Zach saw her coming and rose from the table. Wordlessly he brought a plate from the oven, and a glass. Next to the glass he put a can of beer.

She noted that he'd poured one for himself, also. She raised an eyebrow.

"It's legal," he said defensively. "Private home, parents' consent. No way you could tell me not to, even if you were my legal parent. I guess you're not?"

"I don't know. Probably not."

"Well, I'm not gonna ask her."

"How is she?" Mary never thought she'd see the day when she'd consider her mother neutral territory.

"The same. Seems my visit here last weekend was a major betrayal."

Mary bit into the sandwich. He'd used tons of cheese. It was gooey from the oven and tasted like comfort.

After she'd swallowed and sampled the beer, she said, "Why are you here, Zach? I didn't expect you for weeks." She was fully aware she was skirting around the scene at the party, but she couldn't help that. At the moment, she needed to pretend life was normal.

Her grown-up, handsome son squirmed. "It was sort of bad. There was this thing that went down, it was just a party but things kind of got out of hand. I wasn't doing anything," he said defensively. "But when she heard about the police and all, she gave me hell. Screamed I wasn't living up to *him*. And that if that's the way I was gonna behave, I could get out. So I did."

Mary had stopped hearing anything more after one word. "Police?"

"It's okay. I snuck out the back."

"Zach…"

"Honest. Some neighbors called the cops because of the noise. That's all. There weren't any drugs or anything going down, far as I know."

"Just underage drinking."

"Well, yeah, some. This isn't high school, Mary. One of the guys enlisted. It was a send-off."

Old enough to kill, not old enough to drink.

It was beginning to sink in that Zach was at least as nervous about this face-to-face with her as she was. And that she was the adult here.

"So you left. And came here."

"Where else?" A quarter of his second sandwich disappeared into his mouth. After he'd swallowed most of it, he spoke around the rest. "I'll be moving here anyway pretty soon. I'm not going back. Ever."

"It's okay, you can stay here. But we're going to have to go back. I'm sure you didn't pack your whole life up."

"Left a few things. Nothing important."

114

"Clothes."

"Oh. Yeah, some. I don't know what the guys wear at OSU."

He's nineteen.

"I'm sorry about today."

"So am I. I guess, when I think it through…" He took a healthy swig of his beer, straight from the can. "If I didn't know, then I guess you wouldn't have told anyone else, either. I just thought… I wanted to try it out. See what it feels like, having a real mother instead of… her."

Dismayed, she put down her sandwich. "Oh, Zach. Not that I had any choice, but I thought you were the son they wanted."

"Treated you rotten, didn't they? I didn't really notice, growing up."

Mary finished her sandwich in silence, neither confirming nor denying his assessment, then pushed her plate aside and tipped some beer into the glass. She sipped, then said, "If they hadn't taken you, I'd have been forced to put you up for adoption. I was too scared to stand up for myself. Claude said she'd have kept you, except that her own circumstances weren't so stable back then. Whatever hell our parents created for us, at least I've been able to keep track of you."

"Yeah, I saw the book." Mary had a scrapbook of pictures of Zach from babyhood to now, of every newspaper clipping, every home run Zach hit, every mention in the school newspaper. She'd kept the scrapbook hidden until last week, when she'd brought it out and put it on her coffee table. She'd delved into it numerous times since her father's death, trying to fathom the tsunami of change that had overtaken her.

Zach tipped up his can and came away empty. He set it down in the middle of his plate, rotating it to line up the label. "Isn't there something like an open adoption? Where you stay in touch?"

She nodded. "But I was fifteen. I didn't know anything, and I didn't have any support at all from *them*. I was living a nightmare and scared out of my mind. Claude held me together, but even if she'd been able to keep you, there were cross-border things about citizenship and all… it was more than I could handle. When they learned you were a boy and got excited about keeping you themselves…" She shrugged. "It was the best I could do."

"I guess, that day she told me, it didn't really sink in. Fifteen's awfully young."

From his exalted nineteen.

"I wasn't a slut, Zach. I hadn't even been kissed before that party. I had no idea the punch was spiked, and when this guy showed interest in me – it had never happened before. When you dress like a pauper in shapeless clothes and your parents won't even buy conditioner for your hair or let you use any makeup… I was a waste of money to them. I think they liked keeping me plain, so I wouldn't get into trouble. *Trouble.*" Mary made a sound that marked her disgust. "It was a date rape, plain and simple. When I got home my father took his belt to me. There's still a scar on my back."

Zach stared at her open-mouthed. "That's horrid. That's, like, assault."

"They did send me to the minister, for him to do the fallen woman routine. He fobbed me off on the assistant minister, who promptly hit on me, then condemned me from the pulpit."

Mother and son sat in silence for a few minutes. Mary sipped at her beer, but without much appetite for it. Zach turned his can around and around between his big hands.

"At least they were good to you. I watched as best I could."

Zach nodded. "I got big young. They were still, you know, disapproving of everything I did, but he didn't dare hit me."

"Thanks for the sandwich."

"I'm sorry I messed up your barbecue."

"You didn't." She thought it over. "In a way you solved a problem. I couldn't figure out how to tell people I've known for years, oh, by the way, did I mention I have a son? I knew I had to, but I couldn't find the courage."

116

"That Chris guy. He seems pretty cool. He gets it, I think."

Mary had no answer. She couldn't think of anything to say that wouldn't imply either too much or too little. Her mind still hadn't wrapped itself around his presence here this evening, in her condo, holding her, kissing her half out of her mind. Or the way he'd insulted her, forcing her to drive him off.

She didn't have a clue what to think about Chris Peterson. She'd wanted so much for him to be one of the good guys.

Zach disappeared into his room soon after supper, figuring, no doubt, that since he'd cooked she could clean up. Worked for her. Mechanical tasks like washing the frying pan were about all she was up for, after the day from hell.

Chapter 14

Late Sunday morning Mary received a phone call from Chris. Against her better judgment, she answered. "Aren't you supposed to be doing something saintly on Sundays?"

"Service just finished, and think of me more as a moderator. Nothing holy about it, especially today."

"That robe thing."

"I never wear it. Shirt and tie, usually."

"Why today?"

"Because my mind was a lot more on what we did yesterday than the service."

"Forget it, Chris." She hung up on him.

He could say what he liked with his fine talk of true selves and his wandering thoughts this morning. He'd wanted her, and refused her. Judged her, and rejected her. So much for his exalted moral status.

Hypocrite.

Did he believe her invitation meant nothing? He didn't know how long it had been since she last invited a man to her bed.

Could he be worried he wouldn't measure up?

But no. He couldn't be *that* inexperienced.

From the way he kissed and explored her body, he wasn't inexperienced at all.

She never expected to go for someone like him. Mild-mannered, not ripped… *ordinary.* But he'd felt good under her hands. She'd wanted more. For him to deny her…

She glanced around her once-tidy condo. Zach took up space. Already his books and magazines invaded her living room, his shoes cluttered the floor of her entry closet, his toiletries crowded hers. He'd gone shopping that morning and brought home things like beef jerky, frozen pepperoni pizzas, protein powder. Then he'd disappeared after starting a load of laundry – and extracting a promise from her to do a second load. The physical realities of Zach's presence were starting to manifest.

She sighed as she shuffled a pair of runners out of the bathroom to the closet where they belonged. Without ground rules, this would never work.

She made a plan for supper – pasta, she had the ingredients – because she felt calmer with something, at least, in control. A quick text to Zach confirmed that yes, he'd be there. She pulled cooked chicken from the freezer to add to the dish.

That afternoon she showed houses to a pleasant young couple choosing their first home together. That part of her work kept her grounded and enthusiastic.

Chris phoned again later.

"Just stop trying. I don't want to talk to you."

"Why not?" He sounded on edge, and as if he honestly hadn't figured it out.

"Leave me alone." She hung up on him again. Didn't she have enough to deal with?

Why would he spout those soothing, accepting words, then reject her?

Or maybe… what if that wasn't what he meant at all? Maybe her reaction was knee-jerk, a leftover from her parents' harsh condemnation. But still…

At least her friends knew, or most of them. A few hadn't been at the barbecue. Mel, for instance. She was so immersed in whatever world she was creating with that banker of hers that Mary rarely saw her, unless they got together for a jaunt to Creekside Mall. Everyone *knowing* was easier than having to actually say the words.

Chris told her no one had said anything negative about her, but she'd bet the gossip blanketed Calter Creek by now.

He'd tell her be realistic, and that she was too hard on herself. She knew it. But her parents' lessons and punishments had a life of their own.

Zach bounded in around six o'clock, looking hot and sweaty. "Hey, Mary," he called on his way to the bathroom.

"Hey."

The shower started up. Another thing she needed to consider, the increased power bills.

Later he watched as she served the meal, using a tea towel to hold the warmed dishes. She'd piled his with double her usual serving. "Have a good day?" he asked.

"Not bad."

"Looks fabulous." And Zach looked like a ravenous young man, healthy and wholesome, his hair damp and unstyled. Maybe he'd been able to escape their parents' clutches in time, and no long-term damage had been done.

She grated parmesan. "What have you been doing?"

His fork hit the pasta bowl. "Look. I'm not going to sit here and get an inquisition, okay? I got enough of that at home."

She'd been happy to see him. Shouldn't this be easier? "That isn't what I meant. I was just making conversation."

"Sorry." He was more on edge than he was letting on. "I met some guys from the Frisbee thing over at the Baptist church, where that youth drop-in place is. Got in on pickup basketball. It was good."

"Hot weather for basketball."

"Yeah."

They made small talk about sports and house viewings over supper, then Zach disappeared into his room. She could hear his masculine voice, probably on the telephone. Another thing to check, his phone plan.

Perhaps if she started keeping lists. Mary prided herself on her ability to keep track of her life in her head, with a little help from a calendar. The changes and resultant confusion had fried some of her circuits. But she didn't need support from anybody. Chris, for instance. Just a list, and she'd be fine.

One good thing about Sunday dinner with Rodney and Sadie Bradshaw, Chris reflected, was that no one challenged his vocation. No one teased, no one demanded explanations, no one ran away. It was the last of these options he found hardest to deal with these days.

No trouble dealing with Sadie's pot roast, root vegetables, and apple pie, the kind of food he rarely got anymore. The kind that came with being settled, with having a partner in life.

Could a slow cooker ever be a fair substitute for a wife?

Sadie complemented Rod. Nicely rounded to his razor thinness. Practical and organized while he could be the original absent-minded professor. Leading with her heart, whereas Rod showed mainly his logical side. Baseball fanatics and bird watchers, between them they ran the Renewed Life Center with love and an appreciation for the mechanics of maintaining a healthy community. The elderly couple had welcomed him like a long-lost son when he'd moved to Calter Creek. He hoped when the time came for him to assume responsibility for the church, the Bradshaws wouldn't do the snowbird thing and head south. He loved them both, as if he'd been blessed with a second set of wonderful parents.

Rod had held the conversational reins through most of their dinner, but with the plates removed and the apple pie in front of them it was clearly Sadie's turn at bat.

And Sadie, being the businesswoman of the family, didn't beat around the bush.

"Tell me about her."

The heat rose in Chris's face. Possibly, if he could get his Mary-related thoughts under control, he'd suppress the blushing at the same time.

"My age, give or take. Long, dark hair, straight. Blue eyes but they're almost green sometimes, like when she's mad. Average height—"

"Chris." Sadie stopped him with a word. "I know all that, from Ellen's funeral. After you dumped your vestments in a pile on the floor and hared off out the side door? You shouldn't indulge in atypical behavior if you don't want to be seen."

"Yeah, I guess not," he said sheepishly.

121

"Our boy had a crisis of confidence," Rod said, indulging a chance to put the cat among the pigeons. "Seems he neglected to tell her what he does for a living."

"A fact you've mentioned once or twice before," Sadie said with a look of mild reproof at her husband. "I get that. I might mention that I'd gone out with you a few times before you blurted out you were heading for seminary in the fall."

Chris grinned. Sadie might have been saving their forty-year-old backstory for just this occasion.

"Have you seen her since then?" she continued.

"Yeah. But she's not impressed with me at the moment." He could hardly tell this warm couple that Mary wanted him as much as he wanted her. No way could he discuss his lack of a sex life with Sadie. "There was a party."

"An after-party, too," Sadie said shrewdly.

He shoveled in another bite of pie before saying, "Something happened that upset her. I thought I might be able to help."

"Did you?"

"Marginally." And got himself kicked out for his pains. "I've phoned a couple of times. She hangs up on me."

"The young lady is making a statement," Rod said.

"Statements need to be acted upon," Sadie riposted. "What are you going to do?"

"I don't know." He took in Sadie's gaze, open and compassionate. No judgment there – from either of them, although Rod was more brusque in showing it. "Maybe I should just accept it's not meant to be."

"Uh huh. Do you believe what you're saying, Chris?"

The pie afforded him a chance to think it over. "No. Not really."

"Then you need a strategy. And you be quiet," Sadie said, stabbing a finger in her husband's direction. "However sweet, our courtship was the most hapless thing I've ever witnessed, much less participated in. A little more romancing wouldn't have gone amiss."

"It worked," Rod shot back with a grin.

"Despite, not because of."

Wondering whether he and Mary would one day achieve that level of comfortable banter, Chris put in, "Sending roses and stuff like that seems trivial, especially given her background. Flowers aren't… lasting."

Sadie frowned. "Hold on. If you want lasting, here's an idea." She left the table and returned from the kitchen a minute later with a flyer in her hand. "Did you get one of these in your mail?"

Chris nodded. "I'm involved."

Another of the charities he worked for. The Earth's Bounty Foundation gathered apples from yards and vacant lots throughout Calter Creek and converted them into fruit leather and applesauce. These were sold or donated to centers like the ones where he volunteered his time. The Foundation had been gifted a parcel of land not far from the Renewed Life Center and sought donors for apple trees. The cost was moderate, the payback enormous.

"Would a tree in her name mean anything to her?"

He didn't know. He really didn't know her very well. But it had to be better than roses.

"I'll call in tomorrow. I could get them to expedite the certificate."

"Good. Then what?"

Trust Sadie to cut to the chase. He didn't have a clue what came after the apple tree donation.

"Outdoors and shady," she decreed. "With full summer descending on us, you need shade. And if she's that skittish, she needs outdoors. Romantic, but not too much. Talk more than touchy-feely, if you get my drift."

He did. Sadie could be blunt, and she was right. "You're wise. I appreciate it."

"Excellent," Rod said. "Problem solved."

The look the older couple exchanged suggested they'd just achieved world peace. Chris wondered where he'd misplaced his masculinity, that he relied on them for dating advice. But this was a new world to him, with new parameters.

123

The Chris who would have had Mary in his bed long before now had vanished. The Chris who looked to the future still battled uncertainty. He might have the courage of his convictions, but translating those convictions into action was proving to be more problematic than he'd expected.

Sadie was on her feet again. He sprang up. "I'll help." He carried plates to the kitchen and joined her in tidying, noting with pleasure that she put a large slice of the pie into a container for him to take home.

Chapter 15

Chris tried the phone again Monday morning. He trusted Sadie Bradshaw's wisdom, almost as much as he trusted his sister Abby. If she said to be persistent, he'd be persistent. When Mary didn't answer her cell, he tried the office number.

"Is there a problem about the sale?" she asked him by way of greeting. Cool, no inflection in her voice. Businesslike.

"No, no problem. Mary—"

"Mortgage in place?"

"Yes, ages ago. Look, we have to talk. I don't know…"

"Not now. I'm at work."

The line went dead.

He was running late. Mondays usually brought a heavy load of visiting the shut-ins and seniors on his roster. He did his best to compensate for what often had been a long, lonely weekend. Not the same as family and old friends, but he tried to approach his visits as if he were both. He hated to call it work, but some days, like today, for instance, when his mind refused to focus, that's exactly what it was. He hoped they didn't notice.

Later, he stopped at the Earth's Bounty Foundation, administered from a small office tucked into a suburban garage. There he bought a tree in Mary's name and arranged to pick up the certificate the next day.

He spent the afternoon holed up with Rod, planning the lessons for the upcoming two months. Once they'd nailed the topics and assigned Sundays, he'd spend hours researching, choosing quotes, reflecting on what he wanted to say, making it a coherent whole, and rehearsing in the privacy of his apartment. But his mind refused to behave. If asked to come up with a theme for September, he'd probably have said *Mary*.

And Rod would have understood. But that missed the point. After Saturday she claimed more of his head than ever.

The next evening, Mary stared blankly at the certificate on her dining room table and wondered what she should do with, and about, the thing. No message attached, nothing to identify it as coming from Chris, but Suzanne said he'd brought it in. As peace offerings went, an apple tree in her name had the merit of originality, but still...

She'd brought it home with her. The certificate impressed Zach. "It's unusual. Shows creativity."

"Ever give a girl flowers?" she asked him.

"Nah... well, once. For her senior prom."

"Women like flowers."

"Yeah, but an apple tree'll last a lot longer."

But it didn't leave you with anything to brush with a finger, to sniff, to show off to your girlfriends.

Should she get in touch with Chris? Thank him? And then say what? Please stay out of my life?

Please come back into my life.

No. She wasn't the type of woman to be involved with a minister. It would be wrong.

It felt right.

But she knew herself better than that. Exit stage left, Chris. He'd find himself a sweet churchgoer who'd run bake sales and pray and that kind of stuff. Someone without a history. Someone immune to judgment.

A note would be the best way to acknowledge the certificate, she decided. Words exchanged for words. The symmetry pleased her.

Composing the note took more time and trouble than she'd bargained for. The draft occupied most of Wednesday morning while she fielded phone calls and negotiated a sale that stood no chance of going through, given both the owners' and the prospective buyers' expectations were so far out of line.

In the end, her response was businesslike and formal: *Thank you for the donation in my name. It wasn't necessary. It is both my job and my pleasure to assist you in purchasing your dream home.*

When she signed it, she included her professional credentials.

Nothing personal.

Mary was the last to leave the office, tasked with answering last-minute phone calls and locking up the office. At about six o'clock, she had just slotted her laptop into its case and was about to head for the parking lot – dreading the heat when she opened her car door – when Chris stormed into her cubicle, thunder on his usually mild face.

Slowly, carefully, she placed the case on her desk. "Why are you here?"

Un-Chris-like, he sounded tight, controlled. "Because you and I have to talk. I want to know what the hell's going on."

Hell? She quickly glanced up and down the short corridor connecting the four agents' cubicles, but of course they were alone.

"There's nothing to say."

"Are you kidding? Saturday left me... I mean, what happened? One minute everything's as good as it can be, and the next you're kicking me out. I deserve more than that. So do you."

She snatched up her case and headed for the front door, Chris on her heels. He didn't touch her, but his glower burned into her back, as if he'd connected them with electrical wire.

She locked the office and turned into the lane that led to the parking lot. At her car he said, "Leave your computer in the trunk. You and I are going for a walk. We need to clarify a few things between us."

She registered the look on his face. Mild, gentle Chris was furious.

He'd never physically hurt her. But the words he'd use, the words to tell her what he really thought of her... that was another story.

Better to get it out of the way? Probably. Then it would be one sword no longer hanging over her head.

"I have to move the car. It's too hot for the computer."

"Fine. Be my guest."

He had the nerve to settle into her passenger seat while she shifted the car to the far end of the lot, under a row of trees marking the property line. She stowed her satchel in the trunk, tossing in her suit jacket as an afterthought, and changed into a pair of runners before locking the car.

He took her hand with surprising gentleness and steered them via a side street in the general direction of the park. "You don't really believe the apple tree's about finding the condo, do you?"

She didn't answer.

"Damn it, Mary, after Saturday—"

She shook off his hand. "Yeah, Saturday. That told me all I needed to know."

"About how I feel about you?" He sounded puzzled. "It's more than just wanting you, but we sort of didn't get to that part—"

"Stop it." To her horror, she realized her voice was rising. Thank God no pedestrians were around, it being the witching hour after the stores closed and before the restaurant and club crowd descended, because she couldn't have controlled her volume if she'd wanted to. And at that moment, she didn't want to.

"Mary—"

"Oh, I got it. You figure any male that makes it through my front door has a free pass, don't you? You have me pegged as worthless, some species of whore who'd just invite—"

128

"*Mary!*"

He stopped her in her tracks, both vocally and physically, grabbing her arm and swinging her around to face him there on the sidewalk. "Is that really it?" he shouted right back. "You think I'd treat you like—"

He froze. She turned; two elderly women had emerged from the library across the street.

While from prior experience she might have expected Chris to blush, instead he paled, swallowed, and pitched his voice to a more even tenor. "Eleanor, Rosie, nice to see you. What brings you downtown?" Mary felt his tension through his hand.

Yelling on the street. Not good for the saintly aura.

"A book signing," the shorter of the white-haired women said, giggling. "With one of those romance writers. Altogether too proper, I'd say, given the things she writes. I admit I was disappointed. I wanted to hear where she gets her stories. Graphic, if you catch my drift."

"Her stories," Chris mumbled. The color had returned to his face, in fact had flooded it.

Mary found the idea of seniors actually reading the more erotic romances a little unnerving.

"Now, Rosie," the other woman said. "Seems to me Chris isn't interested in our choice of fiction."

"Might learn something," Rosie muttered.

"Well… I didn't…" The usually glib Chris found no coherent words for these two cheerful seniors.

"Let's go." The taller of the women tugged at her companion. "Chris doesn't need us here. We're interrupting."

"I'll see you Saturday," he said a bit stiffly.

Rosie turned sharp blue eyes on Mary. "Hold onto this one, girl. He's the best."

With that endorsement, the elderly pair moved in a half circle around the younger couple and made their way down the street.

Chris sagged. "Bloody hell."

"You're not supposed to talk like that."

"I'm human, Mary. You keep trying to either sanctify or demonize me." He'd never released her arm. Now he used his grip to turn her in the direction they'd been going, following a road that cut diagonally through the town.

The park was in sight when Chris finally spoke. "If I understand this correctly, you think I didn't make love with you Saturday because you're not good enough for me. Is that it?"

She heard his struggle to speak calmly, but Mary had been kidnapped from her office, dragged through town, yelled at – okay, she'd done her share of yelling, too – and on top of everything else it had to be ninety-five degrees outdoors, and she was in no mood for Chris's attempt at rationality.

"Listen here, buddy. Believe it or not, I'm pretty damn picky. When I invite a man to my bed it's an *honor*, and I don't choose lightly. But oh, no, mister holier-than-thou Peterson's got these elevated standards, and the town slut doesn't measure up."

He stopped walking. Through clenched teeth he said, "Don't ever, *ever*, refer to yourself that way."

"Ask anyone. Mary Boylan." She couldn't help the bitterness. "I'm well aware of my reputation. My *outdated* reputation, but it's not like I'll ever live it down."

"Just shut up." His voice had dropped to a near whisper, which was scarier than if he'd shouted. "I beg you. Just. Shut. Up."

She did. So did he. They stood facing each other and blocking the sidewalk, both of them breathing as if they'd gone ten rounds.

The tension hadn't ratcheted down one iota.

"So the way you see it, not sleeping with you was a judgment on you."

"You wanted me. Don't even try to deny it. There's no other possible explanation."

Chris swallowed and let go of her arms. He held out his hand to her, but she ignored him and wheeled away. Without further words they crossed the road circling the park.

"I can come up with a couple of reasons, besides the right one," he said. "Zach could have walked in, for instance. You were distraught, and it might be construed as me taking advantage of you."

They sought the shade of a massive buckeye tree. Nobody was within earshot, although she could see families with young children near the pond.

"Zach's already concluded I was a teenage tramp. What difference would it have made?"

"A lot. Get a grip. You're building a family there."

"And you'd never dream of risking your saintly image."

"Saintly? Me? Times have changed, Mary. Personally, I'd rather be an ordinary human." A white line of tension formed around Chris's lips; his eyes narrowed.

Mary had had enough of his arguments and excuses. "Just stop. Go be an ultra-moral paragon somewhere else, because I don't need this. I'm not leaving myself open to that level of rejection again." She turned from him and began walking.

His hand landed on her shoulder, spinning her around and pressing her up against him. "So *this*—" He kissed her, hard and fast. "—doesn't lead to making love, because I've assumed the right to judge you? I got news. Come with me."

He strode away from the park, pulling her along behind him.

"Where are we going?" A sheen of sweat bloomed on her skin from the exertion of keeping up with him.

"My place. Closer than yours, and this isn't a conversation we can have in the open."

He said nothing more but maintained his hold on her arm until the door of his fourth floor apartment closed behind them. The boxes and general dishevelment told her he'd been packing. "Am I right about this? You're saying because I didn't sleep with you Saturday, I don't consider you good enough for me?"

"I just—" Words failed her. This harder-edged Chris was unexpected. She didn't like it.

"Despite evidence to the contrary."

No point even nodding. There had been plenty of evidence.

"So if we made up for it today, you'd be convinced that isn't true? But damn it, if we make love now, does that mean I think you're free for the taking? Talk about lost causes."

He was right again. She'd dragged them both into a no-win situation.

The hardness on his face dissolved; under it she saw uncertainty. "Mary, so help me, I'm groping in the dark. However much I want this for us... what do I do here?"

A switch flipped in her brain, having to do with hating to see him so vulnerable and unsure. She stepped into his arms and kissed him. A friendly kiss, no passion in it. But he responded. Slowly, luxuriantly, the intensity built until, without warning, she felt a tremor under her fingers, and the kiss morphed into an irresistible force. The hunger, the need and the determination as his tongue danced with hers, wiped out her defenses. His hands pulled her against him while his mouth continued its assault, breaking away from hers as he twisted her hair into a tight, almost painful knot and nibbled her earlobe before running kisses – my God, were those *kisses*? They felt more like... like... she gave up. He made thought impossible.

She fought his shirt free and ran her hands up his back... smooth, hard. Hot. She raised her arms automatically when he yanked her camisole over her head. A gasp, then his hands cupped her breasts almost reverently through her flimsy scrap of bra.

He shuddered, his eyes flicking toward his bedroom. "Yes?" he asked, his voice ragged. "Or no?"

She almost said yes. Longed to say yes. But Saturday, a mirror image of today... had been different. This felt more like being taken, less like being made love to.

"Wait," she said.

His hand had reached for her, but he hesitated and drew back. "What?" His gravelly voice warned her that waiting wouldn't be an option for long.

But her lens had shifted; a new perspective opened up. "You don't want this, do you?" she asked.

"Seems to me it's obvious what I want," he barked. But he released her and crossed the living room to drop onto the sofa, his face in his hands.

She sat in a chair across from him. "Yes, but..."

Chris raised his head and looked at her. Just looked. Whatever the message in his eyes, she either didn't understand it or was too panicky to read it.

"No," he said quietly. "No, you're right. What I dream of is, when you finally come to my bed it will be for love, as well as desire. But... God help me, I'd take you in a moment. I don't know myself right now."

He stared at nothing. Mary sat still, frozen in place, absorbing the candor behind his words.

He wanted more. Expected more.

But...

He was *so* not her type. And yet his touch on her skin, twisting her hair in his hand, claiming her... And she'd stopped it.

Because a fundamentally good man saw value in her. A value she hadn't been able to see herself.

"Should I go?"

"No, don't. Come over here."

She rose and sat next to him on the sofa. When she risked touching his back, she felt him spasm through the knit of his shirt.

"I'm sorry, Chris. I didn't understand."

Tension played across his facial muscles, his bleak expression. "I guess I didn't, either."

"You don't have any reason to take a chance on me."

He finally sat upright, gathering her hands in his grasp. She could see that his body hadn't recovered; he must be suffering, but he held himself back, touching only their united hands. "Because you had a baby at fifteen? That's no cause for condemnation. Because you've been kind of wild? I told you, I went pretty wild myself. I swear, Mary, if we ever get there, I will not only love, but also honor you, and that includes your body. Right now though… would you mind putting your top back on? This is painful."

She'd completely forgotten that she was sitting half undressed beside him. How was it possible to be so comfortable, at home in her skin, after distrusting her body for so long, hating the way she'd used it?

The camisole on, she stood beside him. "I'm not sure what to say."

Chris glanced up at her, his face serious. Mary longed for him to return to his usual cheerfulness, but that didn't seem to be in the cards anytime soon. "I'm trying to figure that one out myself. Manners dictate that I walk you back to your car, but frankly, it could be awhile before I walk anywhere."

"Same here."

"Want to get us something to drink? There's pop or iced tea."

Hands unsteady, she found the tea, poured two glasses, and brought them back to the living room. By then he'd opened the slider to his little balcony. She joined him there, handing him a glass, and they stared out at his apartment's pool below them.

"Can we talk?" she asked. Chris seemed a stranger, as if she only now saw him clearly. Rather like kissing the frog. Presto, instant prince.

"Sure. What about?" He flashed the original Chris smile, returning the evening to a semblance of normalcy.

"You. How you got to where you are."

Chris pressed the glass to his face. "Why I opted for ordination instead of commercial success, you mean?" He glanced over at her. "There's not much money in ministry. Assuming I take over at the Renewed Life Center, it comes with a little house. I'm comfortable there, it's got that air of a home that's held a lot of love, but it's old and definitely not upmarket."

"You said you'd been in business."

"Second in command in human resources for a corporation with ten thousand employees. The head hunters had noticed me. All that at twenty-eight. Heady times."

"What happened? I don't believe you were active in a church then."

"Wouldn't have voluntarily set foot in one."

"Then what?"

There were no chairs on the tiny deck, so he leaned against the wall. "Simple story, but not easy to talk about. My best friend was always a daredevil. He tested fate one time too many and ended up a quadriplegic. I hung out at the hospital, then at a rehab and extended care facility. When Darren wasn't around or available, I'd visit with the others." He fell silent.

After a minute she said, "Chris?"

He jumped slightly, as if he'd been submerged in memory. "What happened… Darren died. He couldn't breathe on his own, and then he got pneumonia. I lost my best friend. And the visiting.

"I went to the funeral, of course. Methodist, nothing like the Renewed Life Center, but even so I got a hint that there might be something to that religion stuff. Might be," he emphasized. "I didn't have a dramatic conversion on the road to Damascus or anything. But I found comfort in it."

"Baby steps."

"Barely steps at all, at first. Back to my life. But I'd go home and stand in my condo – we're talking Cincinnati, tenth floor, luxurious – anyway, I'd look around and wonder why I was there. I like nice things. I like having a financial cushion."

She thought about the leather sofa, the quality of the furniture in his living room. He'd brought the remains of his high-flying lifestyle to Calter Creek with him.

"But the work, the life… they lost meaning. I missed the positive feeling I'd had at the rehab home. Just listening perhaps, holding the hand of a senior who'd fallen and broken a hip and wasn't sure if the pain would ever go away, or if she'd ever walk again." He paused. "There'd been some fundamental shift, one I didn't know how to interpret."

"So, you took action." Mary kept her voice quiet. She sensed Chris didn't readily share this deeply personal time of his life.

"Volunteering was miles from my world view. But finally, I got it. I went back to the rehab place and asked about volunteer opportunities. And they referred me to their head of pastoral care."

Giving him space, Mary sipped her tea. The ice cubes had already mostly melted. "And from there… next logical step?"

"Mmm. I visited twice a week after work, then three times. And talked to the pastor. Eventually I checked out his church. I literally shook in my boots the first time I attended a service." He chuckled. "It wasn't a good fit, but it gave me the impetus to shop around. I found another church, another minister. Two years later I enrolled at the seminary. For my second-year practicum they referred me here, to Rod… he and I did Ellen's service together. He's been my friend and mentor ever since. Work couldn't believe it," he added, clearly amused by the memory. "They told me I was out of my mind, throwing over such glorious career prospects."

"Do you agree? Regret?"

He idly reached for her hand, intertwining their fingers. Down below, what looked like every child and most adults in the apartment block had converged on the pool to fight the stifling heat. "No regrets, usually." He glanced at her, then away. "No, that's wrong. No regrets, ever. Frustrations sometimes. If I could figure out a way not to blush, I'd have life by the tail."

"I like that you blush. It shows that there's a real person inside."

"It can show more than I want it to," he grumbled, but grinned at the same time; the good-natured Chris was back.

"So now you work at the senior center and the youth drop-in center and… do you do the apple thing, too?

"I collect windfalls from houses. It's amazing how many people have apple trees, but the apples are a little bruised or a hole might or might not be a worm, and they won't touch them. We process thousands of pounds of apples every year."

136

"Is that all?"

"All? There aren't any more hours in the day. Running a church is a business. Besides the expected activities like preparing lessons – you might call them sermons, but to me that sort of implies a my-way-or-the-highway speech, and we're not like that – there's the social and fundraising stuff, talking with anyone who brings a concern to your door, and keeping the building standing from one year to another. It'll be a full-time job once Rod retires."

"Seeing you in that gown thing…"

His mouth twisted. "We almost never use them."

"The folks dragged me to a church, growing up. The minister preached hellfire, and his assistant—" She froze, not yet ready to tell Chris about the nausea at the touch of the man's hands, his voice assuring her that she wanted it.

He missed her cue. "We come in all shapes and sizes, Mary. And all beliefs." His grip on her hand tightened. "I'm dying for you, okay? But I mean this." His half smile deserted him, and he finally turned his gaze from the pool to her. "When it happens for us… I want it to mean something. I've seen it with other couples, but not for me, not yet. Until now."

Chris's honesty released a pent-up dam of feeling. His words washed over her and threatened to swamp her. They were too rich, too meaningful, for what might have happened between them. It pointed out the difference between them so clearly. That he would think of earning the right to make love to her, and she had thought only of getting his clothes off.

But still…

"Church wives run Sunday schools and stuff. That's not me."

Wives? Where had that come from?

He chuckled, a flash of his casual good humor. "In fact, Rod's wife sees to the bookkeeping, as well as keeping the inevitable church politics under control. Rod's more cerebral. It's figuring out where your strengths are… and deciding if you want any part of it. You don't have to be involved."

"Chris, it's time for me to go. I'm overwhelmed."

"I'll walk you to your car."

"No need."

"For you, maybe. I agree we've pushed this far enough for now, but I don't want to be apart from you, either. Does that make any sense?"

She smiled. "Yeah, some."

"Come on, then."

Few words passed between them during the walk through town, but in the parking lot he kissed her. Not the hottest they'd exchanged, not by a long shot, but nice.

As she drove away, she idly wondered how it would be to say goodbye every morning at the door of a dumpy little house that felt like home, watching him go off to help the people he cared about so deeply.

Mary.

Chris's whole body ached. Prolonged arousal, plus reliving the pain of Darren's death, the story of his conversion... it had been a grueling evening... but necessarily honest.

Who knew he harbored caveman tendencies, dragging Mary to his lair? Barry would laugh his head off.

She enflamed him, enraptured him, didn't understand him, and drove him crazy. Whatever his past experience, Mary was in a whole different league.

He'd watched her drive away, then drifted toward home, wishing for the new condo rather than the expressionless apartment. Funny how some places simply refuse to bend to your will, allow you to put your mark on them.

He could throw stuff in boxes. That would help take his mind off Mary.

Sure it would.

Just thinking about her, the temptation lurking under her little shirt thing... heat flooded him again.

Public place, Peterson. Get a grip.

Bad choice of words. A grip... oh, shoot.

He crammed his hands in his pockets, not that that would fool anybody for more than ten seconds.

A dip in the overcrowded pool might cool him off – if he managed to control his baser instincts long enough not to make a spectacle of himself. Which meant *not* going down the only neural path currently functioning in his brain.

So this is what it means to burn.

Desiring her, that was one thing. Today, fueled by the possibility it might actually lead to lovemaking... he'd barely touched her, not the way he longed to, yet when she said *wait* she'd nearly killed him.

Walking along the shadier south side of Main Street, his body more or less under control, Chris twisted his mouth into a semblance of a grin, laughing at himself. More than lust underlaid his overcharged skin, nerves, blood vessels, just about every part of him in fact. But at the moment, lust won hands down.

He wondered what she was thinking right now. And feeling. All his fine words about waiting until they were sure... did it mean anything at all to her? He didn't get to be assistant director of HR, much less an ordained minister, without psychological and counseling experience under his belt, and her self-doubt slapped him in the face every time he saw her. On her own turf, across town, he had no way to counter it... not that he would dare give her advice.

At his apartment Chris headed for the shower. Between external and internal heat sources, he was desperate. When he was a kid, Barry had told him to be careful, or it might get stuck that way. He was beginning to think his big brother was right.

Zach was there when Mary got home. She'd completely forgotten that possibility, focused on stripping off her clothes, taking a cool shower, relaxing with a glass of wine in her summer jammies and lightweight robe. Giving herself a chance to recover from the encounter with Chris and whatever it meant.

He looked up from his magazine when she came in. "Holy crap, Mary. What happened to you?" He sprang to his feet before she'd even kicked her shoes off, coming close and peering at her – and flashing from alarmed to amused. "That looks a lot like whisker burn to me."

"Which you're an expert at?"

"Girls have complained a time or two. I shave before I go out now. Who did that to you?"

"No one."

"Ghosts don't have five o'clock shadow."

"This one does."

"Are we having supper?"

She glanced at her watch. Almost eight thirty. Given the temperature, no way was she cooking, but maybe she should eat. "Want to make a deli run? There's money in my purse."

"Couldn't you go?"

"Whiny baby. No, I got overheated earlier—" She realized what she said and did a Chris, the heat creeping up over her face. She ignored it. "I made the mistake of walking across town instead of taking the car, and I'm ready to die of heatstroke. You get the food."

Zach's protest had been form. He was already rummaging in her purse for the promised funds. "Salami on rye, slaw?"

"Sure."

She hid out in the shower as her brain tried to make sense of the evening.

Couldn't Chris see what was right in front of him? Even if they managed to strike something up – and in the face of the fire that kindled and flamed every time they got within sight of each other they certainly could *strike something up* – even given that, it would burn hot for a while, then lukewarm, and finally fizzle, leaving two people with nothing in common, no real overlap in their lives. She saw it so clearly, surely he must, too.

Unless he planned to try to change her. Mary's lips compressed into a thin line.

But no. Chris wasn't like that. Was he? Nothing about him was as she'd expected.

She let the water pour over her, rinsing the shampoo out of her hair and the heat out of her body.

He'd certainly taught her that dangerous men came in many guises. His story, full of good deeds and morality… she'd learned early and well not to expect lasting respect. And earning Chris's respect… he was just too good for her.

Chapter 16

Passages, the teen youth center, was quiet for a Thursday morning in the middle of summer. Could be the heat wave had sapped all the youthful energy, or lots of folks were away on vacation.

Whatever, the peace completely bypassed Chris. He charged into the office from the small room shared by the coordinators and leaned over Peggy, the receptionist, jabbing his finger at a spreadsheet on her ancient computer screen. "I can't believe they turned us down. Half a dozen basketballs. What is it about six balls the board doesn't get?"

Peggy was well suited to her position by virtue of being completely unflappable. "The budget."

"Damn the budget." He stopped, swallowed, got his voice under control. "The kids need a reason to come here. A bunch of cracked table tennis balls isn't going to do it."

"How many do you have now?"

"Two. One of them won't hold air." Chris held up a half flat basketball. "We can't run a program like this."

"Didn't the board suggest a car wash?" Peggy said.

"The board's next to useless. Remember how much enthusiasm the last car wash whipped up? They don't even help with advertising." Another pause, another attempt to keep his voice and emotions under control. "Funded the snack bar for a month. Talk about demoralizing."

Peggy patted his arm. "You're taking on the cares of the world, Chris. This isn't your concern."

"As the person facing the kids and telling them no basketball tournament because we can't afford another half dozen balls, it's my concern." He ran a hand through his hair. As he did, he glanced up and spotted a young man hunched over a clipboard in the lobby. His mood changed through a hundred eighty degrees.

"Zach!" Chris touched Peggy on the shoulder, thanking her for listening to him, then went out of the office into the lobby. He extended a hand.

Zach stood, and they shook. "You suggested volunteering. I was just filling out the application, since I'm kind of at loose ends at the moment, and it would look good on a resume, and it could be fun…"

"No need to give me excuses to do what I'd hoped you might do. Come on in, I'll show you around."

Zach fell into step with Chris. First stop, a formal introduction to Peggy, then a tour of the gym, the meeting rooms, and finally the equipment room.

"You see why I was ranting."

Zach looked at the worn and deficient supplies. He picked up a table tennis ball. Ran a thumb over the crack. "You've got a problem here."

"A big one. We've put the squeeze on the school board, the city, the county, the parents of the kids who are regulars here. Each time we get a little, enough to squeak by, but what we need is to replace the whole mess. Begging isn't an aspect of this job I enjoy."

Zach surveyed the shelves and chose a battered fielder's mitt, and a softball that had to be ten years old. He began rhythmically thumping the ball into the mitt, which, although their largest, was still too small for his hands. "So, no car wash, huh?"

"Overheard that, did you?" Chris grinned. "Peggy keeps me sane when I get on my soapbox. Come on, let's grab a drink. If we're lucky there's a stale muffin."

Settled in the utilitarian kitchen with pop but no muffins, he said, "What were you thinking about in terms of volunteering?"

"Pretty much anything, especially baseball or basketball. I like kids."

"You'll have to. They can be a handful."

Zach grinned. "I did some coaching in college, just neighborhood league baseball. Twelve-year-olds."

"So, you've already tested out your people skills."

"Yeah, I guess. The kids seemed to be okay with me." His ears reddened; a kindred spirit, Chris thought.

"Do you have any references from those days?"

"I could probably get one. Before I came down here, I wasn't thinking about stuff like that."

"The board makes the decisions, but I'll put in a good word. You're majoring in something sports related?"

"Yeah, management. I'm not good enough to be a professional jock."

"But you wish you were."

Zach shrugged. "Who wouldn't? Doing what you love, earning the big bucks?"

Chris grinned. "As a man who does what he loves and earns next to nothing, I can relate. I've got to run. Finish the form and leave it with Peggy. You'll hear from someone – soon, I hope."

As he left, he felt Zach's eyes on his back. His skin prickled. Zach represented another complication in his quest to win Mary, and the younger man's assessing gaze suggested he was ready to spring to the attack should anything hurt her.

Good. She needed allies. He just didn't want to be the one attacked.

"Are we having fun yet?" Mary asked the women gathered around the table. Libations' Friday night music pounded around them, so they all leaned in slightly, in order to hear each other.

Mel raised an eyebrow. "You're questioning it?"

"I'm not feeling it."

"Care to elaborate?" Bryony asked.

"She's not exactly a barrel of laughs tonight," Mel observed. "Do you suppose something's on her mind?"

"Or someone?" Bryony countered.

"Guys? Sitting right here?"

Mel grinned, but it missed being the trademark grin she and Bryony were used to.

"Enough about me," Mary said. "What's up with you?" She gestured in Mel's direction with her wine cooler.

"That's two of you who're missing the joy," Bryony said. "Makes me wonder why I'm hanging out with you at all."

"Plenty of joy," Mel said.

"Tons," Mary said. "I moved two houses in that new Brandon Caine development this week. Lots of money equals lots of joy."

"Especially with another mouth to feed," Bryony said.

Silence descended. Mary squirmed.

"We didn't want to bring it up until you did," Mel said. "But since you haven't…"

"Elaborate, girlfriend," Bryony said. "No one else need know your dastardly secrets, but we're your best buds. We've got privilege."

Mary sighed. She'd expected the inquisition; she just hadn't been sure what shape it would take. "What do you want me to say? My parents adopted Zach, so legally they're his parents, too."

"We've done the backward math," Bryony said.

"By now most of Calter Creek has," Mel said.

"What were you thinking, having a baby so young? Not a clever move."

"Nothing clever about it," Mary conceded. "I was a kid in a situation I couldn't handle. My parents packed me off to my aunt in Halifax, then raised Zach right in front of me. Like rubbing my nose in it."

"That's not such a big deal. Why didn't you tell earlier? Why the secret?"

Why, indeed. Hadn't she been asking herself the same question ever since Zach found out?

"It's not that easy."

Mel held up her hand. "Enough. What went down years ago isn't at issue. More to the point, what happens now? He's staying with you? What's that like?"

What was it like to finally have your golden son under your roof, have him there for supper most nights, talk to him into the evening, learn his hopes and dreams...

"We're adapting. Zach's big, he takes up more space than I ever dreamed possible. I knew he planned to move here before my dad died."

"So now you've got Zach dealing with this new relationship, starring you as mother instead of sister," Bryony summed up. "And you trying to figure out how to be a mom. It sounds like a mess, Mary."

"Maybe not so much." Mary ran a finger along the rim of the glass of wine cooler, grateful that it kept her throat from drying up completely, as well as occupying her hands. "He's a good kid. He told me he called in at the youth drop-in center up near where they're building Landmark Mall and volunteered. Chris suggested it."

"Ahh," Mel and Bryony said in chorus.

Mary froze. The Zach conversation, she'd expected. This? Oh, no. Enough was enough. "Nothing doing, okay?"

"Defensive much?" Mel asked Bryony.

"Too much, I'd say," Bryony said.

"He's a nice guy. Fun to be with. But that's it."

"Good kisser?"

Mary turned the glass on the table a little faster.

Mel noticed. "Good kisser," she said to Bryony.

"I *wish* you two would stop doing that. It's like trying to relax with a Greek chorus around you."

They both laughed. Mary gave up and laughed with them. "Yeah. Not going anywhere, though."

"Time will tell," Mel said. Mel was inclined to be smug, with her banker drooling all over her these days.

146

"Why not?" ever practical Bryony asked.

"For one thing, turns out he's a minister. A little fact he neglected to share when we met him."

"Get out," Bryony said. "Like, sermons and prayers and stuff?"

"And a long white robe to do them in. I found out when he officiated at Ellen's funeral. You may remember her, she was the receptionist at the office for years."

"The slime. And he never told you?"

"Nope. A deceitful rev."

"And this is a deal breaker?" Mel said. "I mean, if he's good in bed and he treats you well and if you really get off on him…"

Mary shook her head. "Not gonna happen. Anyway, enough about me. There's something you're not saying. Don't think I don't recognize it."

"True," Bryony said. "Come on, Mel. Spill."

Mell shrugged as if it didn't matter. "I talked to the boss lady today. About moving up."

"Promotion?" Bryony asked.

"Bigger pay? More responsibility?" Mary asked.

"Taking work home? Which you swore you'd never do?" Bryony asked.

"Ten to one her banker's behind this," Mary informed Bryony.

"No bet. Why would you want to, Mel? You love your work."

"Yeah, but there's no challenge anymore. I'm not stretching."

Mary and Bryony exchanged an eye roll.

"Baloney for brains. That's what love does to you," Bryony said.

"A mistake. The love and the promotion. Baloney's awful," Mary said. The wine cooler might be getting to her, just a little. Probably because it was such a filthy hot night.

"Lay off Ryan," Mel said. "Nothing to do with him."

"Uh huh."

"Honest."

Poor Mel. Mary called a halt, even though Mel's love life served as a useful deflection from her own. "Find something more cheerful to talk about."

"More cheerful than men?" Which Bryony didn't have one of at the moment.

"Has anyone been out to Creekside Mall recently?" Mary asked. "The new fall stuff should be coming in about now."

"Absolutely no way am I dealing with anything involving long sleeves tonight," Mel said flatly. "The heat out there's suffocating."

Her friends chattered on, sipped at their drinks, and watched the action around the bar. Mary valued these two women, her sounding board and cheering section. But tonight…

Tonight, she'd rather be at home. The more the decibel level ratcheted up, the less she wanted to be here. For perhaps the first time in the last ten years or so, Mary and Libations weren't working for each other.

They'd end up knitting, she thought, a trifle sourly. Chatting on each other's sofas.

Sure.

But maybe she could at least learn how to knit…

She'd be willing to bet Chris wouldn't turn up at the bar tonight. So what was the point?

Chapter 17

"All done," Mary said. "It's yours."

Standing outside the lawyer's office holding an envelope full of legal documents, Chris looked like a man who had just won the lottery, the girl, and the next presidential election with one spin of the roulette wheel.

"My impulse is to grab you up and swing you around. I suppose that wouldn't be politically correct."

"Don't do it. You'd be sorry." She shot him a look, warning him off.

"Funny, isn't it." He took her hand and steered her along the street by the municipal park, toward the heart of downtown. "It isn't like it's my first home. Why this should thrill me so much…" He shrugged.

"Then my job is done. Congratulations."

Walking through Calter Creek was far from pleasant, especially in business attire. Chris had cleaned up really well, so to speak; she assumed his lightweight gray suit dated from his business days. Still, it must be agony to wear, because her skirt and jacket brought to mind words like heatstroke and shade and beer. Today, though, Chris was impervious to not only the heat but any negative vibrations at all. "Want to go over and look around?" he asked her.

"Not this morning. I have another appointment later. You go. I doubt anyone could stop you."

"You're right. Wish we could share it, though."

"When are you moving in?"

"Saturday, but I'll be shifting things all week. There's a team from the church, plus Sven and a few others, coming to help out. The little stuff I can handle on my own." He got that dreamy look on his face she'd seen once or twice. "I want to go over there and throw all the windows open – all the windows that will open, anyway – and sit on the back stoop and have a beer and look at the garden… I expect you think I'm crazy."

"It sounds cool and nice, actually. Go do it."

"I'll see if Rod wants to come over." At her slight frown, he elaborated, "Senior minister, remember? Great guy. Come with me. Just for a minute." Abruptly Chris changed direction, looked up and down the quiet street, then dragged her across it into the park, where he stopped in the shade of a buckeye.

"I really don't have time…"

"Thirty seconds." He dropped the envelope with all the legal documents and put a foot on it. Then he reeled her in and kissed her.

Sometimes she wished he wouldn't do that. Just assume he could kiss her anytime, anywhere. But now definitely wasn't one of those times. She drank in all he could give her, meeting his hands, his tongue and lips, even the length of his body pressed against hers, and ignoring the trickle of perspiration working its way down her spine under her suit jacket and top. Chris had raised her temperature, if that was even possible in the sultry heat.

When by mutual consent they broke apart, he said, "Now that was a mistake. You should have stopped me."

She just looked at him.

"Good to know," he said, reading her unspoken message. "But besides some serious discomfort in my immediate future, now we're both about ten degrees hotter. Is there a water fountain around here somewhere?"

"Over on the other side, near the playground, I think." The words didn't come out completely smoothly. A little breathlessly, maybe.

A little like she could eat him for breakfast, right here on the street.

"You have an appointment. Let's go."

150

He got them safely back across the street and steered them onto Main Street. From there it was six blocks to the heart of downtown and Mary's office.

"Are you going to make it? You've gone awfully red." Chris's concerned face studied her.

"As long as we stay on the south side of the road, in the shade of the buildings." It was still early enough that the sun wasn't overhead.

He nodded but didn't look convinced. "I was going to peel off and go back to my apartment, but I think I'd better see you back to your office."

For once she didn't argue. It had been a fine morning so far, even if it wasn't quite coffee break time yet, and she wasn't in a hurry for it to end. Chris's palpable excitement at completing the handover of the condo, the kiss...

The kiss. And she thought she'd get any work done today?

Chris could become a habit. Somehow, she had to prevent that. But how? When his presence was as smooth and seductive as a hot fudge sundae... involuntarily she moaned.

"Was that for me?"

"That was for ice cream." She didn't need to tell him that the ice cream was a simile, and he was every bit as enticing.

"Come out with me tonight? I want to celebrate."

"Tell me, how does a minister celebrate? Are you allowed to?"

He grinned. "I'm allowed. Tonight I'd like to sit on an outdoor patio and order something Italian and enjoy the evening. And talk about the condo. I'm inviting you to be completely bored, because I won't be able to shut up."

She smiled. "All right. Consider it part of the service."

"I'll consider it part of my courtship, if you don't mind. I'll pick you up at seven."

Courtship?

"Chris, go home. It's not that far to the office, and it's in the shade. I'll be fine."

"You understand. Thanks. See you tonight." With those prosaic words he was gone. Mary pictured him loading up his car with boxes, shuffling his life to the condo in the old house, sitting on the stoop with a beer like he'd imagined.

She couldn't – *couldn't* – allow herself to dream of this man. See herself on the stoop beside him. This had to stop.

Which went nowhere toward accounting for the dance in her step as she made her way to her office and her next appointment.

Mary breathed the air, which seemed cooler somehow, perhaps the effect of the grape arbor over the outdoor patio at the Italian restaurant on the old Columbus road. That the grapes were artificial didn't dampen Chris's spirits one bit. Not beer but a decent Chianti stood between them as they settled side by side, so they could both sit in the shade. Mary might have preferred air conditioning, but this place had attitude; she'd take it.

"So what's next?" she asked. "I'm assuming you can't think of anything but your new home, but you must have other things you have to do."

"Meetings all morning tomorrow. We're planning the fall program at Passages. Did you know Zach's volunteered? They called him today to see if he'd run the basketball tournament in August."

"He told me he was looking for ways to volunteer."

"At the party I slipped him a card. Easier to go someplace you know is looking for help than shop around. Anyway, I think he's planning on using it on his resume down the road. Shows that he has experience, as well as being community minded. He seems to be a good kid, Mary."

"I think he is." She fumbled her wine glass and almost spilled the red liquid on the white tablecloth.

Chris put his hand over hers. "Sensitive topic?"

"Some, I guess." She passed it off with a shrug. And wondered why she suddenly felt defensive, and a little angry, around Chris.

"It doesn't need to be. If he were a hoodlum, we might be having a different discussion, but he's not. He was horrified when he saw the state of our equipment room. He wants to make a difference."

"At least he's doing something. I had a snippy call from my mother yesterday, demanding I send him back home. As if I'd kidnapped him or something."

"Does she have the right?"

"Legally, more than I do, but he's nineteen. No one's going to tell him to go live where he doesn't want to live. That's the reality."

"I think we'll be able to keep him busy. It'll be interesting to see how he relates to the kids."

"Give him a fair chance."

He looked mildly shocked. "Of course. I'm not worried at all. My instinct is he's got what it takes."

"I want to know. Any hassles." God, what was going on? It was as if she'd suddenly become possessive where Zach was concerned. As if Chris was trying to win him away from her.

"As you said, he's nineteen. Although he did list you as his next of kin and contact person."

Chris was studying her, as if he couldn't fathom where her thoughts had gone. Well, he'd never been a parent. She thought about this boy who was turning into her honest-to-goodness son. Suddenly, how Zach presented himself to the world mattered. A lot.

Did Chris's opinion matter? Of course. He'd outrank Zach at the drop-in center, so he was in a position to judge. And she didn't like that. At all. She didn't want Zach judged by anyone.

Perhaps sensing her unease, Chris abruptly changed the topic. "You'll come over Saturday? Help with the unpacking?"

"It doesn't sound as if you'll need me. And I have a couple of house showings booked."

"Afterwards. I'd like you to be there. Assuming the weather holds, I'm anticipating a pizza and beer blow-out in the back yard once the heavy lifting's done."

Saturday evening with his church buddies? Not a thrill.

"Once your stuff's moved in, what do you plan to tackle first?"

"Want to see my list?" He said it in a way that sounded almost like *I'll show you mine if you show me yours.* Suggestive.

Of where this evening might go? Mary was having more and more trouble slotting Chris into the ministerial role she'd assigned him to.

She called his bluff. "Okay. Show me."

He whipped a paper out of his pants pocket. "Here goes. First, be sure the windows are in working order and sealed. I'd like to replace them, but that can wait. The fireplace, of course – the guy's coming Tuesday. I'm thinking about a new kitchen counter. The peeling laminate isn't exactly a chick magnet, and if I want a chick in my kitchen cooking for me…" He raised his eyebrows at her, his mouth artificially pulled into what he probably thought resembled a leer.

It was hopeless. The man was hopeless. She shot a wry smile in his direction, shaking her head.

"Come on, Mary. Come over Saturday. Everyone would love to see you."

The laugh faded. "Give me the third degree, you mean. Who's coming besides your church cronies?"

"Sven and Antonio, last I heard. Danika later, she has something on at the college that afternoon. It'll be fun. You can tell me where to put my cups. Actually, if you want to go shopping for shelf paper after supper…"

She almost said no. then asked herself why not. Shelf paper would be an innocuous experience. Neutral. Not dangerous.

At least she thought not dangerous until they got to the condo. The antique ceiling light in the living room gave just enough illumination to get them to the kitchen.

Where he tossed the shelf paper on a table he'd already moved in, wheeled around, and hoisted her up onto the counter. Mercifully a smooth section where there was no rough laminate edge to snag her clothing. "Kitchens have lots of uses," he said, worming his way between her legs. His hands landed on her shoulders.

She was impressed. He didn't look like he'd have the strength to lift her that way. Chalk up another surprise to Chris Peterson.

"Cooking, making coffee…"

"Pouring wine, washing dishes. I'll bring dishwashing soap from home tomorrow."

"This is home, isn't it?" Her voice, annoyingly, was a little unsteady.

"Not till I'm actually sleeping here. Not tonight. Which means, I suppose, that I'm not sleeping with you tonight."

"No… of course not… I think…"

He was closer, leaning in, his hands now on the counter either side of her. She should have kept her knees locked together, forced him to stand beside her instead of *there* where he could push up against…

His mouth found hers, and simultaneously his hands abandoned the counter to move with pinpoint accuracy to her breasts. His thumbs… oh God… his mouth, his teeth nibbling gently on her lower lip…

One of his hands shifted to the back of her head. They both tilted their heads, improving the angle, then the kiss progressed from nice to the hottest thing that had ever happened to her. Her arms wrapped around him, pressing him closer. If she'd been able to form a coherent thought at all, it would have been that the only reason she wished she'd kept her knees locked together was that if Chris chose today to take things further, it was going to be almost impossible to deny him.

He was the first one to step away. "Mistake," he said. "I seem not to be able to help myself when you're around."

Mistake? She shoved him backwards and hopped off the counter. "First time anyone's said that to me." Clearly her

155

emotions were too close to the surface. She was insulted, again, even though he couldn't possibly mean to offend her.

He gestured. "Look at me. I'm going to be in agony for hours, probably. Definitely a mistake."

She looked. She couldn't help herself.

Looked back at his face. "I could…" She took a step forward, but stopped when he shook his head.

"One day," he almost whispered, "I'd like nothing more than to have you…" He paused and chuckled. "Take care of my problem? Funny how the words don't come easily anymore." He turned away from her, to look out the window. "One day I'll return the favor. I want to, Mary. You don't know how much. But I can't even look at you right now. I'll explode."

"Funny," she said to his back. "I've never thought of ministers actually… doing it."

"We do it. Very prolific lot, ministers. Parsonages full of kids." His shoulders shook; she suspected he was laughing. "Must be all those congregations praying for us. Or maybe it's just that the houses we live in tend to be under-insulated. Long, cold nights. Lack of distractions." He turned back to her, raising a quizzical eyebrow. When she didn't immediately respond he elaborated. "Ministers are men, too. Unless they're women, anyway. What do you think we'd pray for?"

"World peace?" She gave up and grinned. "You're certainly skewing my perception of you men of God."

"Come on. After that, there's no way I can lay shelf paper in here tonight."

He took her home, without much comment. Their kiss at her door was neutral, at least until he shifted briefly to her earlobe. "Thanks, Mary."

"What for?"

"Tonight. You make me happy."

"Oh." Dammit, how did you tell a man he made you happier than you'd been in your life, without leading him on? How was she ever going to get him out of her life?

He gave her a last peck. "See you Saturday."

~

156

Chris ran into Zach as he exited Mary's building. To his surprise, the young man didn't seem exactly pleased to see him.

"Heading home?"

He nodded. "Just dropped Mary off. See you soon, I hope."

"I'll be in Thursday afternoon. They called this afternoon to say they'd approved me."

"Glad to hear it. I didn't expect any problem, but administration can drag its feet, especially in the summer. It's a miracle we get anything done."

Chris turned to go, only to feel Zach's hand on his arm.

"I'm watching out for her."

"Good. Glad to hear it."

"She's my mother."

"And given a chance, she'll be a fine one."

"So, am I going to go up there and find she has whisker burn all over her neck again?"

Chris was grateful for dusk. He was sure his ears were red. "Ask Mary."

The look they exchanged was more like two primo males defining their territory. No camaraderie at the moment. None at all. Zach looked grim, like he didn't quite know how to handle the situation he'd just put himself in, but was going to deal with it anyway.

Chris knew how he felt. He'd never encountered the grown son of a woman he dated, either.

Finally Zach broke the impasse. "Just remember. I'm watching."

"I appreciate it." He could have said a lot more. About how there are never any guarantees in a relationship. How his intention was a long way from hurting Mary. How he was as much in foreign territory as Zach was – and he sensed Mary wasn't any surer of her footing. But he said none of it. One day, maybe, but right now it wasn't his place. He let the young man stake his territory, conceded his right to do so, and sent out a silent prayer of gratitude for this positive step in the forging of a relationship between Zach and Mary.

157

With curt nods on both sides, the men parted. Chris drove back to his apartment, now no more than a shell of a home, thoughtful.

All in all, he concluded, Zach was a complication he was happy for. His presence might heal something in Mary, and he was glad someone besides him had her back.

At the thought of Mary's back, he groaned and hit the shower, then settled in for what he expected would prove to be another restless night.

Chapter 18

Chris watched Zach out in the gym, enthralling the thirteen- and fourteen-year-olds surrounding him. The basketball erupted from the middle of the group and sailed toward the beaten-up net. It bounced off the rim, but that didn't dampen the enthusiasm of the kids around the young man.

The basketball hadn't been here before today. Zach had apparently strong-armed some of his friends in Cleveland into donating money for balls. They now possessed six, if you counted the one that wouldn't stay inflated.

A cheer echoed around the gym as a shot rattled in. Zach grinned. He towered over the other kids, tall and solid. Chris wondered if the handful of girls sprinkled through the knot of teenagers had any interest in basketball, or if it was the new coach drawing them closer.

Hormones. Something he could do without, here at Passages. Theirs, and his too.

He left the gym and finished stowing flats of pop in the fridge. He was just checking the ice supply when Peggy stuck her head in. "Want a drink with more oomph?"

"Thanks, but I'm already over-caffeinated." And had been for the last twenty-four hours, not that he'd needed it. After finalizing the condo purchase, and that incredible episode with Mary in the kitchen, he didn't need a boost to his energy supply. His body was firing on all cylinders. It was more important that he calm himself down, not rev himself up.

Getting Zach in here so quickly had required a phone call, a verbal recommendation, and a request to expedite the interview. Had he done it for Zach, or for Mary, or for

159

Passages? Good question. When the threads of his life converged this way, they defied disentangling, like some of the knitting he witnessed at Silver Threads. But it felt right, as if these particular threads were meant to come together into an intricate, if disorderly, pattern.

He opened a bottle of water and wandered out into the gym.

"Watch out, Priest!"

The girl's shrill cry got through to his instincts. He ducked to the side just as one of the new basketballs landed in the previous location of his chest. Laughing, he set the water on a table and shot the ball toward the cluster of kids.

"Well fielded," Zach called out.

In Peggy's office he settled into her guest chair for a few minutes, watching the activity through her open door. "Think he'll work out?"

"Seems likely, based on this afternoon." Peggy stopped fiddling with her coffee maker and sat. "Where'd you find this guy, Chris? He's what we need around here, and they're few and far between."

"I know his… some of his family. He just moved down from Cleveland to go to OSU."

"You did good. I suppose when school starts, we'll lose him again."

"Maybe not. He's interested in sports management. I looked it up. Doing this kind of volunteer work would play well. He might even be able to get course credit for it, if we give him more responsibility."

More yells and shrieks from the gym. Zach had the kids organized into two squads now, mixing up the boys and the girls. No one could say the game was skilled or even followed rules, but everyone seemed to be enjoying it.

Zach blew a whistle, and for a moment silence prevailed, other than his voice rumbling over the kids.

"I'm hoping word about Zach will get out," he went on. A couple of the guys out there are on the edge. If they're happier here than hanging out with… well, what should I call them?

Thugs? Dangerous anyway. Might be sexy when you're fourteen, but it's not safe, especially given the drug situation in this end of town."

"All we can do is keep trying. Don't get discouraged, Chris. You're a big help."

"Thanks. And me, discouraged? Not on your life." He launched into a description of the condo's wonders, omitting the things he now knew he could do with the kitchen counter.

Not that that wasn't on top of his mind these days. His meeting with Rod tomorrow would get him back on track. He'd already juggled the Sunday lesson schedule so it would be Rod, not him, on stage this week at the Renewed Life Center. He didn't expect he'd have much left to give after the Saturday moving party.

More whoops, as the kids tried to emulate whatever Zach had shown them. Chris chatted with Peggy and listening to the chaos in the gym, daydreaming about his new home and the woman he increasingly wanted to share it with.

Chapter 19

Late Saturday afternoon, Mary ignored her instincts and made her way to Chris's condo, but stopped in the open door, hesitant to join the chaos inside. About twenty adults milled around, filling the living room. She could smell the pizzas, in fact had passed the delivery car when she turned onto his street.

An elderly couple appeared behind her. "Hello," the woman said. "Are you moving in?"

"Oh, no. I'm just a friend."

The man smiled at her. Grand-parental, she thought. Both slightly overweight, she wearing a cardigan, slacks, and a perm, he with iron gray hair and glasses. "We live up on the second floor," he said. "Got the invite, so we came down to see what's happening."

"It's moving day," Mary explained. "Chris arranged a work crew."

"If those women are unpacking for him, he'll be a week before he finds anything," the woman stated with ominous good humor. "We're the Franklins, Ross and Shirley. Ross here works for the city, I babysit."

"Mary. Calter Creek Real Estate."

"Thought I'd seen you somewhere," Shirley said. "Probably the picture downtown in the window."

"So, which one's Chris?" Ross Franklin asked.

"The guy over there." Mary gestured toward a crowd gathering around the pizza boxes spread across the dining table. "In the blue t-shirt."

Looks good in a t-shirt...

"Nice looking fella."

"I suppose. He works at…"

She trailed off as she became aware of a hush, an air of expectancy, falling over the room. All three of them turned toward the pizzas.

Then Chris's voice rang out, alone in the silence. She didn't remember the words later, something about blessing the food, and friends, and his home. But she remembered his assurance, the way his tone conveyed conviction about the efficacy of his words.

Voices murmured amen, then the noise and chaos returned.

And there it was. The other side of Chris, the one she'd done her best to pretend didn't exist. She'd seen him conduct a service. She'd heard him talk about his occupation, even joke about it. This was different. Not a rattled-off prayer over meals such as she'd been subjected to, growing up, but a public statement of faith. The day-to-day reality, the life of a minister.

There was no dodging the truth anymore. Not when her experience with ministers and churches still made her queasy.

"I have to go." She squeezed past the Franklins and fled to her car.

Praying? Getting tangled up in all that religious stuff? No way. *No damn way* could she become a part of all that. They might as well live on different continents.

Never.

She drove home in tears.

Much later that evening, Chris kicked aside a sheet of packing paper and stepped into the main foyer, opening the outer door to find a fuming Zach looming over him. "Hi. What brings you here?" he asked.

"What did you do to her?" Zach growled, then stormed in and spotted Chris's open door. "That yours?"

Chris followed the younger man, quietly closing the doors behind them. "Tell me what you mean. I haven't seen her today."

Mary's absence had been the only downside to an otherwise perfect afternoon. While the men got sweaty shifting the furniture, he'd given the women carte blanche in the kitchen, saying a small, private prayer to be able to make sense of it later. His belongings were stowed, his bed was made, the hot water heater had produced a decent shower a few minutes earlier. The only mystery was Mary. Why hadn't she come? He'd have sacrificed the rest for it to have been her hands unwrapping his plates and smoothing out the stacks of linens.

"Is she okay?" Chris continued. "Not hurt or sick?" Anxiety bit at him, wiping out the lingering glow from the party.

"She's shut up in her room. Look, I warned you, I'm not going to let you—"

"Whoa." He herded Zach to the sofa and sat on a chair across from him. "You haven't talked to her?"

"I tried. She shouted at me to go away."

"Not because of me."

"Then what the hell?" As his righteous indignation faded, Zach sounded bewildered.

Chris fixed him with a level look. "I'll phone her, but no offense, not with you sitting here."

The young man bristled. "I don't want you saying things to my sister you wouldn't—" He caught the ridiculousness of the statement before he finished.

"I say a lot to Mary that I'd rather keep private. You know I'm seeing her. Would you be thrilled to have little brothers horning in on your conversations?"

Or sons.

"I just don't like it, is all," Zach mumbled.

"Because now she's not only your sister but your mother. That will take a while to sort out."

"Oh, it's sorted. After everyone *finally* told me the truth."

"The facts, but the emotions behind those facts won't be that straightforward, for either of you. I expect she'd be happy

164

you're defending her. I'd personally rather not get beaten up because of it, though."

"Yeah, well." Zach seemed not to be able to find a place to put his hands. "That's not how I operate. Usually my size is enough to make people back down. I don't like fighting."

"Good, neither do I. What I propose is this. You head home. I'll phone Mary. If I can't help, you'll be there for backup. You don't need to say anything. All you have to do is be there."

The tension on Zach's face lessened slightly. "What's with women, anyway?" he blurted. "I thought it'd get easier. But what's going on now... I don't get it."

Chris didn't fully get Mary's mood swings either. But he could present the straightforward explanation. "We're simple. Women are complex, Mary especially. It'll sort out."

He hoped. Because his resolve was growing stronger by the day. Despite everything that conspired to keep them apart, he intended to draw them together.

Love.

The word filtered unbidden into his consciousness.

Which is why he chose to avoid an audience when he talked to her. Partly. The other part had to do with what didn't happen in his new kitchen a few days before.

He slapped down the memory, fast. Zach *really* shouldn't pick up on how much Chris desired his sister-mother.

With the teenager on his way home, Chris called Mary's cell, then tried her landline. Her voice told him to leave a message, which he did.

He debated going to her condo but rejected the idea. Instead he fired off two texts. To Zach: *"No answer. Over to you."* To Mary: *"Feeling desperate to talk to you. Missed you today. You okay?"*

Then he waited. But other than a call from a parishioner about rescheduling a blessing ceremony, no one disturbed his uneasy quiet.

Chapter 20

"We keep doing this. You must know by now I'm not going to let you hide forever." Chris propped himself against the divider wall of Mary's cubicle and glared. By Monday, a weekend of frustration, fueled by her refusal to take his calls or to answer the buzzer at her condo, had left his nerves on a short fuse.

"I'm not hiding."

"You're not talking, either. At least tell me what I did. I'm going crazy here."

She got to her feet and glanced at the other three cubicles. The office was deserted except for Jean at the front desk, leaving them effectively alone.

"Whatever you imagined was happening, it isn't. End of discussion."

Wondering what to say next, he heaved a breath. "I can't just walk away from you."

"Irrelevant. It takes two, and you haven't got a second. I'm busy, Chris." Her arms folded across her chest, a classic defensive posture.

He didn't move. In fact, he wasn't sure movement was possible. After a Sunday in which he'd barely been present for Rod's service – the congregants at the Renewed Life Center noted this and took it in their stride, even with a note of sympathy – followed by an afternoon of tearing his hair out and twice going over to her condo to lean on her buzzer, he was so on edge that if forced to movement he would probably rip the fabric on the divider wall to shreds and pitch the thing across the office.

He took a breath and began again. "Why didn't you turn up Saturday? I kept watching for you."

"I…." But whatever she was going to say, she decided against it and shrugged.

He frowned. There was something in her face, the line of her jaw… was she clenching her teeth? With difficulty he shoved aside his rising frustration "We can go to a coffee shop or to the park, your choice. Just tell me why. Tell me what happened."

She sighed, sat, moved her hands to the keyboard, then to her lap, then tapped her fingers on the edge of her desk. Nerves? Her voice, when she spoke, was carefully uninflected. "It's no good, Chris. One of us has to face up to that. We live different lives. There's no common ground."

"But that's the whole point of courtship. We enjoy being together, we want each other – oh, no, don't deny it." He held up a hand when she opened her mouth to speak. "It'll take time to learn each other's ways."

"Our lives don't intersect. They never will."

They stared at each other. He was certain he saw indecision, masked by a stubborn refusal to talk to him, and wondered if his face reflected his desperation to stop this on-again, off-again seesaw of their relationship.

"Please, Mary."

She shook her head. "You need to get this through your head. I'm sorry, Chris, but we're finished. We're wrong for each other. And I want you to leave me alone.*"*

At last their eyes met. Reading what he didn't want to see in hers, he gave a curt nod, turned on his heel, and left.

Parish business occupied his day, along with a couple of hours at Passages. His mood had soured, if that was possible, by late afternoon. Mary was driving him crazy, but at least this latest unexplained retreat helped clarify his feelings. Every buzz, instinct, and thought pointed straight to her.

And didn't he sound like every moony, hopelessly-in-love, you're-my-baby pop song he'd ever laughed at?

167

But she'd closed the doors. Slammed them shut. After her rejection, he had no avenue left to approach her.

And that left the ball in her court. All he could do was get on with his life and hope against all rational hope she'd change her mind.

Chapter 21

Mary watched the Friday night crowd in the bar without enthusiasm. Next to her, Bryony dug a nacho into the little pot of guacamole in front of her. "Energy's not great tonight," she said.

"Blame me, Bry. I'm off my game."

"You've been off your game ever since you started mooning about the preacher man."

"I'm not mooning. He's history, anyway. I've got my commission, I don't have to babysit him anymore."

Bryony treated her to a can-the-bullshit look. "That wasn't babysitting. The flush you'd get when his name came up... was he the pits in bed?"

Mary tried for indifference. "Never went that far."

"Then what happened?"

Bryony bore an unfortunate resemblance to a pit bull when she sank her teeth into a topic. Mary did a short now-or-later debate with herself, then surrendered. "Reality, is all. He's not my type."

"Uh huh. The sparks are flying everywhere, but he's not your type." Bryony rolled her eyes and dug another nacho into the dip. "So how are the man's moves?"

Chewing required concentration. Mary took her time. "Not bad. But come on – a minister? Me?"

You? Why not you? What are you so afraid of?

Why are you semi-lying to one of your best friends?

Nachos absorbed them for a few minutes, then Bryony glanced up, did a double take, and said, "Well, look who's here."

The man walked up to the bar with that confident stride of hot guys who scored more often than not.

Chris's brother.

"Barry? Was that his name?" Bryony interrupted the confusion in Mary's brain.

"Yup."

Barry – and a chance to prove Chris meant nothing. A little flirtation would send a clear signal and end the Chris thing once and for all. Barry's rough edges, clothes that showcased his muscles, a hairstyle more tousled than upmarket... and his interest.... She watched as his eyes scanned the room and landed on their table.

End it... assuming that's what she wanted. Really wanted.

Of course it was.

He sauntered over. "Hello again," he said, looming over them but focusing on Mary. "Dance?"

"Sure." Even though every instinct in her screamed no. *Wrong*. The hell with instincts. If anything would convince Chris to leave her alone... even though the one she needed to convince was herself. Or possibly both of them, because this uncertainty was driving her crazy.

Barry put down his beer and nodded to Bryony, who nodded back and shot Mary a be-careful glare. Taking her hand, he led them into the maelstrom of the club's dance floor.

The nagging sense of wrongness wouldn't leave her, though. The band switched to a slow number and she found herself swaying... but wait. His hands on her hips didn't press her against him as she'd expected. He kept his distance; they barely brushed against each other.

When the song ended, he reclaimed her hand and growled over the bedlam, "Come with me for a minute."

She resisted, wondering what he wanted from her. Did loyalty exist between brothers? Would he try.... But at least she knew, suddenly, irrevocably, that she would not be intimate with Barry. Not now, not ever. "Where?" she shouted.

"Somewhere quieter."

She allowed him to navigate through the milling bodies to the front door, where he said to Enrique, the doorman, "Just stepping out for a breath of air."

She shot a glance at Enrique, silently asking him to watch her back. He nodded. Barry led her down the street to the next storefront.

"So, Mary, let's talk." He released his grip on her hand.

"What about?"

"Chris is real pleased with his condo."

Of course, he'd know that much. Chris had let her know more than once how close he was to his family. "I'm glad. That's my job." She phrased her sentence with care, keeping it all business.

Barry leaned against the brick column dividing the plate glass windows in the lawyers' office. "So why'd you dump him? What did he do to you?"

She ignored a flare of anger and spoke without emotion. "What's *not* going on between Chris and me doesn't concern you. And Bryony's waiting for me." She turned toward the door to Libations.

"Not till you hear me out. You don't listen very well, do you?" He straightened and touched her arm, effectively stopping her flight.

His voice was relaxed, conversational. "The thing about Chris is, seems I spent most of my teen years bailing him out of scraps. He'd be in the middle of some argument or other and I'd have to throw some weight around. Then he got into college and learned to take care of himself. But since he began this new spiritual lark – hell, I shouldn't say that, he's dead serious about it – it's scrambled his social life. Then he finds you and falls ass over teakettle, and suddenly you freeze him out. What's with that?"

Mary turned to him. "Not that it's any of your business, but I'm hardly the kind of woman who goes to church every Sunday."

Barry barked a laugh. "That's what you think Chris expects of you? Don't kid yourself. If you never set foot in that church of his, he'd roll with it."

"I find that hard to believe." Arms akimbo, she glared at him. "Bottom line is, maybe I thought there was something, and maybe I decided I was wrong. And it's frankly none of your business."

"Same as all the others," Barry muttered under his breath. Then he said, "The way I see it, running from Chris because he's a minister is rotten, especially before you even know what his expectations are. When he told me about you, I thought, great, perfect match. Be honest here... has he ever tried to convert you?"

She was silent.

"Has he made a single move to change your life? I bet not. Do you call that a fair chance? Because I don't like to see my baby brother hurting."

"I'm going in."

She'd turned for the door when he spoke again. "Frankly, this scene doesn't appeal to me anymore. It gets old. I wouldn't mind a home and family, if it came my way. That ring any bells for you?"

She ignored him and kept moving, past the doorman, joining the throng in the club.

Bryony greeted her with raised eyebrows.

"Turns out I'm not in the mood for this tonight. Are you ready to go?"

"Works for me. Next time let's try the new wine bar. Quieter."

When they stepped outside, Barry was nowhere to be seen. They parted at their cars. Mary drove home, thoughtful. If even Barry, an obvious player, could consider settling down... if the whole bar scene bored her and her appetite for sleeping with strangers had long since disappeared... if Chris really wouldn't try to change her… change her into what? What did he see, and might that be better for her? Could she learn to live with the minister part?

Zach had gone out. Mary heaved a sigh of relief to find her condo empty, although she wondered what he was doing – and reminded herself to mind her own business.

Was Chris waiting up for Barry? Did he know his brother had picked her up in Libations and lectured her on his sterling qualities? Probably not. She'd bet that encounter had been entirely Barry to the rescue, like when they were kids.

Had she rescued her own brother? Was Zach better off with her? Hell, yes.

Thoroughly confused, Mary got ready for an early bedtime.

There was no point hoping that his seniors would be quiet and well behaved. They never were. Having Chris around to be the butt of their jokes and the object of their matchmaking gave them a reason to turn up on Saturday mornings, so he'd take it.

This morning he expected to take it right on the chin, absorbing the blows.

He checked in with Wanda, the manager of the center. "You heard about Lily?" she asked.

"Yeah. I went to the funeral. We'll miss her." The downside of working with seniors; loss always waited around the corner.

"They may be a little subdued today."

What he wanted, but wished it weren't because of Lily's death. She'd been one of the quiet ones, but everyone there would sense the hole in the atmosphere.

"It's fine with me if we keep it low key."

"Good luck," Wanda said. "They get a kick out of trying to rattle you."

He chuckled. "I'm their favorite grandkid. Talk to you later."

As usual, Nadine was the first to wave him over and comment on the circles under his eyes. "That isn't happy tired," she said. "Something go wrong?"

"You might say that. We're starting with 'Bye Bye Love'. I'll find it for you." He reached for her songbook, thinking to himself, how appropriate.

"Bosh." She whacked his arm. "Love life not firing on all cylinders, I bet."

He sighed. No way could he joke about Mary today. "Let's call it a near miss, okay? I really don't want to go there."

For once she didn't announce his condition to the others. Instead she fixed the sweetest grandmotherly smile in the world on him and said, "It'll get better. Sometimes God tests the good ones before He sets everything to rights."

What could he do but smile back? "Thanks, Nadine. You're one of the good ones yourself."

"I was thirty before I found my luck. That was old in my day. Give it time. You'll see."

"Hope so."

He wove through the room, stowing walkers, bending over wheelchairs to find the place in the songbook, focusing on a senior who could no longer speak clearly, hearing the intent if not the words. What mattered was that he listened, heart and soul.

Chapter 22

Zach had been volunteering at the teen center for about two weeks. So far, he seemed to enjoy it. He was talking before Mary was fully in the door.

"I get a real kick out of those kids."

She dropped her purse on the table in the entry, then, with a sigh of relief, toed off her work shoes. "Tell me more."

He was sprawled on her sofa with a beer – *don't comment* – looking more content than he had in a long time. "Passages is gonna look good on my resume, and the staff is solid. Besides Chris, a couple others organize things. There's this one bunch of older kids, though..." He trailed off as if debating the wisdom of telling her. "Troublemakers. They've been banned, but they turned up again today. Hassled some of the younger ones. Into drugs, as a guess."

She tensed. "You're not in danger there, are you?"

His laugh came easily. "Of course not. The supervisors deal with them. Don't fuss, Mary. It's a good place. Well run, even if they are always broke."

"Glad it's going well. I'm heading for the shower."

"So, why'd you dump Chris?"

Sucker-punched. Glaring at Zach, she said, "Too many people think they have a right to stick their noses in my business." She disappeared down the hall.

"Want me to make sandwiches for supper?" he shouted after her.

"Great, thanks."

But when she returned to the living room, comfortable in shorts and a loose top, Zach hadn't given up. "The story with Chris? Don't say you aren't interested, Sis. Food's on the table."

Mary sat across from him, wondering how to avoid this conversation. "Yes, he's a good guy. It doesn't follow that I have to be into him, just because he likes me."

"But you are. Or you were." Zach took an enormous bite of his chicken and mozzarella sandwich.

She shrugged before trying a much more moderate bite. Zach made sandwiches three inches thick. "Things change," she said once she'd swallowed. "It wasn't working out, that's all. Mutual agreement."

"Bull. You're so restless you're twitching. And he looks kinda... I don't know. Forlorn?"

She put the sandwich on her plate. "Please, Zach. Drop it."

Zach frowned at his plate. After a pause, he said, "Look, we've both got the scars from our shitty upbringing, but you need to get a grip on reality. He's not a sleaze. He's interesting, he works hard. And you ditch him? Honestly. He deserves another chance. So do you."

This was her son talking? He sounded more like an older brother.

Barry preached the same line. As did Bryony.

Zach disappeared into the kitchen, returning with a glass of milk. "I met some guys at the park today. They're at OSU, we're getting together to shoot the breeze." He chugged the milk, finished his sandwich – she'd never understand how a member of the male sex could gnaw through food so quickly – and eyed hers. When she nodded, he snatched up her second half and carted it to the kitchen along with his plate and glass. He emerged, chewing. "Forgot to mention, my car's acting up. I'm taking it in to a mechanic in the morning. Any chance of a ride to Passages tomorrow?"

Mary did a quick mental review of her schedule. "Sure."

"Gotta go."

"Be safe."

"Think about it," he commanded. The front door closed behind him.

Like she didn't spend most of her waking hours, and a fair number of her sleeping ones, thinking about it.

Mary curled up on the sofa, idly scrolling through the empty offerings on the television, gave up on that and tried a book, tossed it down and stepped onto her balcony. No matter how she fought it, Chris permeated her mind. Her home, her work… her life, leaving her empty, hollowed out, when he wasn't in it.

Was she just scared?

Maybe.

No Chris phoning or dropping by tonight.

Nothing at all. The words echoed in her brain.

Abruptly she rushed back into her condo, snatched up her purse, and headed for her car.

The past weekend hadn't been ideal for coming to terms with the Mary situation, if that was even possible. Barry's flying visit, ostensibly to check out the new place, meant that they'd done a ton of home repair work together, scraping layers of wallpaper, patching walls, and tinkering with plumbing, leaving Chris aching in newly discovered muscles and with a hefty list of finish-up tasks.

Maybe Mary had preferences in wall colors?

He shoved the thought away. Like it or not, he was on his own.

This evening he'd put on a shapeless pair of shorts and a paint-stained t-shirt and escaped out the back door. Nobody had paid any attention to the side garden in years, it seemed, other than to keep the strip of lawn mowed. If he wanted a decent view from most of his windows, it fell to him to deal with the weeds.

He made a mental note to check on the gardening services contract.

And to buy more equipment. The trowel and dandelion extracting tool he'd purchased earlier did their job, but his knees were taking a beating. Perhaps one of those pad things, and a rake... and with storage at a premium, how about a garden shed? He could tuck it in the back corner of the lot, where it wouldn't bother anyone, and then stock up on whatever tools he liked.

At least the mechanical process of removing identifiable weeds gave him space to mull over the enigma of Mary.

It was the kind of evening Ohioans dreamed of and too rarely got. The mosquitos held off on their nightly assault, and the humidity had dropped, making the heat bearable. Chris tackled his weeding with an enthusiasm that almost countered the disquiet in his mind. Halfway along the bed, he wiped his dirty hands on the seat of his shorts, sat back on his heels, and admired his handiwork. Then he straightened as he heard the buzzer through the open window, signaling someone at the outside door.

Standing, he considered the picture he must present, and shrugged. Gardening was an honorable activity; they could take him as they found him, dirt and all. He circled to the front of the old mansion and stopped dead.

There, five steps above him, Mary waited. Fighting the rush he got at the sight of her, Chris said in his most normal voice, "Hey."

She whirled. She looked so clean, so fresh, so... scared?

"Come around this way. I've been weeding. You can probably tell."

"Yeah, a little."

"The bed gets morning sun and it should be a feature, not an abandoned junkyard. I cleared out a garbage bag of pop cans and wrappers." He waited until she made her way down the steps and across the lawn to him before he led her along the side of the house, resolved to act as if her appearance was an everyday event. "Plants are a new challenge," he rambled on, "despite the parents assigning us chores all summer, including weeding."

"You're making progress," she said.

"Half of what's left is weeds, most likely. My sister will turn up one day, and she's the expert." He'd stuck the dandelion thing in the dirt, freeing his hands. "I'm filthy. Want a pop? I have ginger ale."

"Thanks. That would be nice."

As he walked with her to the back door he thought, okay, something's weird here. Normally confident, tonight Mary was tentative. He'd have to feel his way through whatever was going on.

"How about fixing the drinks while I wash up. Am I smelly?"

"You smell fine."

"You'd tell me?"

"Damn straight. Who wants to hang out with a guy who stinks?"

More like herself. Good.

"Back in a minute."

Hands, face, and knees scrubbed and wearing a respectable t-shirt and shorts, Chris found Mary standing at the window of the living room overlooking the side garden. With the sun almost set, deep shade only hinted at its potential beauty. Mysterious, like the woman occupying his condo. Filling it up.

She turned as he came into the room. Glasses of ginger ale, paper toweling wrapped around the bases, waited on the pass-through separating the living area from the kitchen. He flicked on the miserable excuse for a ceiling light, then walked over to her. "Replacing that thing is high up on the priority list." He nodded at the feeble bulb. "But it is sort of soft. Does it work for you?"

Silent, she slipped by him and switched on the table lamp beside the sofa.

"I'm glad you're here," he said, picking up the glasses and following her. The furniture saved from his corporate days made the space comfortable despite the remains of his work with Barry cluttering the room.

On closer inspection, her eyes had a haunted expression. After a silence that triggered a clench in his gut, she blurted,

"People keep telling me I'm crazy, I don't know what I'm doing."

The hint of a smile he'd carried with him ever since she'd appeared at his front door vanished. He set the ginger ale on his glass coffee table. "Because...?"

"Because of you. Dammit, why'd you have to be a minister? Even Zach's on my case about you. But—"

"Whoa." He touched her arm, stopping her words. "Ignore them. Only you can decide what happens between us. Only you." Cautiously he felt his way into the conversation. "Nice to have a fan club, but in the final analysis it's up to you."

"I know," she whispered. "But after what happened..."

"Don't overthink. Just say it."

Simultaneously, as if there were ESP communication between them, they sat on his sofa. Not touching. Mary reached for her glass; he watched her swallow the fizzy liquid, almost greedily. Her face changed, grew harder, as she peered into a past he couldn't share.

And then it all tumbled out, words piling on words. "He was the youth pastor at our church. Nice guy, youngish, cool, wife and a couple of kids. Played guitar. Everyone loved him. When I got pregnant, they sent me to him for counseling."

A chill run up his spine, in anticipation of what he suddenly knew was coming.

She paused. "We were alone in in his office. He said some stuff about it not being the end of the world, then he—" A gulp swallowed her voice, followed by a hardness in the set of her mouth.

"He touched you, or wanted to," Chris said gently.

Moving with enormous control, Mary rested her glass on the coffee table and buried her face in her hands. Her voice came to him muffled, but her hands couldn't mask the pain, the betrayal. "He said he'd make it so good for me, and I obviously liked it, and... oh God."

"He wasn't worthy of his role, and he should have been reported, but I suspect nobody believed you."

"I never told. There was no point. I'd already been beaten for getting myself raped." She looked up, but not at him. "When it happened, I froze. But then, when he… I panicked, I guess. Somehow I got out of there. But his expression, watching me go… smug, and vindictive. The next Sunday he denounced me from the pulpit as beyond redemption. A week later, my folks shipped me off to Halifax, to Aunt Claude." She paused, lost in the past. "That was better. Claude took care of me. Gave me a sense of my own value."

Chris had felt his body recoil at the word *denounced*. Nothing like that had ever been a part of his background, or of his beliefs. But her story had ended on a positive note. "Sounds like the right move for the wrong reasons."

Mary sat up, swiped at an errant tear working its way over her cheek, and nodded.

He'd kiss away that tear in an instant… but it wasn't his time. Not yet. "So now you stay as far away as possible from churches and ministers."

"Wouldn't you?"

"Yeah, I would." Chris let the silence build before he risked saying, "But I'm not him."

"No."

"I'd never undervalue you. Or under-respect you."

With her gaze focused across the room, she said, "But there's more. I… Friday, I saw…"

"You saw Barry."

Mary tensed and sat up straighter. "What did he tell you?" she demanded.

Chris snorted a laugh. "That he tried to interfere in my business and got his ass handed to him."

The tension released its grip, but she blushed and looked down. "It's so dumb. I thought I could flirt a little, to prove there's nothing between you and me." She reached over and picked up her glass, tracing her finger through the moisture above the paper towel. "Guess it didn't work. Chris, I wouldn't have—"

181

"It's okay, Mary." He rested his hand on her free one and gently squeezed. "We'll be okay."

And then it was over. It was time to build, not destroy.

He tightened his hold on her hand. "You and me," he said. "I don't see any way out of it now. Do you? I'm learning what it means to be head over heels. Jeez, that sounds corny." He chuckled. "But that's how it is for me. I've found a woman who's independent and gutsy and speaks her mind, and won't let me become sanctimonious. Who gives me a run for my money. Who has this capacity to love she's barely tapped into – although I think you've always felt it for Zach."

"He's my son."

"Not everybody loves their children."

He watched it sink in. "True. Or never show it."

They sat staring into the cold fireplace, holding onto glasses of pop as if their lives depended on them. Both of them waiting.

At last she nodded. Chris suppressed a sigh of relief.

"Let's toss these." He lifted his glass. "They're mostly melted ice. And talk. Curtains, for instance. Bare windows are creepy." He was babbling and didn't care. "Nothing prevents the couple next door from wandering over to my side of the lawn, or the gardeners. I'd like a semblance of privacy."

"Stop." She put a hand on his chest and, to his chagrin, hastily moved it away again. "You're trying to convince me everything's normal, aren't you? Nothing's normal."

"Possibly not." But the outspoken, take-no-prisoners Mary was back. That mattered a heck of a lot more than curtains. "But stay anyway."

She stayed. She shifted to a chair, putting distance between them, and drank ginger ale, and chatted about showing the horrible, box-like condo and how she hoped to pull off a sale of a mini-mansion south of town. Suggested blinds for the windows. Neutral subjects, but she stayed.

Later, when he walked her to her car, he risked kissing her. Not a high-octane kiss, but one that established his presence. Hope flooded over him for the first time in days.

182

Every minute of watching this reserved, uncertain woman settling into his heart while she filled up his condo, every minute was worth it.

And maybe, just maybe, he'd given her the peace of mind she so needed.

Chapter 23

Mary pulled into the Baptist church parking lot a little after two o'clock and swung toward the back, where Passages was located. Another new experience, running Zach around, giving him a hand. That hadn't happened since very early days when she'd occasionally helped him with multiplication tables and other academic mysteries.

She frowned as she drew the car into a parking space. Something was happening outside the glass doors to Passages. It was another hot day, made hotter by the blacktop pavement. She had a feeling this was more than irritation fueled by the heat, though.

A dozen or so teens, mostly boys, formed a loose, raucous circle. As she opened her car door, she heard a girl crying, *"Don't! Let me go! NO!"*

Zach sprang from the car but didn't approach the teenagers. *Not my job,* he'd told her, but she could sense his conflict: obey the rules or follow his instincts. Mary darted around the car and grabbed his arm. "Call 911," she shouted over the din.

In counterpoint, several male voices began a chant: *"Slut, bitch, slut, bitch."* One voice emerged: *"I get her next, Jarrod!"*

Chris charged from the youth center. He shouted something, she couldn't hear. Without hesitation he plunged into the milling teenagers, pulling smaller ones from the outskirts of the throng and ordering them into the building.

To her right, Zach yelled into his phone. In front of her the racket intensified. Somebody shoved the girl; her voice broke off as she fell. Before Mary's eyes, the scene morphed

184

from crowd to mob. From where she stood, it was evident that the ringleaders were three older teens now surrounding the downed girl.

Chris elbowed his way toward the center of the trouble. Everyone was shouting.

Zach finished his call, shoved his phone into his pocket, and darted into the melee.

Mary took a single step forward, then retreated. Much as she longed to straighten out a few of the rampaging teens, she recognized her limitations. She'd only be a liability.

Sirens, some distance away, added to the chaos. A few of the less involved kids heard the sirens and bolted.

She saw it, then. The sun flashing on a knife.

Then Chris's voice, rising above the cacophony. "Dammit, Jarrod, put that down. *Now!*"

The fighting surged, and both Chris and Jarrod disappeared from sight. The girl screamed again, "*Priest!*" A shocked silence settled over the teens.

Everyone scattered. Through the gap, Mary spotted Chris on the pavement. The blacktop shone wet, and a red bloom spread across his pale blue shirt.

Rational thought fled. She bolted toward Chris.

The sirens cut off as the vehicles swung into the lot. Two police cars and, thank God, an ambulance. The girl lay whimpering nearby. Chris's face contorted with pain, but to Mary's astonishment he reached out and brushed the girl's hand. Then he groaned and his own hand fell limp.

Off to the side, Zach held the boy who had wielded the knife in an armlock. An older woman stepped out of Passages and spoke to a policeman, then crouched next to the girl. The ambulance attendants nudged Mary aside and surrounded Chris, who was stark white and seemed to be fading in and out of consciousness.

Two police officers claimed the boy, and Zach materialized at Mary's side, wrapping an arm around her. After a few seconds, she turned her face into his shoulder. "Chris...."

185

"Shh." Her strong, competent son kept her pressed against his side as the sounds penetrated her brain; they were transferring him to a gurney, taking him away. He'd cried out, once, as they moved him.

When Zach released Mary, after the worst of her near hysteria had dissipated, she looked around. A second ambulance had pulled up as the one carrying Chris departed. The attendants assisted the fallen girl, who by now had struggled to her feet with the older woman's help. Only a couple of teens lingered, and the boy, presumably Jarrod. He stood slumped between the police officers, his hands cuffed.

The whole thing probably hadn't lasted longer than a minute or two. It had felt like several eternities.

The woman waved toward Zach to attract his attention, then disappeared into Passages.

"Peggy needs backup," he said to Mary. "And we'll probably have to talk to the police. Let's go."

"But Chris…." She pulled against his insistent hand.

"Yeah, I get it. But we've got a roomful of traumatized kids. I have to stay. You could help, you know. It'll be a while before they'll tell us anything at the hospital."

As her mind cleared, she weighed it in the balance. Sit in a waiting room, or be useful? There was no doubt at all which Chris would prefer she do. She followed her son into Passages.

It wasn't that bad, they'd said as they stitched him up. But he had bled enough that they were keeping him in overnight, and just as well. His head… he couldn't focus, much less pull himself into a sitting position. The police had turned up soon after the stitching; it had been all he could do to report the situation, and his actions, accurately. Rod and Sadie had dropped by soon after the police left. However much he loved them, he was grateful they stayed only a couple of minutes.

Chris's side, where Jarrod's knife had sliced, hurt enough that he felt like swearing, even with the painkillers. His stomach churned over the green gelatin dish they'd allowed him, and

186

cramps in his muscles provided a constant reminder of the afternoon.

He'd lain still for half an hour, enduring multiple affronts to his body and listening to the bustle in the corridors. If only he could force his mind to focus on last night, when the future shone bright. Mary. And now this.

He had a vague memory of her hovering over him, before the paramedics got to him. Surely a hallucination. Zach had been there, though, he remembered that, collaring Jarrod before he could hurt anyone else.

No, that green stuff hadn't been a good idea. Should he call the nurse?

His mind wandered.

And a vision appeared beside his bed. Mary. There, with him.

"I'm not coherent," he whispered.

Her hand touched his where it lay limp by his side, avoiding the tube bandaged to his skin. "They said to tell you your parents are on the way," she whispered back.

His eyes drifted from her to the ceiling, to the darkening window. "They said," he repeated. "Mary…?"

"What is it?" She leaned closer.

He forced his head to turn away from her and shot a quick prayer to the heavens. It didn't work. There was a call button somewhere; he'd never find it in time. "Get the nurse, please."

With that, his system rebelled, and he threw up a green stew of gelatin and bile, all over the sheet.

Chapter 24

Why doesn't he call?

Mary had spent hours reflecting on her reactions from the day of the fight, and one feeling always came out on top. When things got bad, when the knife appeared, her heart had lodged in her throat with fear – for Chris.

His parents had arrived, and he had been discharged the next day, according to Zach. So she knew he was home and on the mend.

She couldn't escape the uneasy conviction that Chris was avoiding her. But why? Underneath his undoubted physical misery, his expression had lit up when she appeared at his hospital bedside.

And now, nothing.

When she'd phoned, her call bounced to voice mail, and he never responded. Would he refuse to answer his doorbell, too? It was high time to find out.

Mary arrived at the old mansion around seven on a sunny August evening. She buzzed; there was no reply. As she stepped down from the porch, intending to circle the building and pound on Chris's back door, the elderly couple she'd met at his moving-in party strolled from the parking shed tucked against the left-hand property line. The Franklins, Shirley and… Ross? She smiled and walked over to meet them.

After exchanging pleasantries, she explained her visit. "I haven't heard from Chris and there's no answer on his phone. I'm worried. Any chance you'd let me in, or knock on his door for me?"

"Sure, honey." Shirley gave her a quick hug as they followed the path to the front door. "He's had company the last few days. Parents, unless I miss my guess. You heard about those drug addicts at the youth center?"

Mary nodded reluctantly. "I saw the news reports." In fact she'd snipped and saved them. No need to mention she'd been there; she wasn't ready to talk about it yet. "Are his parents still here?"

"Drove off yesterday afternoon," Mr. Franklin said. "Never got a chance to make their acquaintance. Seem to be a tight family."

The couple unlocked the outer door, and Mary crossed the lobby to Chris's entrance. "Thanks. I appreciate your help." She knocked, internal fingers crossed he would answer.

"You take care of that young man," Shirley cautioned. "Injured and all."

"Good neighbor," Mr. Franklin affirmed as they made their way up the elegant staircase.

At the sound of a click, Mary turned. Chris stood framed in his doorway.

Pale. Thinner.

Neither of them spoke for an eternity. Then he said, "I guess you'd better come in."

Fazed by his lack of enthusiasm, she slipped past him into his comfy living room and blurted, "How are you?" *God*, was it possible to sound more stilted?

"Improving. Lots of parental fussing. Please, sit."

She did, on the sofa, hoping he'd join her. But he chose a chair instead. In fact, Chris acted like a pale shadow of himself. His trademark charm and confidence seemed to have seeped out along with his blood. Unsmiling, he sat awkwardly, favoring his side, and didn't look at her but at his hands, resting lifelessly on his thighs.

"Chris?"

His expression was bleak. "Sorry. It's just that I've been dreading this conversation for days. But it has to happen."

"What do you mean?"

189

"I'm grateful you came over." He smiled, but without any underlying happiness. "You're not the type to put up with loose ends. And I've become a loose end."

This wasn't the man she knew. The man she was...

Could this be real? Had she fallen for a minister?

"And after that..." He gestured. "What shall we call it? Stoned teens? Hazard of the job? Anyway, after that, you'd never—"

A minister who was doing his best, in his kind way, to dump her?

"Never what, Chris?" she interrupted him, seizing control. Because he couldn't be serious. He couldn't be giving up on them, not now.

At last he focused on her. His voice was quiet. "I can't ask you to share my life, Mary. I pretended to myself it could work. But lying there in the hospital, I finally faced reality." He sighed and looked back down. "I know I've been driving you crazy. It won't happen anymore."

He didn't watch as she rose and crossed the room to kneel by his chair. "Are you nuts?" she demanded.

That got a smile. "Yeah, probably." But then he said nothing more, just waited.

She swallowed, hard. "We agreed to see where it went."

"Yes, but that was unfair to you. At its best, my life must seem boring, at least if you're not the one living it. And now we've both experienced the worst of it."

She reached across to claim one of his hands. After a gentle squeeze, he rested her hand on the arm of the chair, releasing it, and leaned back, changing his gaze to the ceiling.

This, when finally she was ready to screw up her courage and seize what she wanted?

Time to bring out the big guns. "Did you read in the papers a week or two ago? Somebody murdered a real estate agent in Cincinnati when she met clients at an empty house. They don't know who did it, or why." She poured conviction into her voice. "There are never any guarantees. You were

190

nothing short of a hero that day, tackling the guy with the knife—"

"Zach did that. All I did—"

"Was charge into the fight to break it up, after you got the younger kids to safety. I was..." She'd spent hours reviewing her reaction to the scene at the youth center. "Everything happened too fast to think. I was terrified and... I wanted to help. Maybe I should have gone straight to the hospital..."

"Instead of staying at Passages and helping calm things down?" When she raised her brows in surprise, he added, "Peggy told me you were a big help. Thank you for that."

After a few seconds, still not looking at her, he said. "Mary, for my sake, let's not drag this out. Tell me where we're going."

Her hands tingled – an adrenalin rush? – and her heart thudded uncomfortably in her chest. Whatever her next words were, they would seal her immediate fate... and Chris's. Not that there was any question any longer what her answer would be. "I want to try."

He looked at her. "You don't want to end it?"

Not as big a moment of truth as declaring undying love, but big, nonetheless. "No."

He used both hands to push himself up out of the chair. "Come look." His voice sounded choked. When she glanced up, his eyes glistened in the failing light.

Mary stood and followed him to the bay window facing the side garden. "I've holed up here since the folks left. Afraid to talk to you. Afraid of what you'd say." With his right arm, the one on his good side, he rubbed her back, then circled her waist. "Pretty neat, huh? Mom finished it."

The flower garden lay pristine in the evening shade, its soil smoothly cultivated, its plants, perhaps surprised not to be choked by weeds, reasserting their dominion. A few shrubs had been planted, and no unwelcome vegetation dared show its head.

"It's late in the season now, but it's going to be gorgeous," Chris said with only a hint of his earlier uncertainty. After a minute he added, "It didn't seem fair to try to tie you to me. But you don't know how much I've hoped we'd be here in the spring to see the garden."

"No promises," she said cautiously, an instinctive response to the intensity behind his mild words.

He shook his head. "One promise. I know I'm not exactly your dream man, but I'm willing to do everything in my power to be what you want."

The honesty in his words pierced her, driving home the weight of the decision she'd made. "Me, too."

He pulled her against him, but didn't hold her tightly – not a surprise, given the healing gash in his side. His head rested against hers. "I was sure I'd lost you," he murmured.

So she kissed him. Gently, because it felt like a time for gentleness. His lips returned the pressure. Then he said, "I need to sit down. I'm weak in the knees."

Together they moved to the sofa, side by side this time, and talked, always touching, as the soft summer night descended over the garden.

Chapter 25

"So, I've told you the seniors think I'm their favorite grandson or something, and they're always trying to embarrass me, right?"

"Right."

Chris had met Mary at Joe's for a pizza slice, filling in a lunch hour that was uncommitted for both of them. Not something that happened with any regularity, given their erratic and busy schedules. They sat side by side on an outside bench, leaning back against the building in the sun. "What did they do this time?"

He ran a finger over her hand. Just to touch her, briefly, to be sure the connection was still there.

"They set up a competition to see who could make me blush most. You don't know how lucky you are, not going pink if someone so much as looks at you."

"It's sweet." Mary spoke around a bite of pizza.

Tempting. Mary, with him, relaxed and so, so tempting.

Enough of thoughts like that. Chris pulled his mind back to their conversation. "Anyway, I got there Saturday, and everything seemed fairly normal at first, maybe a little subdued. Then Ralph and Bernice called me over to the sofa they usually claim."

"I think I see where this is going."

"Well, I didn't. Biggest patsy in the room. Ralph's this hearty, hail-fellow kind of guy, booming voice, all that. The two of them have been hanging out together ever since I started there, so I didn't think anything of it, I just went on over.

Usually they want me to bring them another song book or something like that. Bernice uses a walker so she's not entirely mobile."

He stopped and took a bite of his pizza slice.

"Go on." Mary nudged his arm with an elbow.

He took a breath. "He announced – ostensibly to me, but of course the whole room could hear – he announced that since I still seemed to be short in the nookie department – that's their shared code word for the seeming absence of a woman in my life, not that that's the case anymore, but they don't know that—"

"Are you going to tell them?"

"Sure, sooner or later. I need to have a few secrets with that bunch. Anyway, he said they'd been talking, and he reckoned my problem was that I needed lessons."

"Oh, no." Her eyes danced. She was getting a kick out of this.

"Oh, yes. The pair of them started making out right there on the sofa. Mary, he's eighty-two and she's in her late seventies. And they're going at it. I'm sure tongues were involved, and his hand was inside her blouse…"

He trickled off as he yanked his mind away from the appalling image. Mary was convulsed in laughter beside him on the bench. "I bet they won the competition, right?" she barely got that out, then waved a hand at him and dissolved into giggles again.

"He was feeling her up. When she started on his waistband, I admit I fled."

"Poor Chris."

He felt her hand on his arm. Almost the first time she'd initiated contact between them.

"Wanda, she's the director there, told me to take it like a man and sent me right back out there. They gave me a round of applause. All three of us, actually. Ralph and Bernice and me."

"Now you're wondering how you'll ever live it down."

"Not really. They're wonderful. But oh, God, Mary. It was like catching your parents or something."

Her hand tightened. "I think I'd like your seniors. It proves there's hope."

"Life doesn't end when we hit seventy, for sure. But I promise, when we're seventy and I grope you, we'll be in some very private place."

That got through to her. She stopped giggling. He watched as the implications of what he'd just said swirled around in her head.

He leaned closer. "I admit, it's hard to picture you now with a pot belly and sagging boobs."

Spell broken. She used the hand that had been resting on his arm to punch him. But she didn't say anything, which was unusual for Mary. He'd sort of hoped she'd give him a lecture, question his assumptions.

Because, after all, he had only a tactile knowledge of her body. Not a visual one. Not yet.

Soon.

"Come over for supper tonight?" she asked.

"I've been coming over for supper every night for days."

"So we'll keep it simple."

"Salads. I could pick up something."

"One of us should learn to cook."

"Okay. Let's learn." He gathered up the papers that had held their pizza slices, crumpled them in one hand, then used his napkin to blot a patch on her upper lip. "They make 'em messy."

"For this kind of thing, Joe's is as good as it gets." Mary stood and brushed off her skirt. He chucked their garbage in the can, and they walked out toward Main Street.

"Where are you heading this afternoon?" she asked.

"The Renewed Life Center. Planning for the big bazaar coming up in October. It's massive. Dozens of tables, everyone in the congregation volunteering, food. It's worth going for the food alone."

"I bet," she grumbled, the smile gone. "Frumpy second-hand dresses and electronics that don't work."

195

"Your experience of bazaars is a long way from mine. Come October, we'll see. What are you up to?"

"Closing on a sale, and a viewing later. It's been a good summer."

"It has."

His words had meaning, and she caught it. They stood awkwardly on the corner, then he squeezed her hand. "Back to work. Talk to you later."

She returned the squeeze, then she was gone. And this was better. This was okay. Just being able to say 'talk to you later' meant that there *was* a later, in both their minds. And that she'd welcome hearing from him, later.

With that much resistance to the bazaar, though – and the thing was a many-tentacled monster he could never escape from – could he hope for a positive response if he ever invited her to attend a service? Because he'd never pressure her to join his congregation, that was for her to decide, with no help from him unless she asked for it. But he would like her to see what he did for a living, even though he'd probably be nervous enough to make a wreck of the service if he knew she was there.

Chapter 26

Autumn hadn't announced itself yet, though Labor Day had flown by on a wave of barbecues and toasts to the end of the summer. Mary felt pretty good about life as she and Zach puttered companionably in her kitchen. She could tell he was wired from his first day at OSU by the way he whistled under his breath as he put together a salad, so although he didn't say much she concluded things had gone well. Time enough to question him later. A rotisserie chicken from the deli waited in the fridge. With the potato salad Chris had promised, they had the makings for a casual late summer supper.

In fact, she'd felt good since the night two weeks ago when she'd turned her fate over to Chris. *Chris and herself*, she corrected. They'd become a team, oddly enough, spending much of their free time together, learning each other's ways. They had walked, worked in the garden, shared meals and movies, talked, touched – Oh, how they touched. Every chance they got. The intimacy of changing the dressing over his wound…

Only two hurdles loomed – how she'd handle the church thing, and the major question of *when*. It wasn't *if* anymore, and the interminable delay only heightened her desire for him. He'd become a fact of her life, and for all intents and purposes a part of her family. Her fears were fading. The closer she grew to him, the more palatable his spiritual commitment became.

More than once his jaw had clenched as he pulled himself away, but he'd committed to waiting for her go-ahead, and she… well, it had to happen soon, or they'd both go mad.

When the phone rang she eyed it, then sighed – Zach never received calls on her landline, so the odds hit a hundred percent it would be for her. She wiped her hands and went to the table by her front door to answer it.

"Ms. Mary Boylan?" an unfamiliar male voice said.

"This is she." She matched his formality.

"Constable George Woskowski here. We're outside your building, assisting a woman who got lost trying to locate your address. Her name's Betty Boylan. She says she's your mother."

A hard, frozen lump developed in Mary's stomach, but she kept her voice level and controlled. "Thank you, Constable. I'll buzz her in."

"We need to come up, ma'am. She also says you kidnapped a minor and may be holding him against his will."

An unladylike snort punctuated her reply. "Hardly. This should only take a minute or two to sort out."

She hung up the phone, pressed the downstairs access buzzer to let them in, then turned to Zach. "The fun and games are beginning. That's Mom, with the police."

He looked up from his salad fixings. "Shit. You're kidding?"

"All we have to do is tell them the facts and be polite. Don't worry."

Zach frowned. And to be honest, she wasn't ready for this confrontation. The last thing she'd expected or needed was her mother on her doorstep.

With a might-as-well-get-it-over-with attitude, she opened the door. The constables appeared a few seconds later, her mother looking very small between them.

"Come in." Mary stepped aside and made a parody of a welcoming gesture. The taller of the men showed her his credentials and handed her a business card.

Her mother headed straight for the sofa. "I'm parched. The least you could do is fix me a drink."

"Certainly, Mrs. Boylan. Coming up." Zach disappeared back into the kitchen.

"*Zach!*" Their mother's heartbroken cry at his intentional distancing resonated in the room.

Perhaps already tired of the power games, Constable Woskowski called them to order. "Could we all sit down and go over this situation?"

Mary suspected he'd as soon escape their unwonted family drama, but rules were rules. She'd cooperate and hopefully get the two large men out of her condo. "Certainly. What do you want to know?"

"Please. Sit."

Mary took one chair and the second constable chose the other, leaving a narrow space on the sofa beside her mother for Constable Woskowski. He appeared to be huddled against the arm, putting as much distance as he could between himself and the older woman claiming the sofa's center.

The other constable whipped out a notebook and a pen. When he signaled his readiness, Constable Woskowski said, "For the record, you are Mary Boylan?"

Mary nodded, caught the beginning of a protest in the other man's face, and said, "Yes, I am."

Zach came in and put the glass of iced tea in front of their mother, then grabbed a dining room chair and straddled it.

"And I suppose you are Zachary Boylan?"

"Yup."

"And this woman, Betty Boylan, is your mother?"

"Mary's natural mother, my adoptive mother," Zach said.

"And you are under twenty-one years old?"

"Nineteen."

The buzzer rang.

"Leave it, please," Constable Woskowski commanded.

"I can't. He's expected." Because the whole situation had her feeling on edge, she added, "If I don't answer, he'll probably call the police." She buzzed Chris in, left the door ajar, and returned to the family pow-wow happening in her living room.

Constable Woskowski scowled and spoke in a way that commanded attention. "Now, here's the crux of the matter. Mr. Boylan, can you explain the exact nature of your stay with your sister." His tone made it a command, not a question.

"Sure," Zach said, loose and easy. "Since I have a choice of mothers, I pick Mary. I was moving down here anyway, for school. I just came a little early."

"And what do you mean by a choice of mothers?"

Mary heard the door move behind her. "I'm here," Chris's cheerful voice called. "Where shall I put... oh."

She turned in time to see his puzzled frown at the group around the coffee table.

"In the kitchen," she said. "Then you may as well come join the party."

Chris nodded to Constable Woskowski. "George."

"Hey, Chris. What brings you here?"

"Supper. Hang on a sec." He turned into the kitchen, returning a moment later without the bag he'd been carrying, then sat in the one remaining vacant place, next to her mother.

"I've met everyone here, except..." He extended a hand. "Reverend Christopher Peterson, ma'am."

Mary nearly cracked up at his subtle emphasis on his title. She shot a quick glance at Zach and saw the same reaction on his face. Chris had put it together in record time and was pulling rank. Bless him.

Mary's mother touched her fingers to his. "Reverend, huh? I hope you're planning to find a way to save her. We never could control her base impulses."

"What on earth are you talking about?" Mary asked.

"You know what I mean," her mother said, giving first Chris, then Constable Woskowski, a knowing look.

"Well, I don't," Zach said. "Care to elaborate?"

"If we could get this discussion back on track," Constable Woskowski interrupted. "The question on the table had to do with having a choice of mothers."

"I'm Zach's natural mother. My parents adopted him as a baby. Choice." Mary was growing irritated by this whole charade and wished she could be lounging on the balcony with something tall and cold, winding down the day in a more civilized manner.

Both constables faced Zach. "True, as far as I know," he said. "Since I was two months old, I don't remember much of it."

Constable Woskowski actually rolled his eyes.

"And you are living here of your own volition? No coercion?"

"Hell, no. I'd pick here over there any day."

"That's because the boy thinks he's entitled," Mary's mother piped up, her voice shrill.

"Zach wasn't happy in Cleveland, Mom," Mary said with a restraint that amazed even her. "He's too old for the kind of restrictions you put on him."

"You can't tell me he wasn't out drinking and womanizing every night. I insist on a moral, law-abiding home."

Zach shrugged. "I've had the occasional beer at friends' houses. As for womanizing? Hell, I'm nineteen. I wish."

"Precisely." Mary's mom settled back, her arms crossed. Mary noted dispassionately that she hadn't touched her tea.

"George, Zach volunteers at Passages," Chris said. "He was instrumental in stopping the rumble a couple of weeks ago. The kids adore him. I'll put in a good word, if you need one."

The two policemen looked at each other. Constable Woskowski shrugged. "This strikes me as a situation you need to work out among you. No point in escalating it." They stood, the second constable pocketing the notebook and pen. "I will caution you to behave quietly and civilly. I won't be happy if I get a call for disturbing the peace later tonight."

Chris walked the two men to the door, where they exchanged a few quiet words. The policemen nodded politely to the room and left.

Zach swung his chair back around to the dining table and returned to the kitchen. Mary watched him go, sensing he was more shaken by the encounter than he let on. Then she stood and joined Chris. When he draped his arm over her shoulders, she didn't shy away, letting her mother know in the least subtle way possible that he was more than a family friend. That he belonged here.

"Mom," she said, "Chris is a minister at the Renewed Life Center, and he works with Zach at the youth drop-in place."

"I don't suppose you're prepared to feed an old lady," her mother grumbled. "That drive was enough to tax a saint."

Mary let that one go, but she saw a smile tickling the edges of Zach's mouth as he returned to the living room.

"Let's all eat," Chris said. "Then I'll get lost if you prefer. It doesn't seem to me this should be that difficult to straighten out."

"Optimist." Mary took Chris's hand and led him into the kitchen. "What are we going to do with her?" she whispered.

"Put her up overnight," he whispered back. "One of you can come sleep at my place. Flip a coin."

She raised her eyebrows.

"Okay," he said in a more normal tone, "I do have a preference." His voice dropped again. "Better send Zach, because if I have you under my roof, we're both in for an uncomfortable time."

Their eyes met and held. Mary was subliminally aware when Zach poked his head in the kitchen, but he scrammed as the force field they radiated reached him.

She straightened and pulled away. "Given what's waiting us in the living room, my energy's a little mixed up tonight."

"Yeah." He laughed. "So we're on the same page, I came over here intending to get you alone later and make a statement, but since that's not likely to happen I'd better tell you now. I love you, Mary."

The floor fell out and dropped them a story or two, while simultaneously her eyes went fuzzy and her stomach practiced every Girl Scout knot she'd never had a chance to learn, because the woman sitting on her sofa thought the Girl Scouts were some kind of cult.

Chris. Love. Her. Saying it.

Putting words into full, complete sentences ceased to be an option.

"Now, let's make nice with your mother, shall we? I suspect the sooner we can convince her to go home again, the happier you and Zach will be."

With an effort, she put Chris's declaration aside in favor of semi-normal conversation. "Shouldn't you encourage me to welcome her with open arms?"

He shot her a mock horrified look, then grinned. "You're kidding, right? Given what you've told me... no. I don't think so."

The supper inched painfully along. Mary tried her best. Zach didn't try much at all but ate at a speed typical of a young man still growing, announced he was outa there, and left.

She couldn't tell if Chris was trying, or just being his charming, *ministerial* self. He said a simple grace, something he'd never done in her house before – pandering to her mother's probable expectations? He was polite, asked innocuous questions, and passed dishes. Once, when her mother launched onto the theme of her daughter's dissolute ways, she caught him swallowing an exasperated sigh. He didn't hesitate to pour them both a second glass of wine.

When the supper clean-up was finished, Chris drew her mother into the living room and said, "So, you can see that Zach's well settled here. At the youth center, we're more than grateful for him, and OSU's a top school. I hope you won't worry about him anymore."

All this with his mild eyes fixed on her mother, who squirmed like a bug when he didn't give her a reason to complain.

Finally, she huffed and said, "It's fine for you to say. You aren't a member of this family. You don't know—"

"I know enough."

Something in his manner stopped her mother cold. Mary couldn't quite peg what it was. Ministerial influence, perhaps? Whatever, his tone brooked no further nonsense.

"I'm heading home." Chris drew her with him to the door and kissed her soundly. He whispered, "I suspect she's going to rant. If I stay it'll only delay it. Let it bounce off, sweetheart. Okay?"

203

"I'll try."

"Call me. Any time."

"You meant it?" The words flowed unbidden; she could have kicked herself.

He caught her meaning instantly. "Of course. I love you. It's been growing for a while, as you know. Be tough."

Not brave. Tough. Brave implied going against nature; tough *was* nature. He had that much faith in her.

They whispered good nights, and Chris left. Wearily, Mary turned to face her mother.

The woman on her sofa was a shell of the one who had raised her. Although only sixty years old, she looked as if life had chewed her up and spat her out. Limp hair straggled around her face, which bore a network of frown lines. Her lips more or less disappeared into the tight, pinched expression that had become habitual. Her shapeless dress hung on her gaunt frame. And Mary couldn't remember the last time, during her occasional visits home, that friends or neighbors had phoned for a chat or dropped by for coffee.

As the two women stared at each other across the small expanse of Mary's living room, an emotion suspiciously like pity crept into her awareness.

"What happened to your stuff?" she asked. "Where's your car?"

"Where do you think it is? I wasn't about to leave it in a convenience store parking lot."

"So Constable...," she consulted the card she'd stuck in a pocket, "... Woskowski drove it over? Good. Why don't I go get your suitcase—"

"And trust you with my keys?"

"Mom, I'm thirty-four years old and my car's newer than yours. Give me the key, and I'll bring up your bag."

"Rob me blind," her mother mumbled, but dug into her ancient purse and put a key – which she carefully removed from the ring – on the coffee table. "If you're not back in ten minutes, I'm calling the police."

"You do that, Mom," Mary said wearily. "You just do that."

At least the short trip to the street, where she spotted her mother's car parked a few doors down, gave her a brief respite. She quickly retrieved the battered case from the trunk, but before she returned to her condo she allowed herself a minute to breathe in the warm night air.

It didn't take long to install her mother in her bedroom. Mary cruised the room quickly, gathering necessities for the next morning and confirming there was nothing snoop-worthy. Then she changed the sheets, said good night, and retreated.

Alone in the kitchen, she took out her cell and phoned Chris.

"Reception's not great."

"I'm not risking the landline. My room has an extension, and she used to listen in, every call I got."

"Wish I could be with you. But since I can't, tell me what I can do to help."

He'd be holding her now, his skilled hands creating all manner of pleasurable reactions, if her unexpected visitor hadn't turned up. She shivered with unrequited desire as the memories invaded her consciousness.

But that was for another time. "What am I going to do with her, Chris?"

"Well… do you have early hours at work?"

"Not until noon. There's paperwork, but I'm mostly free."

"How about taking her out for breakfast? She doesn't look like she's been eating much."

"I noticed. Why does that make me feel guilty?"

"Your mother's problems aren't your fault, Mary," he said gently. "And you can't solve them. Think of yourself as a sympathetic ear. When can I see you?"

"First thing tomorrow at the Madison Inn?" she asked, more as a joke than anything else, although the hope that Chris might join them for breakfast lightened the prospect.

"Depends on how early you go. Wednesday morning is a social club at Silver Threads. Call me, and I'll try to be there.

Besides," he added with a chuckle, "the old folks get happy-excited when I'm late. Nookie and all."

"You're amazing with them, putting yourself through that for their amusement."

"If it were only amusement, I'd save myself the pain. I've become an important person in their lives, and their way of showing it is this over-the-top teasing. One day they'll learn about you and it'll stop. I hope."

"It might get worse."

He groaned on the other end of the phone. "Oh, Lordy. Anything goes, with that bunch. But I love them."

Mary hung up, vaguely reassured. Chris did love his seniors. Even when they tormented him, he spoke about them with humor and fondness. He cared about the kids at the youth center, too, despite the challenges they presented. They had given him the nickname *Priest*, which he accepted with resignation if not pleasure; that seemed to indicate affection on their part, too.

His parents had rushed to his side when he was wounded. Barry watched out for him. His dominating sisters clearly adored him. He lived in a world of caring and stability. He'd never experienced anything like the harridan ensconced in Mary's bedroom.

The key turned in the door. Zach stepped in and looked around with a frown. "She gone?"

"My room. I've got yours, and you're going to Chris's, if that's all right with you."

He dropped a small sports bag on the floor and came toward her, shaking his head. "I don't like leaving you alone with her."

"I can cope. She's harmless."

"Bullshit. You stay with Chris."

Touched, she passed the cell phone from hand to hand. He was trying to protect her. Somehow Zach had survived the hell of their family home. He'd emerged a good kid.

Except…

"You fled down here a month ago," she said. "Neither of us wants to deal with this, but she's here, so there's no choice. Go on. I'll be fine."

And I'm the adult, she thought grimly. For all his size and maturity, her son was still finding his feet in the world.

"I'll manage on the sofa."

Their eyes locked. With Zach doing the immovable male thing she'd seen in him once or twice, capitulation suddenly seemed easier than another battle tonight. "In that case, you keep your room and I'll sleep on the sofa. It's too short for you. I'm taking her out for breakfast. Want to come?"

Predictably, his expression brightened at the mention of food. "Believe it."

As she went to gather bedding, she heard him on his cell, telling Chris about the change of plan.

Chapter 27

Nobody had slept well. From the moment she emerged, Mary's mother had produced a steady stream of complaints about the hardness of the bed, the city lights coming in through the curtains, and the size of the tiny ensuite bathroom. Now she sat in their window booth with arms folded, having taken one sip of her coffee and declared it far too strong. Their mother's idea of coffee was akin to dishwater. The harried waitress hadn't yet arrived with hot water to dilute it.

The only bright spot was Chris's presence at the table. Because her little family had risen with the dawn, he would have plenty of time to eat and get to Silver Threads.

Mary hid behind her coffee and watched as he struggled to keep a semblance of conversation going, but she sensed ripples of strain on his face. Periodically he glanced at his already empty mug with longing.

"Have you decided how long you'll be staying in Calter Creek, Mrs. Boylan?" he asked.

Her mother glared. "Don't see what it is to you. Not that anyone else is making me welcome here."

"With a little advance notice, we could have made better arrangements for your comfort," Mary said. Even to her it sounded stilted.

Chris tried again. "If you expect to stay for any length of time, perhaps you'd like to come by the senior center. There are some great folks there. Usually someone's got a board game or a jigsaw puzzle going." She noted that Chris's mild Kentucky accent came through more prominently than usual and wondered if it was a sign of stress.

208

Her mother ignored him. "Appalling service. You see that you don't leave a tip, you hear? Show these people who's in charge, or they'll walk all over you." Her voice carried; a few heads turned.

"Shut up, Ma. You're making a scene," Zach snapped.

Everyone shut up. Please.

"I wanted to give you a treat," Mary said neutrally. "Would you rather go home? I can ask the waitress to package up—"

"Isn't that just like you? Offer something then snatch it away? And I suppose you plan to abandon me in that tiny place of yours all day."

Mary sighed. "I do have obligations at work later. Chris, what's on at Silver Threads?"

"The Social Club, an informal gathering for games and sing-along this morning, then on Wednesdays there's an afternoon tea. You might enjoy that, Mrs. Boylan." Chris's voice held a note of questioning hope.

"Charge an arm and a leg, I bet. Waste of money."

"It works on a donation basis. The food's good."

"You've all pigeonholed me, haven't you? I'm not that old."

Chris instantly reframed the afternoon, casting her mother as assistant rather than attendee. "What I find satisfying is supporting the older folks. Seating them, serving their tea. Many of them aren't very mobile or strong, and we can always use extra helping hands."

Her mother snorted.

Blessed silence fell.

"Here you go." The waitress, a cheerful if overworked young woman who probably depended on their tips to get through college, put a fresh, half-filled coffee cup and a small silver pot of hot water on the table. She poured fresh brew for the rest of them. "Your orders should be up in a minute. It's been crazy."

"Thanks," Mary said with a smile designed to counteract the effect of her mother's scowl. "We can see how busy you are."

The girl returned the smile and disappeared. After a couple of minutes of silence, during which her mother pointedly ignored the hot water and even Chris seemed flummoxed, their meals arrived. Without the need to make further conversation, the tension relaxed. To Mary's amazement, her mother put back a giant plate of eggs, bacon, and hash browns, with a fruit cup. She'd never done more than pick at food, ever.

She was starving, Mary realized. Why? Had eating become too much trouble? With no family close, did she lack motivation to care for herself? Was she slowly dying of loneliness?

Abruptly, completely without her planning or wanting it, the hostility bordering on hatred she'd lived with for so many years evaporated. Across the table from her sat a lonely woman, fighting the world in the only way she knew.

Mary's eyes met Chris's. His half smile and nod told her that whatever conclusion she'd just reached, she wasn't alone.

Which was good. Because her thoughts terrified her.

Chapter 28

Provide it, and they will come. Grand Central Station, Chris thought as he set up the coffee maker. He'd invited Abby and Susan to see his new place. Barry's appearance, on the other hand, had been a surprise.

Amiable bickering emanated from wherever they happened to be. His plan was to put his sisters in the spare bedroom. Barry's arrival probably meant he himself would end up on the sofa.

What on earth was he going to do with his entire passel of siblings? Show them his church?

At least the morning at Silver Threads had been relatively calm, the Saturday crowd perhaps concluding that last week's demonstration might have pushed him too hard. They had overwhelmed him with kindness, spiced by sympathy for his nookie-less state.

He had to do something about the absence of nookie, soon, or he'd go out of his mind. His sibs didn't need to know that.

"So, when do we meet her?" Susan appeared at the door to the kitchen, blocking him in until she got the answer she wanted.

"Her?" he asked, in mock innocence.

"Her." Abby was in the living room with Barry now, but the open hatch between the two rooms eliminated privacy. All his siblings joyfully participated in this conversation.

"Don't think we haven't heard about her," Susan added. "Barry blabbed."

211

His hand jerked and coffee grounds spilled onto the counter. "Thanks, bro," he called as he swiped it up and tipped it into the filter.

"She's hot," Barry informed his sisters.

The familiar heat crept up his neck. But what the heck. His family had lived with his blushing all his life.

"When, Chrissy?" Susan demanded.

He flicked the switch to start the coffee, hoping thereby to pacify the natives. "Dinner. She's working this afternoon."

"Come on, brother. Details." Susan kept him pinned in the kitchen.

"Long hair. Blue eyes. My age."

"Hot," Barry said again. "You got any Danish or anything?"

"In the middle of the afternoon?"

Of course in the middle of the afternoon. This was Barry, after all.

He dug a box of cookies out of a cupboard and tossed it through the hatch. His brother fielded the box as if they'd been doing it all their lives. Which they had.

"Is she okay with you being a minister?" Susan demanded. "Not everyone would be."

"Let's say she's working on it. She expected me to be a judgmental prude. I think I've proved her wrong on that score."

"I bet she's great in the sack," Barry said.

"Lay off," Abby said, a little sharply.

"Are you kidding? Who else is gonna keep the kid in his place?" Barry spoke around a mouthful of cookie.

Abby's natural compassion bloomed – or maybe she read his face. She hurried into the kitchen, throwing an arm over his shoulders. "Love life's off limits, guys."

Dramatic sigh from Barry. Chris turned away, but he'd bet on an exchange, a wink perhaps, between Abby and Barry. Sometimes, being the youngest in a tight family was its own kind of hell.

Good thing he loved them.

212

❖

Which wasn't to say he felt completely calm and collected as he met Mary at the door later that afternoon. Nor, he could tell, did she. She'd finagled a few nights for her mother in her condo building's guest suite, giving herself much needed breathing space, so the undercurrent of tension he sensed probably had more to do with the room full of boisterous adults behind him than with her own family situation.

"Am I glad to see you. They outnumber me." He stopped on the threshold and draped his arms over her shoulders, shielding her for a moment of shared peace. "How's your mom?"

"Good, relatively speaking. Says she loves the way the suite's decorated."

Chris guessed she'd had more to say than that, somehow casting Mary in a negative light, but he didn't pursue it. "And so?"

She swallowed. "I suppose I have to do this," she whispered.

"Yup," he whispered back. "I'll vouch for them. A little rambunctious, but they've never bitten yet."

"Not true," Susan called from across the room, proving that their moment of privacy was purely illusory. "Remember when Barry bit Abby's finger when he was about two?"

"I hadn't been born for that one," Chris retorted.

"Hey, I've grown up," Barry growled.

"Prove it." Susan, having dispensed with Barry, added, "Don't keep her to yourself, Chrissy."

"But I want to," Chris whispered to Mary, then gave her a quick kiss and stepped aside, keeping an arm around her as he ushered her into the maw of his family.

Abby assumed the role of hostess. "Welcome," she said, descending on them. As soon as Mary took her extended hand, shooting an uncertain look at him, Abby reeled her in for a hug. Everyone's mother, that was Abby. "We've been dying to meet you."

213

"The rest of us, anyway." Susan joined the huddle. "We gather you've already had the dubious pleasure of running into our other brother."

"Delightful it was," Barry said, sprawling on a chair and stretching his legs. "Nice to meet you in daylight, Mary. Beer?"

"No, thanks. Not right now."

"Let us get in the door, guys." Chris had lost his hold on Mary when Abby swept her up, but he regained it – and noticed that she sort of sagged against him. "She only just got here." Together they negotiated the furniture and his siblings. "Everyone, this is Mary." He named his sisters and brother.

Abby perched on the arm of a chair and Susan, wire-thin and athletic, sank in a tangle of arms and legs on the floor. Barry, who had staked a seemingly permanent claim to one of the chairs, gave Chris a grin and a thumbs-up, then raised his beer can – whether to him, a compliment to his good taste in women and alcohol, or to Mary, he wasn't sure.

Then they stared at him. "You're the host, baby brother," Susan said. "So talk. Make us feel right at home."

"Like you don't already," he countered.

"I'm not convinced Mary does," Abby said, ever the voice of calm reason. "Hon, you want to leave this mob behind and find you a drink? Ballast is recommended when you're faced with the Peterson kids all at once."

He felt Mary relax next to him, responding much as he always did to Abby's version of practical kindness. "Sure," she said. "Sounds like a good idea."

Mary left him in favor of the kitchen. Conversation died in the living room; thankfully, the open pass-through between the rooms precluded commentary.

Other than sign language. When Mary's back was turned, he got a thumbs-up from Susan, matching Barry's.

"Coffee, Chris? Or beer?" Mary called.

"Coffee, please."

The unnatural silence lasted until Mary and Abby returned, glasses and mugs in hands. And then, predictably, everyone talked at once. Words climbed over words; Mary politely answered their barrage of questions – her work, her family. Until, after about half an hour of his siblings' good-natured natter, she turned a look on him that said, plain as day, *Rescue me.*

"You clowns enjoy yourselves. We're going out to start up the barbecue." The barbecue he'd bought two days ago, anticipating Abby and Susan's visit. He and Mary had settled on the sofa; he pulled her up, and they made a hasty exit.

Safely outside the back door – he didn't expect it to last longer than a minute – he said, "Mind if I kiss you?"

She shot a wobbly grin at him. "I'll try to tolerate it."

"Good. You're going to be tolerating it a lot over the next lifetime or two."

Wasting no time, he followed through.

Then Barry and Susan invaded their space – he figured Abby was in the kitchen tidying. Before they separated, she whispered, "There's something I want to discuss with you."

"Tonight?"

One of the nicest things about kisses was that they left you with your hands on your woman. He let his settle on her shoulders, then run up and down her arms while they talked and Barry and Susan, pointedly ignoring them, got the barbecue going.

Another nice thing – her hands stayed on him, too, comfortably resting at his waist.

"Doesn't have to be. But soon."

"You're worried?"

She nodded.

"Later, then. We can make a break for it."

Mary liked them, especially Abby, the oldest and the one Chris referred to as his second mom. She couldn't detect even the faintest thread of tension or hostility among them. They yammered and teased and squabbled and generally enjoyed each other's company – and seemed more than willing to include her in the tribe.

Finally, they gathered around the dining table. Chris blessed the food, and they dove into the steaks. This time the blessing thing didn't trouble her. Lots of families said a blessing before meals. His brother and sisters apparently accepted it as a matter of course, so she did, too. It mattered to Chris, she was sure of that. When they went out together or shared a meal at one of their homes, there was usually a short pause before he ate; she suspected he was saying the words to himself. Alarm bells no longer clanged at Chris's gentle approach to his spiritual life. In fact, she'd begun to speculate that it might not be a negative on her balance sheet.

What balance sheet? The very fact of Chris blew all her calculations right out the window.

Later, he walked her to her car, pulling her tight against him. "Opinion?"

She smiled. "I like them."

"I knew you would. Despite the similarities to being trapped in a litter of puppies."

She chuckled.

"So. Tell me what's troubling you."

Her smile faded. Mary looked down, watching their feet moving along the sidewalk. "It's my mother."

He said nothing, but his hand tightened on her arm.

"She's... well, you've seen her. She never mentions friends. She's way too thin. I doubt anyone's keeping an eye on her."

"Makes you wonder how a person ends up in such a lonely place, doesn't it?"

"I hated that church of hers, you know that. But shouldn't they give her emotional support? Bring casseroles? I don't see how I can let this go on."

"What are you thinking?"

"Chris, should I move her down here?" As she spoke the words, the proposal rose before her in all its awfulness. Surely she had lost her mind.

She felt him flinch, but he said, "I'd wondered about that myself. Not if it means sacrificing you, though, living with her hostility for the rest of your life."

Her spirits sank. "What else can I do? I can't just send her back."

His arm tightened around her shoulders. "This needs more time and thought."

"Come over tomorrow night? How long are your sibs staying?"

"Everyone's clearing out after lunch tomorrow. Things don't always go according to plan in the Peterson clan, but there's a reasonable chance I'll be free."

"I'll feed Mom, but then she'll go to her suite to watch her TV shows. So come after dinner. I can predict Zach's reaction. I need someone in my corner."

"We'll figure it out, Mary."

After a highly satisfying good-night kiss, which involved his mouth's detour to the spot under her ear that always sent her into shivers, she drove off, reflecting on how fortunate Chris was in his siblings, and how privileged his upbringing had been compared to herself and the burden she and Zach shared.

Chapter 29

"Have you completely lost it?"

The next afternoon, Mary watched as Zach sprang from his chair. Any possibility of discussing this like sensible adults was blowing up in her face, big time.

"You saw her," she said, forcing calm. "If we don't do something, she won't be alive in a year."

Zach folded his arms over his chest and glared. "Do what you have to. I don't want anything to do with her."

Mary had figured out by now that Zach was as desperate as she had been at the same age to get out from under the parental burden of expectations and demands. As they'd eased into their new relationship, she'd found him to be a reasonable man, generally mild mannered. Not this raging male stomping around her living room... their living room, she corrected.

"We can't let her just wither away."

Her son settled into a silent, fuming lump of manhood.

"We can't, Zach."

He wore a pinched-lip, immovable expression that was, had he but known it, reminiscent of her mother. "Let's be clear about this," he said. "If you've got some bleeding-heart idea of rescuing her, fine. Go ahead. But count me out. And don't expect me to be around if you start inviting her here for cozy family chit-chats. This week's been bad enough."

In fact, Zach had been conspicuously absent from most of the meals she'd served her mother.

"I can't predict the future. I'm not even sure of the best way to handle this. But we can't pretend it will ever go away on its own."

"You, Mary. You. Not we."

"Chris is coming after dinner. We'll get his opinion."

"That'll be useful," he sneered. "You know what he'll think."

"Doing the right thing isn't always the easiest."

Zach shot her a disgusted look. "I'll see you later."

She watched her son storm out of the condo, then sank into a chair.

Of course, her mother might refuse to move. Mary felt a lightening in her spirit and shook it off. Too easy. She was facing the unthinkable… and dreading it, and strengthening her resolve at the same time.

As it happened, that evening Chris proved to be lukewarm on the whole scheme.

"Because I'm worried about the cost to you," he said bluntly. "It might be too high."

"Might be?" Zach said, dripping sarcasm.

"Yeah."

Chris and Zach had lined up on the sofa. Mary remained standing, arms folded. "No one's saying she'd be in our pockets if she moved here," she said. "With a little poking around we'll find things to keep her occupied."

"Like Sunday dinners?" Chris asked.

"There'd be some expectation," she acknowledged. "Moving her to Calter Creek and then abandoning her… that wouldn't be right."

"But at the cost of you becoming a sacrificial lamb?"

"Isn't it up to me to avoid that?" She'd tied her hair back in a ponytail to keep it off her neck. Now she flipped the tail and stared down at the two of them.

"Point. You're a strong woman. You'd be able to do it. I hope," Chris muttered.

"I don't suppose I get a vote in this?" Zach said.

"You've made yourself perfectly clear." Mary bit back her frustration. "And if we – okay, if *I* – do this, you choose how much you see of her. You can't shut her out completely, though. We're younger and more flexible. And who knows? Perhaps putting her in a new environment might improve her outlook."

"I'm not gonna sit around every Sunday enduring that woman's judgmental attitude," Zach stated.

"I'm not asking you to."

Chris's eyes followed the discussion like a table tennis match, finally lighting on Zach. "How about another way to look at it? You needed escape. You're strong and young, and you escaped. Now, it could be she needs the same thing. But she's neither strong nor young. She needs help."

"Next you're gonna tell me there's a nice woman under all that nastiness. I don't buy it, Priest."

"A nickname I'd prefer to leave at Passages, if you don't mind."

Zach shrugged. "Just pointing out that your profession makes you a sucker for every sob story that comes your way. Some people don't deserve a second chance."

Chis shook his head. "Everyone deserves a second chance."

"Ax murderers? Terrorists who blow up daycares?"

"We're getting off topic," Mary interrupted. "Mom's neither an ax murderer nor a terrorist. Focus, please."

Both men shut up.

After a blessedly silent pause, Chris said, "Why do you want to do this, Mary? Really, deep down, why?"

She sat, choosing a chair facing them, and leaned forward on her elbows. "Same reason a person rescues kittens, I suppose."

"Kittens are sweet and fluffy," Zach grumbled.

"Kittens have claws and shred furniture." That wasn't an answer, though. She thought it over. "Okay, I'm selfish. It's taken me years to realize how the past colors your present. I refuse to live with that burden any longer. The same for you," she said to Zach. "By not trying, we condemn ourselves. The house in Cleveland's toxic. I can't go back there, and perhaps she shouldn't, either."

Chris nodded. "Makes sense."

They both turned to Zach, who said nothing.

Sensing an impasse, Mary stood. "Enough for tonight. Who knows if she'd even consider moving, so for the moment it's moot, anyway."

Zach gave them his terse nod. "I'm off." He scooped up a pile of textbooks and disappeared into his room.

"Volatile," Chris said. "More than I expected."

"You think I'm crazy." Mary slumped on the sofa, not snuggled up but within touching distance.

His hand immediately claimed hers. "You're not crazy. You're acting from a place of the heart. But I want to be the one who safeguards that heart." He leaned over and kissed the corner of her eye.

"Chris…"

"Hmm?"

His mouth had moved on, working its way down her cheek. If he reached her neck, they'd never manage a serious conversation. She sighed and gave him a shove. His expression, once she gained enough distance to see it, made her giggle, a mixture of intent, frustration, and…

Adoration?

Oh, come on, she admonished herself. Yeah, he claimed to love her – he *did* love her – but…

"You'll support me, won't you?" she asked. "Whatever I decide?"

Catching her mood, he sobered. His hands framed her face. "Yes. What you're contemplating is one of the most amazing, noble things I've ever witnessed. Truth to tell, in the same circumstances I'm not sure I'd have your courage."

221

She shifted to rest her head on his chest. "It's not courage. It's self-preservation. Or… I don't know. Seeing her out of her environment, maybe I've got fresh eyes."

"Maybe you're a compassionate person who doesn't want another human to suffer." Chris pulled off the elastic, freeing her hair. His hands combed through it, lifting it, allowing it to fall.

Once again she freed herself, sitting up so she could study him. And in the honest depths of his gaze, her remaining doubts evaporated. It was time.

"Invite me for supper tomorrow." Her voice choked, so the last words came out as a whisper.

He read her meaning. "Mary?"

Unable to speak, she nodded.

He pulled her against him. Under her ear, his heart pounded, strong and steady.

Funny how things play out, she mused as she relaxed into his gently caressing hands. Even a few months ago, she'd never have dreamed of encouraging her mother to move to Calter Creek. She had changed… or Chris had changed her. Through him, she'd given herself a chance to explore the caring side she'd kept hidden for so long, aware of how easily she could be shattered.

He chuckled. "Not till tomorrow, huh? Hard sell, followed by twenty-four-hour cooling-off period?"

Only Chris could draw a giggle from her at a time like this. She punched his chest. "This is a major purchase, Bub." Then she grew serious. "It's been an emotional evening, and I'm drained."

"You're sensible." He shifted, separating them, and stood. "And I'm going home. I need to regenerate a few fried brain cells. Not to mention," he added, "planning a dinner worthy of tomorrow, if I can tame my lust long enough to think straight."

At the door he turned to her. "Mary? You're sure?"

"Yes," she murmured. "Very sure."

He kissed her, long and luxuriously, then disappeared down the corridor to the stairs.

222

Alone, she leaned against the closed door, belatedly realizing he'd probably hoped to hear her say the words.

Well, that would come. In the meantime, she texted him.

I love you.

And so it was done.

Chapter 30

Mary arrived at the old mansion to find Chris outdoors, prowling the grounds. His shoulders were hunched, as if he was troubled. "This is crazy," he said as he caught her up in a hug by her car door.

"Why?" She squirmed; he'd pinned her arms, making it impossible to grab her purse, never mind the overnight bag she'd loaded into the trunk. An assumption – the possibility of overnight hadn't been discussed.

When he got the message and let her go, she studied him, frowning. Chris radiated uncertainty. "You okay?" she asked.

"Yeah, but…" He rubbed the back of his neck, not a characteristic gesture. "Today feels all wrong."

What on earth was he talking about? She stared at him blank-faced.

He blurted it out. "As if we'd made an appointment to make love. Which is ridiculous, isn't it? Is this a game changer? Should we have… I don't know… maybe sort of discussed it? But we didn't really, did we? Help me out here, Mary. What should we do?"

He was babbling. She put a finger on his lips to stop the flow.

He shuffled from foot to foot, his hands idly stroking her sleeves. Predictably, the weather had turned; for the first time since they met, Mary wore a long-sleeved top. That didn't block the tingle creeping along her skin at his light touch.

Sure, she was nervous. But the gravity of the situation failed to reach her. "Um… eat?"

"Supper. Of course. Good idea." With a shake of his head, he produced a more natural smile. "I'm a wreck. My thoughts haven't been on food today."

They crossed the grass, skirting the well-tended side garden, and entered through the back door. As she walked down the hall past his bedroom, she noted candles and fresh flowers. All that attention to detail... she suspected to Chris it made things seem even more staged, when tonight should be about spontaneity.

Chris turned from the fridge as she reached the kitchen, holding a plate of sandwiches. "Tuna. Best I could come up with. If I'd tried to cook, I probably would have burned the house down. Not what you'd call focused. Do you want potato chips? Ginger ale? Wine? A pickle?"

She grinned. "Takeaway?"

"And risk garlic?" he countered.

Planned to the nth degree. Weird. And so unnecessary.

The slightly manic light left his eyes, leaving him crestfallen. "I'm acting like an idiot, aren't I? I want everything so perfect, then I mess it up." He fiddled with the plastic wrap covering the sandwiches. "Did I mention I have obsessive tendencies? Just tendencies, I'm not really obsessive, I just want—"

"Chris."

He looked up.

She took the plate from him and returned it to the fridge before he dropped it. "Forget the sandwiches."

A heartbeat, and she stepped into his arms, breathing the clean, male scent of him. Another heartbeat, and their mouths joined. Spontaneously. The odd unreality he'd cast over the evening fell away, leaving nothing behind that wasn't natural and right.

Around midnight, Mary was just beginning to be hungry for something other than Chris and the amazing sensations he brought out in her, the thrill of his body. She lay sprawled on the bed, while he sat next to her, idly trailing his fingers over her breasts, her tummy. Sated, they both needed to catch their breath. "Tell you a story?" he murmured.

"Sure."

"It's about a woman I know. I've known her for a while, actually. This story takes place a couple of weeks ago, at the park. We had hot dogs."

"I remember that." Mary's matched Chris's hushed tone.

He smiled. "Did I say my story was about you?"

"Isn't it?"

He settled back against a pillow, pulling her close. "Maybe. Anyway, we had these hot dogs, and they were messy. In fact, she ruined a shirt. Mustard."

"Dry cleaners. It came out."

"Good to hear. So we'd challenged each other to see who could tell the corniest jokes. I won, by the way."

"You did not." A part of her mind wanted her to sit up and poke his chest in mock indignation, but instead her body succumbed to the lassitude brought on by deep lovemaking. Why disrupt bliss?

"Are you kidding?" he asked. "The one about the clown and the cannibal?"

Mary shifted to explore his nipple with her tongue.

He gasped. "Unfair tactics." When she didn't stop, he swallowed, then said, "I concede, you win. Anyway, the most amazing thing happened."

In the silence that followed, she pulled herself upright to study him. "What?"

Chris's face became serious as his eyes locked on hers.

"Chris?"

"She laughed." After another pause, and never taking his gaze from her, he continued, "She laughed, and it was the most perfect sound. That's when it hit me full force. I was – am – in love. Because with me, she finally laughed."

Warm, soft arrows shot through her heart.

"It's happened since then, most notably when my mysterious woman thought my seniors embarrassing me was the funniest thing she'd ever heard. But that's where it began. And equally important," he added, "I knew then that we could make it. Even with all our differences, if we could laugh, we'd be okay."

The last barriers collapsed. And really, it was easy, once she got out of her own way. "I love you, too," she whispered, then she kissed him, holding his head as her fingers burrowed in his hair, her thumbs brushing his cheekbones.

Heaven on earth, as she'd never known, never imagined possible.

Nor, she reflected later, had a man ever shared tears of joy in her arms.

Chapter 31

A couple of weeks later, Chris was knee deep in his seniors. The administration had procured new songbooks, and suddenly no one had a clue how to look up number fifteen. He ricocheted from person to person, finding pages, chatting about the new book and the probable quality of the muffins, and dodging commentary on his love life.

Just another Saturday at Silver Threads.

The morning was approaching teatime when a ripple, then a silence, blanketed the room.

Ralph, that old codger, let loose with a penetrating wolf whistle. When Chris looked up, he saw Mary hovering at the entrance with a plate of what looked like cookies.

There was no need to excuse himself. They virtually pushed him toward the door.

"Hi," he said, leaning against the jamb as if her appearance were an everyday occurrence.

"Hi."

"Nice to see you here."

She shrugged. "I wanted to check out whether it would be a good fit for Mom."

They stood there like idiots for a moment before Ralph got into the act again. "If this is how slow you are around the ladies, it's no wonder you aren't getting any."

At that, Chris turned his back on their audience, screening Mary from sight. "I did warn you."

"The energy's fantastic. They love you."

"I'm fond of them. But when I think about love, I think something else entirely." He took the plate and put it on a nearby table. "Are you okay with this?"

"With what? Their teasing? Sure, why not?"

"No, with giving them their money's worth."

He framed her face with his hands and kissed her. Quickly, not deeply. "More?" he asked quietly.

"Go for it," she whispered back.

The next kiss, which began hot enough to give him curly hair for a decade, fell victim to their shared urge to laugh, especially when the catcalls started.

"No more," she gasped, and rested her head against his shoulder. He felt her struggle to stay in control. The two of them were in danger of becoming hysterical.

"Shall we take a bow?"

"Oh, let's."

Fully in the swing of things, and happier than Chris could remember being in years, he took her hand and swung around so they both stood framed in the doorway, facing his disorderly seniors. He bowed, she curtsied, and the place erupted. Even Wanda stepped away from the reception desk to join in the applause and cheering.

"Want me to introduce you?"

"Sure. Is there anything I can do to help?"

"Serve tea? The kitchen's short-handed today."

"Happy to."

He picked up the plate and led her into the mob.

Mary worked the room like a pro. When she finally disappeared into the kitchen, he had another five minutes of *very* pointed comments to endure before he got them back to the music.

Forget 'Bicycle Built for Two'. They demanded something called 'To Know Him Is to Love Him'. One of them ruffled his hair, like a ten-year-old.

They'd never served as much tea, or as many muffins, as they did that morning. The two dozen or so elderly people took their time at the counter, checking Mary out.

Several of them hugged him as they left; an equal number hugged Mary.

Over lunch at a local snack bar, he asked, "Not so bad?"

"Not bad at all." Mary was beaming. "I think Mom would like it, too. She's looking forward to better times."

"Zach?"

"Not saying much, but I think he'll come around. The nonstop criticism has died down."

"How did the house-hunting go?"

Mary's mom had grumbled her way into admitting she liked Calter Creek and didn't want to return home. They had been browsing condos, with a second visit to an adult oriented facility planned for earlier that morning.

"Done deal, one bedroom, ground floor, garden patio. It's that new complex southwest of town. The hook is, if you move in before the furnishing and landscaping are finished, you get to join committees and help with the decision-making. Mom's nervous but excited. She's already met another early purchaser. When I left, they were talking a blue streak. Oh, and Chris…"

As usual when Mary's expression turned serious, a small knot developed in the pit of his stomach. "Tell me."

"She wants me to take her to your church."

"Wonderful. When?" he asked, aware of his own reluctance to probe, find out how she felt about it.

"I thought we might go to the harvest festival service, after the bazaar, so she can see it in full celebration mode. From what you've said, that's the day."

A wave of relief rushed through him. She was willing. "Celebrating the end of the bazaar is how I look at it, but you're right, good choice." He didn't voice how much he looked forward to seeing her there, too.

They both worked on their sandwiches. Two of his seniors stopped by their table to chat for a minute before leaving.

"It's nice, the way they care about you," Mary observed, reaching over to pluck a sprout from his lip.

"I kind of dread next week, though." Because now they had ammunition.

She chuckled. "Good thing pink suits you."

He groaned. "You're as impossible as they are."

Mischief danced in Mary's eyes. "And for all your saintly appearance, Reverend Peterson, you're not half bad at naughty. Maybe with more practice…"

He grinned. "Around here it's called nookie. And just say the word."

She grinned back, turning a little pink herself. "Oh, I will."

Chapter 32

Chris's capacity for creative naughtiness amazed her. Since their magical night, he'd found ever more imaginative ways to lure her away, to tease her, explore her. Sexiness exuded from his every pore, and she was insatiable... not only for his body, but for the joy of being with him. Laughter as well as sheer physicality had pervaded their times together over the last week.

There was no room for joking about Chris's penchant for imaginative seduction tonight, however. Mary prepared for a challenging evening, because dinner with Rod and Sadie Bradshaw didn't qualify as her definition of a good time. Despite Chris's reassurances, she dreaded the solemnity and holiness that was sure to pervade a minister's home.

Sadie, a grandmotherly woman with gray hair and a warm smile, greeted them at the door. "Chris said you're pretty, but he understated the case. You're perfectly lovely. Come in." She held out both hands, which Mary felt she had no choice but to accept.

"Did I say pretty?" Chris asked from behind her. "Obviously I meant stunning. Hi, Sadie. What's cooking?"

After a squeeze, Sadie dropped one of Mary's hands and used the other to lead her through the out-of-date but comfortable little home, chattering all the way to the kitchen. "Chris said you eat anything, so I whipped up a Stroganoff type casserole. I hope that'll be all right? If you're vegetarian or anything, I could..."

"No. No, I'm not."

"That's good. And I made a pie. You know Chris loves pie? Can't get enough. I usually bake two, so I can send one home with him. It's a miracle he's as slender as he is."

"Lucky metabolism," he said, while Mary's thoughts irrepressibly strayed to the body underneath the casual slacks and shirt. Suppressing a grunt, she focused on Sadie. The Minister's Dreaded Wife.

"Or youth," Sadie said. "I gave up on all that years ago. Hard to believe I had a passable figure once. A necessity, since Rod's always had an eye for the ladies. Have a seat. Let me grab the wine."

Chris winked, grinned, and wandered away, abandoning her to her hostess, who produced a bottle of Cab and glasses as Mary settled at the old table – metal legs, laminate surface, similar to her mother's. Sadie poured without asking. "Rod snared beers a few minutes ago. They've got budget points to review – projections, how much we can spend on Christmas decorations, that kind of thing. And the eternal planning for the annual harvest bazaar. Have you ever dealt with a gaggle of volunteers and a bazaar? Not always fun, let me tell you."

Mary had arrived ready to be meek and endure sanctimonious platitudes. She hadn't set foot in a church, other than for her father's and Ellen's funerals, since her parents' congregation pointed a massive, judgmental finger at her when she was fifteen. Even Zach's baptism happened without her participation. This cheerful woman bustling around her old-fashioned kitchen, pouring wine and grousing about the parishioners, defied the mold she'd expected.

"Is the bazaar big? Lots of people?"

Sadie sighed, but not unhappily. "Ten to four, six long hours, and hordes, including local commercial and charitable organizations like Earth's Bounty – that's Chris's apple people – and the natural foods store out by Creekside Mall. Problem is, someone always volunteers who's convinced that because she's done it for years, she's the expert. Others take exception, and you can imagine the result. Then we end up sorting things out, clinging to diplomacy by a thread. You'll see – I challenge you to identify the wannabe dictators. More interesting than picking through piles of old clothes and jewelry."

"I doubt I'll be there—"

"Oh, come on by, at least once. No obligation. Chris and Rod make it fun, too. Neither of them is any use when it comes to handling the dragon ladies, so they drift helplessly and wait for the excitement to die down. Generally, they hide near the food."

Mary snickered at the image of Chris peering out from behind a stack of cakes. "Speaking of which, that smells fabulous."

"Family recipe. And I'd better get the vegetables going." Sadie sprang to her feet and rooted in the fridge. "Broccoli or green beans. Any preference?"

"Beans, please." She studied her glass and noted that half the wine had disappeared. Under the force of Sadie's rambling discourse on church politics, she'd relaxed and not even noticed.

Fifteen minutes later, Sadie shooed Mary out of the kitchen to call the men for supper. She found Chris and Rod in a dark cubbyhole of a room clearly used as a study, given the shelves of books and oversized wooden desk. They huddled by the window, poring over a piece of paper, but looked up when she knocked on the doorframe.

"Sadie sent me. Mealtime."

Chris had been speaking. He broke off and smiled. "Thank heaven. We're going in circles anyway. Rod, this is Mary."

The older man was thin, with graying hair, twinkling brown eyes, and a smile that demolished any remaining uncertainty about her welcome at this meal. "I'm delighted to meet you at last. Chris has spoken of you."

Chris looked mildly embarrassed, but for once didn't blush. Mary took that as a mark of how comfortable he felt around the older couple. "All positive, naturally," he said.

"And no secrets revealed," Rod confirmed. "Let's go eat." He dropped the paper on his desk and picked up their beer cans.

"Agree to disagree?" Chris said to Rod, casting a frown at the abandoned document before he followed Mary to the small dining room crammed with old-fashioned furnishings.

"One day I'll teach you not to be so soft-hearted," Rod retorted, making Mary long to know what they'd been discussing.

Instead of tying her in defensive knots, Sadie's grace before the meal felt almost peaceful, a simple, short thank you. Mary relaxed – until Chris's hand landed on her thigh, dangerously close to the hem of her skirt. She slipped her hand into his, removing it from danger. As they murmured amen, Mary surprised herself by joining in. Then Rod served them each a healthy portion of the casserole while Sadie poured more wine. The beans made the rounds.

They ate, and Mary listened. As Chris had promised, in the good-natured banter she heard the vibe of old friends, trustworthy and important in his life.

As for the evening overall, she'd never guess she was in the presence of two ministers. It felt as if they were... ordinary people.

But could she deal with dragon ladies in the congregation?

She shut down that line of thought, vowing never again to be embarrassed by her past. She'd hold her head high, introduce Zach with pride...

Whoa. What was she thinking? She might be stuck with taking her mother – once – but after that she had no intention of ever setting foot in Chris's church, much less dragging her son along... did she?

And that led her to a new set of repercussions. If this thing with Chris followed to its logical end... not only would she be a minister's wife, Chris would be Zach's stepdad.

"Don't you dare ask her," she heard Chris say, penetrating her tangled thoughts. Mary forced herself back to the conversation around the table.

"Wouldn't dream of it. If we're shorthanded, you're heading up the cash box, kiddo," Sadie said.

"If," Chris said gloomily. "This thing's a hydra. It keeps getting bigger than our active congregation."

"A monster," Sadie confirmed, a note of comfortable smugness in her voice. "And worth a mint to the Center. I expect you to whip them into a volunteering frenzy over the next few weeks."

Chris groaned.

"We don't whip," Rod said with a chuckle, "although it may come to that if we don't get more volunteers."

Sadie laughed at their shared reaction. "Stay tuned. We're not short of recruits yet."

Over dessert, the conversation shifted to a person Mary didn't know.

"We found a place for Teresa," Rod said.

"Good," Chris said. "Has she decided what she wants to do?"

"Tough decision, kid her age."

Chris turned to Mary. "Trouble at home, and hassles at school. Fourteen, early bloomer. Word's out she's a tramp, which she isn't. In fact, you saw her, the fight at Passages. The Center's been looking for a place for her where she'll feel safe. Zach knows about it."

Because Zach had remained at Passages, Saturday afternoons since classes started. His decision to hang onto the volunteer position surprised and impressed her. There was still a lot to learn about her son.

"Found someone to lead the Sunday school?" Rod asked.

Chris shook his head. "No such luck, so far. Any chance we can rope Sadie in to take the kids?" He shot a hopeful look across the table.

"One of you do the kids. I'd rather deal with the adults."

Chris made a warding-off hex sign. "Bite your tongue, woman."

"Sorry, gents. I got landed with the kids most of last year. It's someone else's turn."

Mary's eyebrows shot up. The wife of the minister, turning down the Sunday school? Shouldn't Sadie be a bastion of Sunday teaching? Who knew?

The role of minister's wife looked less and less like what she expected.

"In case you're interested, I do the books for the Renewed Life Center as well," Sadie told her, no doubt having picked up on Mary's momentary befuddlement. "I come cheap."

Mary laughed out loud at the incongruity of the last comment, as did the two men. "Nowhere near cheap," Rod said. "You're an expensive proposition, my dear."

"Bear that in mind next time you suggest I take on the kids' Sunday school again," she shot back, grinning.

No. Nothing like her expectations.

This new way of looking at church intrigued her. Just a little.

Later, driving home with Chris at a modest hour, she said, "I guess it was okay to talk about Teresa in front of me? It sounded as if it might be privileged information."

Chris shook his head. "There'll be things I can't tell you, but this isn't one of them. Her situation is common knowledge in the congregation, with the permission of both Teresa and her social worker. The Center's always stepping up to help. She'll board in a home that offers her stability, but outside the foster system." He glanced at her. "It's what we do, Mary."

"I never heard of anything like that." Or possibly she had, she realized, but dismissed it as a bunch of do-gooders with no clue about real life. Mary was beginning to wonder how many of her ideas were based on fallacies.

"A nice evening, I thought. How about you?"

She picked up a tinge of concern in his voice. "It matters to you, doesn't it?"

He nodded. "First, I'm very close to Rod and Sadie. When I started out, they got my feet under me, and they've been there ever since. Second…" He took a breath. "This is what I do. This is who I am. I feel sometimes that we're skirting around the fringes of real life, you and I. My reality is, I'm a minister, I work for a church. I'm tied up every Sunday morning, I help with things like this blasted bazaar. I find places for people like Teresa."

She mulled it over. He'd never concealed facts about his vocation. But… perhaps he had a point. He did lead a life outside the one they shared, although he rarely, if ever, spoke about it or let it intrude on their time together.

Except the funeral. When his robes and his preaching had smacked her in the face.

The Chris she knew was smart, funny, surprisingly sexy. Ministers were… well, not like Chris. Dour, dogmatic. Weren't they?

The picture wouldn't reconcile.

"Talk to me, Mary. How was the evening?"

She twisted in her seat, looking at him through the darkness. "They're nice. They made me feel comfortable."

"But?"

"It's not what I expected. You've met my mother. What do you think made her the way she is?"

"Life? Things not working out, and having nowhere to turn." He swung the car into her condo's guest parking.

She couldn't keep the bitterness from her voice. "I told you what her church did to me. Can you imagine they showed any more kindness to her? With a toe-the-line creed, never set a foot wrong, and under no circumstances have a fallen daughter? And even if you obeyed their commandments to the letter, your chances of salvation were slim."

At her words, the past reared up, and tears flooded her eyes. Before she could stop it, her throat choked with sobs. "When they threw me out, my parents got phone calls calling me a whore," she blurted through what was fast becoming a sobbing jag. "They were damned for having a daughter like me."

"Oh, God." No sooner had they parked than Chris bolted from the car and wrenched open her door. "Come here."

He pulled her up and held her tight while she cried. A lifetime of pain... all the pain she'd kept hidden, even from herself. His hands made circles on her back, his fingers raked through her hair and pressed her face into his neck. And still the tears flowed, until she was empty.

She heard a click as Chris used his fob to lock his car, then he turned them toward her building. "No," she gasped. "I can't go in. Zach..."

"Then let's walk. It's a lovely night."

Their footsteps took them away from the lights on the main road, along a cross street leading into a darker, residential neighborhood. She heaved a shuddering sigh.

Chris's hand tightened on hers. "The reality... that's not who we are. We don't deal in blame, much less condemnation."

"I know. But it's hard for me to believe." She snuggled against him, finally catching her breath. His arm circled her, keeping her close.

"I'm not asking you to join the Renewed Life Center," he said, the slight quaver in his voice alerting her to pay attention. "Or even turn up occasionally. I'd be happy if you did, just so you'll have context, because it's a part of me and it isn't going away. But if we have to separate us and my work, we'll do it."

"Aren't you afraid you'd come to resent me?"

"I don't believe so. You might resent me, because the church does eat up my time and energy."

"A job," she said slowly, thinking it through.

"And that's what it is. A commitment, yes, but also a job. What might be harder... I guess we should have talked about this sooner. Mary, I'd want to see our children raised in a positive, life-affirming faith. Believe it or not, the stuff your parents got isn't that common anymore. That might be the Renewed Life Center or somewhere else, if my church isn't right for you. A friend of mine's a Methodist minister. His wife's Jewish, and the kids alternate between church and synagogue. Somehow they make it work... and so will we."

In the middle of a residential block, halfway between two streetlights, he drew them to a stop and turned to her. "Think about it?" His hands cupped her face as he kissed her, his

239

thumbs wiping away the residue of her tears. A kiss that conveyed the essence of this gentle guy who'd stormed her defenses and shattered them.

Then her mind snapped to his words. *Children?* Suddenly, more was implied than occasional attendance at his church.

"Was that a proposal?" she asked, her voice not quite steady.

He grinned. "Not yet. Since I almost muffed the grand seduction scene, I think I'd better go all out when I pop the question."

She giggled, and the past fell away. Her miserable childhood might always lurk in the background, but it paled beside the reality of Chris.

"Let's head back."

He again claimed her hand, his thumb tracing patterns as they returned to her building. Not for the first time she noted his constant need to touch her – even during grace.

At the door, they stood beneath the canopy, still holding hands. "I shouldn't have said anything about kids and the future," Chris said. "Lousy timing. I love you, Mary."

"I love you," she whispered. As if saying it out loud might break the spell.

He smiled, then leaned in and kissed her again, gently.

When they broke apart, she echoed his earlier gesture, framing his face with her hands. "You're a good man."

"Not perfect by a long shot, but I try." He pecked another quick kiss on her lips. "Thank you."

"For...?"

"Everything. Filling the hole in my life."

Zach was out when she entered the condo, sparing her an explanation for her red eyes. That night, she lay awake reflecting on Chris, the complexity underlying this man who seemed so simple on the surface. Tomorrow he'd be up early, he'd lead a service and give a lesson, a scary, alien world.

It couldn't be that threatening, could it?

Would it be easier if she just turned up, not giving herself time to overthink it? Or would Chris want advance warning?

On overload, she finally dozed off into uneasy dreams of bazaars and congregations and dragons.

Epilogue

Mary arrived at the Renewed Life Center mid-morning to find organized chaos. A team of men marshaled cars in an adjacent field. Kiosks, tables, and food stalls covered the church parking lot and grounds, and an inflatable castle had been set up for the kids. At her rough estimate, several hundred people milled around, chatting, eating, or sitting in the folding chairs facing the bandstand where a bluegrass group contributed to the cacophony.

Not cacophony, she told herself. Merely pleasant bustle. The Ohio State Fair in microcosm.

The day had dawned sunny and mild, with leaves in full display and every table decorated by a pumpkin. Although a lingering chill penetrated her cotton sweater, she suspected it would be too warm by afternoon. Aromas from the food stalls awakened her digestion, even though she couldn't imagine wanting barbecued anything so early. Instead, she ventured cautiously through the crowd, in search of a coffee kiosk.

She spotted Sadie hastening down the outside steps to the church basement. A quick scan revealed Rod holding forth with a group of men, apparently discussing golf swings. On the far side of the church grounds, Chris had been captured by a large woman who waved a shirt around, gesticulating. Mary guessed it was a second-hand clothing stall, and the woman had to be one of the dragon ladies; Sadie's description fit. Trapped, Chris squirmed but couldn't escape.

Sadie spotted her and gestured from the basement steps. As Mary reached her, the older woman's grin plumped out her cheeks.

"See what I mean? Audrey's got hold of him and he's helpless. Unfortunately, I need Chris, too. My volunteer runner is at home with a sick child."

"Could Audrey run?" Mary proposed tentatively.

"Not a chance. She has too much to 'see to'." Sadie made air quotes with her fingers. "Besides, if I let her anywhere near the money, she'll be in the basement telling the volunteers how to count it."

"Rod?" Mary asked.

Sadie snorted. "That husband of mine doesn't have a practical bone in his body... or not many, anyway. No, he's better off schmoozing. Leave him alone, and he'll be happily convinced this was the best bazaar ever. Don't worry, I'll abandon Chris to his fate for a while, then bail him out. Most men shy away from the Gently Used table."

Mary closed her eyes for a moment. Then, before she could question herself, she asked, "What does a runner do?"

Sadie beamed but didn't look surprised and didn't hesitate. "Come on into command central. You can stow your purse while I explain."

By noon, Mary knew the layout of the bazaar inside out and had made numerous trips around the stalls, transporting cash and change, restocking, and carrying messages. The most she and Chris had managed was a wave – accompanied by his expression of pleased befuddlement when he noted her volunteer sash.

Following Sadie's instructions, she tracked down Audrey and politely but insistently commanded her presence at what she now knew to call the Gently Used table, as Chris was needed elsewhere.

A noticeable dent had been made in the stacks of clothing. She walked up to him and stated, "I've brought your replacement. You look as if you could do with a break."

"Could I ever." But he was smiling. "Who... oh."

243

Audrey virtually gave him a hip check, maneuvering him out of the way, and assumed command, arms folded, as if daring customers to approach her treasure trove. Chris grabbed Mary's hand as they made their escape, neither of them laughing until they were well out of sight.

"That was priceless," he told her.

She brushed her hands together. "My work is done."

"Um… not quite."

He drew her attention to the basement steps, where Sadie awaited them. "You're lifesavers. Would you mind handling the 50-50 tickets for a while? We need to hustle more sales. And with the pair of you as a team, they'll be so enchanted they'll virtually throw money at us."

"Do we have to?" Chris mock-moaned.

Mary kicked his ankle. "Can we grab lunch first? I'm starved. The smell of that chicken's been driving me crazy."

Sadie nodded, but it was clear her attention had already turned to the next problem to be solved. "Just be sure to take along a roll of tickets to sell. Everyone's curious about you two."

"I'd thought maybe we could hide out in here?" Chris asked. At Sadie's look, he sighed. "Guess not."

"Isn't this the fun aspect of ministry?" Mary asked him.

"Only if you haven't been on Gently Used for two hours."

The afternoon resembled the morning, except for the crowds. Mary suspected that the entire population of northwest Calter Creek had turned out. The bands rotated, the crowd ebbed and flowed, stock was replenished. She ran errands, sold tickets, and met dozens of people, many of them members of Chris's congregation, as she dodged gentle probes about Chris and herself.

At not quite four o'clock, she watched from the cotton candy kiosk – she'd been trying to get there all day – as Chris approached the bandstand, holding hands with a small blonde girl in a long dress. They appeared to be deep in a conversation involving the doll she carried. He squatted and sketched a cross-my-heart sign on his chest, then gave the child a hug. Hand in hand they mounted the bandstand.

Aware that it was time for the 50-50 draw, Mary balanced her cone of cotton candy as she dug her string of tickets out of her jeans pocket. The child screwed her eyes tight closed and chose a stub from the box. Chris announced the total collected and read the number on the ticket. When a woman shrieked, "I've got it," Mary shrugged. Another day, another windfall lost.

Never mind. Her own windfall jumped from the bandstand and swung the little girl down, to her delighted laughter.

Around her, although a few diehards still shopped and chatted, the grounds team began packing up. Mary tossed out her paper cotton candy cone, detoured via the basement to retrieve her purse, and worked her way out of the crowds.

Rod found her collapsed on a bench overlooking the small graveyard, shoes off, massaging an incipient blister on her heel. "This, my dear, is the hardest you'll ever work," he assured her. "I hope you enjoyed yourself. Sadie doesn't admit it, but she's formidable when she needs someone to do something."

Mary grinned. "I never stood a chance, did I?"

"No indeed." The smile evaporated. "You didn't mind, did you?"

"Not in the least." Mary had expected to spend an hour and leave. Instead, she had hastily arranged for her colleague Suzanne to handle a scheduled house viewing that afternoon. Next time she'd keep the day free.

Next time?

Oh, yes. The thought pleased her, the same way that a resolution long avoided felt good when you finally acted on it.

Chris rounded the corner of the church, carrying a bundle in tissue paper. "For you," he said, handing it to her.

Rod excused himself as she peeled back the wrapping.

Inside she found a doll dressed in satin and lace, conveying a sense of times past. Mary held it up, admiring the finely wrought porcelain face, straight dark hair and blue eyes, the delicate stitching of the long dress. She laid it on her lap, then looked up at Chris. "She's lovely."

He sank onto the bench next to her. "Did you see Noelle up on the stage? There were two matching dolls, and she had to choose. Leaving the other doll behind bothered her, so I promised to take care of it. Perhaps you could bring this one to church tomorrow to show her? And we'd better give her a name. Noelle's doll is called Poppy."

"That's a story to remember." Because it was so typical of Chris, purchasing a doll to assuage the worry of a child, and entrusting her with it.

"Anyway, this one's obviously meant for you, since she looks so much like you. Clearly a descendant."

She nudged his ribs with an elbow – gently, because the knife wound was still sensitive. "Goof."

He returned the poke, then said, "You were fabulous today."

I felt like I belonged. She didn't say it, but he must have read it in her face. He placed a casual arm around her shoulders, absentmindedly waving at a group of people who passed the graveyard on the way to the parking field.

"Why don't you go to my place and make use of that bubble bath you brought over? I should get home about six. There'll be plenty of leftover food, so I'll bring dinner. And you're due for a foot massage."

"Okay," she said quietly, half hypnotized by fatigue and the delicate doll in her arms.

He gave her a quick kiss and stood to leave.

"Marigold," she said.

Chris turned back, puzzled.

"Her name is Marigold." She pointed to the border of orange and yellow flowers still in bloom along the edge of the graveyard.

He considered it, then grinned. "Good choice. But don't expect to get all the say when we name our own."

A tiny thrill went through her at the mention of children, their children, but she said nothing.

He bent to pluck a flower. "Our garden committee would murder me, but this is a special occasion of sorts." He tucked the bloom behind her ear. "See you later."

After Chris left, Mary treated herself to a few minutes resting in the peaceful ambience of the late afternoon, gazing out past the graveyard to the surrounding woods and fields. The solid little church guarded her back, the Bradshaws' cheerful home was just up the driveway, the doll lay on her lap in a bed of tissue paper.

Then, because everything was exactly right, she nodded once, toed on her shoes, and limped toward the parking field.

❖   ❖   ❖

To My Readers

Hello, and thanks for choosing *Mary*. I hope you'll be inspired to check out what else is happening in Calter Creek, where Amanda, Pat, and Mel have their own stories of romance and discovery.

If you enjoyed this book, well, I don't need to tell you how much reviews mean to writers.

I invite you to visit my website, http://lizanncarson.com. I also write fantasy and poetry; you might find something that tickles your fancy.

Happy reading,
LizAnn

About LizAnn Carson

It's interesting, trying to condense who you are into a paragraph or two. I live in Victoria, British Columbia, a smallish city that's large enough to have all modern conveniences, but not so large as to have hours-long traffic jams or heavy duty pollution. I can follow a trail to my local supermarket, or I can be downtown in twenty minutes.

Yes, I spend much of my time writing (and editing, formatting, critiquing for other writers, battling computer problems, and occasionally tearing my hair out). But beyond that, I enjoy a variety of crafts. I play early music on a baritone ukulele and struggle to produce attractive paintings in oil pastel. I walk a lot and enjoy weight training and yoga. Once, a long time ago, I owned a yarn shop, and for a while I taught English as a Second Language. My career, on the other hand, was in the world of computer systems development.

And sometimes, I just watch my cats sleep.

www.ingramcontent.com/pod-product-compliance
Lightning Source LLC
Chambersburg PA
CBHW022159170626

46807CB00005B/2278